Shadows of the Mountain

Bev Pettersen

Published by Bev Pettersen, 2017.

Editor: Pat Thomas

Cover Art Design: Vivi Designs

To the Liverpool Ladies: Cathy, Lauren, Jackie, Suanne, Lorna, Nancy, Ruth Anne. Great trip, great times, great friends!

CHAPTER ONE

The Mustang River Ranch had hosted a variety of guests, from nature enthusiasts to skillful hunters, but never had Kate Miller witnessed such unnecessary violence.

"Don't shoot the rabbit," she repeated, knocking the boy's arrow to the ground before he followed up with a second shot.

"Think I nicked him," his older brother called, his voice jubilant.

"Stop it, now!" she snapped, her voice much too angry to use on pampered guests. But these two boys had been uncontrollable all week, chucking rocks at the cattle, scaring the horses and laughing uproariously when a rider fell off. Placing them in Kate's survival class had been her boss's last attempt to keep them occupied and out of trouble. No one had anticipated they'd find anything to hurt on the deserted archery range.

"You're here to learn how to carve a bow and arrow," Kate said, smoothing her voice. "Not to hunt."

"What's the sense of making this stuff if we can't kill something?" Luke, the older boy, asked. He gave a disgusted snort and flung his bow on the ground. "You wouldn't let us shoot the groundhog or those noisy squirrels. We're not even allowed on the skeet range. My dad said this ranch would be fun. But it sucks."

His brother, Johnny, followed suit, flinging his bow and arrow aside. "Yeah, I'm glad we're leaving today. This place is the worst."

Kate knew she had to keep her mouth shut. Early in their stay, the boys had been flagged as high maintenance, and staff had been cautioned not to lose their temper. But they were difficult to entertain.

Most of the ranch's activities centered around riding. However, these boys sneered at horses. They flatly refused to go on a trail ride and scorned anything involving "stinky" animals. Even learning to rope a steer didn't catch their interest. Still, the hefty price that guests paid for a week's stay meant they needed to be entertained. The ranch's mantra was to provide anything the guests wanted. And Kate needed to justify her job, especially since her survival classes seemed to have been relegated to the spot where frazzled parents sent their disinterested children.

"Look," Luke crowed. "I really did nail him. He's bleeding!"

Kate wheeled, not quite believing that one of his crude wooden arrows had actually hit something so small. Most people couldn't reach the massive canvas target and even she had trouble landing in the bulls eye. But the rabbit was hopping awkwardly, a splotch of red on its shoulder.

"I'll catch him," Luke said. "Smash his head in with a rock. Then make a lucky rabbit's paw, just like Dad's."

"No!" Kate leaped sideways, blocking his path. She might not be able to teach them to respect the wildlife, but she wasn't going to stand back and let them brutalize a helpless bunny. At least not any more than they already had.

"Get out of my way," Luke said, shoving at her arm. "That rabbit is wild. Anyone can claim it. It's my kill."

"You're not going to hurt anything else on this ranch," Kate said, speaking through clenched teeth. "Or scare the horses or cattle or any other animal, wild or tame. Or I will be very annoyed."

"Oh, yeah," Luke said. "What can you do about it? You're not the boss of me."

Both boys snickered but they must have caught something in her expression, because for a rare moment they stopped talking. Luke even backed up a step.

"I don't understand why everyone here cares so much about dumb animals," he muttered, no longer meeting her eyes. "I don't want a stupid rabbit's foot anyway."

And that's all the rabbit was to them, Kate thought, despite the best efforts of staff to foster—if not a love for animals—at least a certain degree of respect.

"You can both go to the pool now," she said. "But listen to the lifeguard... I'll be dropping by later to see how you're getting along."

She knew the boys didn't care about swimming. They'd complained about the lack of a diving board and how there were no small children to dunk. But the pool area was one of the few places with cell phone reception—the best place to log on and watch more of their gory news videos. And while she didn't want to reward their behavior, she and the lifeguard were the only two staff members who could be trusted not to strangle this bloodthirsty duo.

"Finally!" Luke crowed in triumph, patting his pocket, checking that his phone was still there. He wheeled and bolted for the pool, followed closely by his brother. Neither boy gave the suffering rabbit a second thought.

Kate hurried toward the scatter of spruce trees, scanning the grass as she ran. She spotted the arrow, then the rabbit's tracks and a deeper imprint where he'd dug his nails into the dirt, trying to flee. Unfortunately she could also see specks of blood. Not red, more of a brownish stain. Blood didn't look as stark on grass as it did on a less porous surface. On rock, it didn't absorb. It just...pooled.

She faltered, but quickly shoved aside her reluctance, driven by the thought of the wounded animal. If she could find him, she might be able to patch him up. The barn had plenty of first aid supplies, and an empty box stall was always good for convalescing.

The rabbit's tracks didn't go far though and when she saw his motionless body, it was apparent he was critically injured. He never would have stopped in the open like this, not when he was so close to the trees. He lay motionless with thumping sides and widened eyes. Judging by the streak of blood, the arrow had pierced his back.

Kate slumped, heavy with remorse. She hadn't wanted to take the boys to the archery range but their father insisted. So had her boss.

She placed a piece of brush around the dying rabbit then eased back, not wanting to scare him but not wanting to leave him alone either. The least she could do was stick around and protect him from scavengers. Let him die in peace.

Already a crow cawed from a nearby tree. Another landed, followed by three more. Blood had a smell of its own, a coppery stench that tainted the air, clogging one's nostrils, drawing predators... And memories.

She shook her head, determined not to revisit last year's tragedy. But it was impossible not to remember.

The howls were her first warning.

"What's that noise?" Danny asked, blood trickling from his mouth. "Is that Dad again?"

"Nothing to worry about," Kate said, wiping his mouth and adjusting her jacket over his chest, careful to avoid the broken bone jutting from his shoulder. "I'm going to climb down again and check on him."

"Do you think he could come up and wait on the ledge with us?"

"I'm not sure," she lied. "But I'll be back soon."

Danny's dad wasn't climbing anywhere. He'd fallen to the base of the cliff, along with his three horses. The man was no longer conscious. It was amazing he was still alive considering the pulpy mess of his head. His horses were in equally bad shape. Falling a hundred feet off a mountain tended to do that. Danny had been the luckiest, caught up on a ledge thirty feet above. Even so, his injuries were grave, with blood leaking from his mouth and ears.

She eyed the darkening sky as she half slid, half scrambled down the steep slope. Her boyfriend had gone for help hours ago. She didn't know how far he'd have to hike before he found cell phone coverage. It was probably still too early to expect a helicopter, no matter how hard she prayed. However, Danny and his dad needed urgent medical help. Judging from the howls, they might also need protection from predators.

She fell the last few feet but rose and scrambled across the rocks, ignoring her exhaustion. It had been more than an hour since she'd last climbed down and she already knew what she would see.

The first horse, a chestnut with a light mane and tail, had mercifully died on impact, her neck twisted at an odd angle. She'd been Danny's mare.

The second horse, a bay gelding with a white blaze, lay prone on the ground, his eyes glazed. Two of his legs were broken and a *saddle was twisted beneath his belly. One stirrup had been ripped off, but she knew where that was. Still wrapped around the man's mangled leg. She hadn't been able to remove the saddle earlier—the horse had been thrashing too wildly—but he was quiet now, passive with shock.*

The third horse, a stocky buckskin lifted his head when she hurried by, his eyes still alert. Danny said the accident happened when the pack slipped. The buckskin had panicked and leaped sideways, dragging the other two horses and their riders over the cliff. Why Danny's dad thought it was a good idea to have the animals securely tied together, she'd never know. It didn't matter now. Both horses were dying, and probably the man as well.

"It's okay," she said, aching for the horses and her inability to give them any sort of relief. Surely someone on the helicopter would bring a gun. Hopefully help would arrive soon. At least the crows had vanished, driven away by the approaching darkness. She hated how they'd gathered. Cawing. Waiting. Prepared to peck at animals before they were even dead.

Danny's dad lay thirty feet past the buckskin. Smitty, she reminded herself. Danny said his father's name was Smitty.

She followed the same routine as before, saying his name, checking his pulse and assuring him Danny was fine, guessing the man couldn't hear but desperate to comfort him anyway. He didn't appear to have an ear on the crushed half of his face. She wasn't sure about the left side.

At least he was warm. She'd managed to gather some clothing, ripped from their pack and strewn over the mountainside. Basic first aid wasn't going to help Smitty and he shouldn't be moved, judging by the grotesque angle of his neck. But the mere act of covering him up made her feel less helpless. At least it had until she'd heard the howls.

She pulled out her knife and desperately began gathering more wood, enough to serve as both a signal fire and protection. It was a challenge looking after two emergency sites, but neither Danny nor his dad could be moved. Besides, she assured herself, wolves were howling but they were far too smart to bother campers. On the other hand, it was hard to ignore the blood staining the rocks, the horses and even the reddened shirt she'd wrapped around Smitty's head. Its coppery scent filled the night air, acting as a dinner bell.

"I'm building a fire," she called up to Danny, her voice falsely bright. "Be back soon."

She thought she heard his weak reply but the wind was always gusty on this side of the mountain. She couldn't stay here for long. Danny was conscious and she could still help him. She'd come down every hour, check the fire, add wood. Make sure nothing bothered the helpless man and the two surviving horses. Now that she knew the spots for the best toe and handholds, the climb was getting easier.

The buckskin jerked in alarm, struggling to rise, but only able to drag his hindquarters a few feet before collapsing.

Broken back, Kate decided clinically, as she hurried to his side. "Easy boy," she said, gently stroking his neck. "You're okay."

But this horse wasn't ever going home. She didn't know what made him suddenly try to rise. She wished she could persuade him to lie still. It would be less excruciating, easier still if shock took over and helped numb the pain. But seconds later she caught a blur of gray and realized why he was trying to flee... The wolves had arrived.

"What are you doing?" a voice behind Kate said. "Is your class over already?"

Kate turned, grateful to be pulled back to the sunny meadow but needing a moment to compose herself. Sharon Barrett stared with raised eyebrows. And while Sharon was a fair boss, the woman didn't tolerate idle employees. Regardless, there was no way Kate was walking away from this dying rabbit. Not yet.

"Can you please lower your voice?" Kate asked. "Those boys shot a rabbit. I put some brush around him so he'd die in peace. I'm just waiting so I can bury him."

"Those brats," Sharon whispered, her voice much softer. "Any chance he'll live?"

Kate shook her head.

"Well, you're the expert," Sharon said. "I owe an apology to you and all the staff. I should have refunded that family's money and asked them to leave days ago. You're the only one they even half-listen to."

"But I wasn't able to control them either," Kate said.

"This is the least destructive day they've had," Sharon said dryly. "You did better than anyone else."

"I don't think I was able to teach them much," Kate admitted. "They weren't interested in learning how to build a shelter."

"Not many guests are. These classes seem to be a waste of your talent."

And that was the big problem. The ranch couldn't keep employees who didn't contribute to the bottom line.

"Of course I'm happy to continue helping with the children," Kate said. "Or in the kitchen. Or with the trail rides. Anywhere at all."

"That's what I wanted to discuss," Sharon said. "We have a special group coming in for a three-day overnighter. To ride in and see the mustangs. Donna broke her wrist when she fell yesterday so I'd like you to take her place. Look after the meals and anything else they need."

"Certainly," Kate said quickly, relieved Sharon hadn't walked out here to rehash the low demand for her survival classes. If employees were flexible about helping out, they had a better chance of keeping their job year round. Fortunately Kate was experienced with horses as well as cooking over a campfire.

A year earlier, she'd been a Montana Park Ranger and a dedicated volunteer with the search and rescue team. She'd tried working in the office but had felt so stifled she'd left after three weeks, needing a position where she could work outside. The Mustang River Ranch had been the only one to offer employment. Fortunately Sharon accepted that Kate had some geographic limitations.

"I assume we'll be sticking to the Mustang River trail?" Kate asked. "Where it's good grazing?"

"Absolutely," Sharon said. But the empathy in her blue eyes showed she knew Kate didn't want to go near the mountains. "It'll be an easy in and out," Sharon added. "Very little climbing. And Monty will be the guide."

Good news. Monty was a backcountry veteran. He'd lost very few horses in over four decades—and more importantly he'd never lost a rider. But it was surprising Sharon was freeing him up to lead such a routine trip, especially since the ranch was booked a year in advance.

"How many riders?" Kate asked, mentally calculating their food requirements. She'd have to meet with the cook and Monty. Figure out the meals and number of pack horses. Sometimes a vehicle made a drop camp, setting up tents and leaving caches of food so everything was on location at the end of the day. But the trail they'd be taking was crisscrossed by the Mustang River, so this group would be limited to whatever their horses could carry.

"Not sure of exact numbers yet," Sharon said. "But I'll be personally meeting with the group's rep to review their menu...and other specific needs."

Specific needs. So not a standard three-day ride. Possibly a glamping package? The food wasn't that different for the pampered rides. However, the presentation involved more work. And riders wouldn't be expected to cook their own meals. But the way Sharon said "specific needs" raised a flag. And Monty's services were generally reserved for experienced trail riders, the hardy folk who slept with no tent—only a bedroll—and preferred to grill their own steak.

"The group will come in tonight," Sharon went on, "and ride out before dawn tomorrow. Competence as well as discretion is critical. Which is why I want you."

Sharon's trust was reassuring. Last month, a famous actor had visited the ranch, leaving several employees star struck, snapping countless selfies and posting them on social media. Sharon had been furious. Her prominent cousin, a respected horse trainer for the movies, had recommended the Mustang River Ranch for a private getaway and had been similarly displeased.

"I appreciate your flexibility but we do need to fill your hours better." Sharon glanced pointedly at the piece of brush Kate had placed over the rabbit. "Other than the occasional difficult children, do you like working here?"

Kate gave a vigorous nod. She appreciated the ranch, her easygoing co-workers, and being able to live close to nature. Occasionally the guests were a little quirky. But it beat working in a tiny office, surrounded by concrete buildings, frazzled commuters and cloying car exhaust.

"This place already feels like home," Kate said, throwing in a plug for winter employment. "And I'd love to stay long term. I'm happy to work wherever you need me."

"Good to hear," Sharon said, her eyes twinkling. "Because next year I was considering offering some sort of tracking challenge. Where we'll give participants a head start and then mounted staff will try to hunt them down. Guests want more than survival classes. They prefer immersion. Monty is good at tracking, and it would be beneficial to have someone with your background."

"Sounds like a great idea," Kate said, squeezing her hands so as to refrain from giving Sharon a highly inappropriate hug. But that kind of gig would be a dream job. No worrying about riders who lacked proper trail knowledge, no pressure to find injured campers, no sitting on a dark lonely mountain waiting for a rescue helicopter to arrive. She'd still be outside using her search and rescue skills, but it would all be in fun.

She enjoyed working with Monty. He was the perfect trail partner, a grizzled veteran experienced with all types of terrain, both high and low. Then Kate sighed. Because of course if the guests headed up the mountain, she'd have to follow. And that was something she didn't want to do.

"Lots of time to decide," Sharon said. "But we have to find more to keep you busy. Your survival classes simply aren't drawing the numbers." She smiled beneath her white cowboy hat, but her words carried a clear warning.

Sharon Barrett was first and foremost a businesswoman. Her ancestors hadn't held on to their vast land holdings by being soft.

They were tough negotiators, and history showed a Barrett rarely lost a fight.

"I understand," Kate said, squaring her shoulders. "I'm going to help in the kitchen soon. And of course I'll hang around for the music tonight."

"Good," Sharon said. "Make it fun in there. Guests always need dance partners, and positive last impressions mean better reviews. It's important for things to run smoothly...especially this week. And I'm glad you're joining Monty on this trail ride. I don't expect trouble but it's good to know he'll have support."

For such a confident woman, Sharon sounded rather conflicted. Maybe travel agents were visiting, making it more important to socialize in the dance hall and make it look like fun, even if that was the least interesting aspect of Kate's day.

She preferred mellow campfires to ear-splitting music, and the smell of piney woods over men who dressed like urban cowboys and splashed on too much cologne. At least tomorrow she could look forward to a break. A relaxing three-day ride with guests who'd be tired enough to crawl into their tents and sleep as soon as the sun dropped. And they must be animal lovers or they wouldn't want to ride all the way in to see the wild mustangs.

"No kids like the ones today?" Kate asked.

"No way." Sharon actually laughed. "This ride is all about two horse-loving girls. Absolutely no killer mentality."

Kate gave a happy nod, shifting slightly so she wouldn't have to look at the hungry crows. A peaceful trail ride in remote country would be like a mini-vacation. And it couldn't come quickly enough.

"Sounds perfect," she said.

CHAPTER TWO

"Gluten-free flour is like gold," the head cook scolded. "So don't spill it."

Kate nodded and continued with her careful measurements. She usually liked working with the woman but today the cook was edgy, hovering and giving unnecessary instructions.

She glanced wistfully out the window to where wranglers were returning horses to the corrals. Helping with the livestock was preferable to being inside, but nearly every employee was good with horses. Not everyone could cook.

"We also need everything gluten free for a trail ride tomorrow," the cook went on. "So make two dozen rolls along with some pita wraps. Then make that chocolate flourless cake you did for the birthday party last week. Monty can pack that in as well."

Kate reached for the recipe rack, hiding her surprise. Cake was never sent in the saddlebags. It didn't pack well so granola bars were the dessert of choice. "I didn't realize any of our rides this week were gluten free."

"The cake is for a special group," the cook said. "Boss wants these girls treated like royalty. Poor Monty will have to take two packhorses to handle all their requests, and he isn't as young as he used to be."

The cook's voice always softened when she mentioned Monty. They were both longtime Barrett employees as well as close friends. And though Sharon Barrett hadn't revealed much to

Kate about tomorrow's trail ride, it was obvious the trusted cook knew far more.

"Is all this for the two girls who want to see the mustangs?" Kate asked.

"There will be two teens and two adults," the cook said. "Or maybe three adults. We won't know that until later. Depends how everything checks out."

"Checks out? Do you mean with their horses?"

Riders were assigned horses at the beginning of their stay and then given a chance to get to know each other. But with this group arriving so late, there wouldn't be time for the usual introductions, something Kate knew would leave Monty irritated. Horses and riders had a safer and less stressful experience if they understood each other before hitting the trail.

"I better tuck in some extra whisky," the cook said, ignoring Kate's question. "Monty will need it. And before you stick anything in the oven, take a few more cases of soda outside. Those two boys have emptied the pool fridge again. It'll be a relief to see their backsides."

Kate covered the rolls, happy to leave the gluten-free section of the kitchen and escape for a moment. Besides, Allie, the lifeguard, appreciated her help with keeping the boys in line, especially if there were other children trying to swim.

Kate stacked four cases of chilled soda on the trolley then added a case of water, aware Allie never drank pop. And after enduring Johnny and Luke for a couple hours, she was probably hot and thirsty.

Kate heard the boys long before she tugged the loaded trolley through the side door and onto the pool deck. They were snickering at something on Luke's phone, their heads bent over the tiny screen. At least they hadn't smashed any chairs and they weren't fighting.

"I hear you boys are thirsty," she said.

"Put our drinks on the table," Luke muttered, not bothering to raise his head.

"Sure," she said crisply, still a little peeved after burying the rabbit. "Two waters coming up."

"Not water, stupid." Luke jerked in annoyance. "We ordered Coke. Oh, it's you... Sorry." His eyes narrowed on her head. "Why do you have your hair like that?"

Blaring from their phone pulled the boys' attention off her hairnet and back to the newscast.

"They can't threaten us," Johnny said, his gaze intent on the screen. "If I were the President, I'd just shoot all those terrorists."

Kate placed two cans of Coke on the table, surprised when both boys mumbled thanks. They were definitely trying to behave, or perhaps they were just distracted by the news. Two suspected terrorists had been captured by American troops, resulting in ISIS demands that they be released. Over the last month, threats against major U.S. cities had escalated, making Kate doubly relieved she lived on a remote ranch.

She picked up the handle of the trolley and continued along the pool deck toward the swim station. Allie doubled as the afternoon lifeguard and evening dance instructor. Like everyone at the ranch, the woman worked long hours. And right now, Allie was staring at the trolley, obviously in desperate need of a drink. Her lips were parted, her eyes wide with appreciation.

Kate waved, glad she'd thought to replenish the water. But, Allie didn't give her usual infectious smile. She still gaped, her mouth open, and it was apparent she wasn't looking at the water but at something behind Kate.

"Could I have one of those, please?" a man's deep voice asked.

Kate turned, surprised she hadn't heard his approach. In the back country, she could hear the tiniest rustle, but working around all these guests seemed to have dulled her senses. A shame really. And then she quit thinking about anything but him.

This man had the most piercing eyes, brown with flecks of yellow and gold, rather like a wolf's. And he had that same aura: powerful, confident, aloof. At a ranch where nearly every guest donned a cowboy hat, this man's was different, as if the hat truly belonged. Better yet, he smelled of fresh pine, not sweat or beer or cologne.

Probably not a guest. Maybe a long-lost Barrett relative? He had that family's stunning good looks although he didn't have the Barrett blue eyes. He certainly was no chatterbox. He studied her, just as she studied him. And the boys and their loud phone and the clattering from the kitchen faded away.

Someone pushed past her.

"Hey," Allie said, splendid in her tanned skin and striped cover-up with the ranch logo. "Come with me. I have some water in the cooler, already chilled."

The man inclined his head, but his eyes remained locked on Kate's. "Need any help unloading those cases?" he asked, his velvety baritone voice sending a little shiver down her back.

"No, thank you," Kate said, surprised she sounded so normal when his sheer masculinity left her breathless. And when did a guest ever offer to unload her trolley?

"Over here," Allie prompted, urging the man toward the tall cooler on the other side of the pool.

Kate followed more slowly, pulling the rattling trolley and grabbing the chance to study the man. He was just as spectacular from the back, his powerful shoulders tapering to long muscled legs. His jeans, a perfect fit, were slightly faded in spots, as if he were accustomed to being in the saddle. The heels of his leather boots were clean but well worn. And while he might have a cowboy's clothes and good manners, he also had the self-assured walk of an esteemed guest. Not a swagger exactly, just an abundance of confidence. As if he wouldn't be afraid to walk in a dark alley. Or anywhere really.

She gulped, yanking her gaze off him and back to Allie. At some point, Allie had slipped off her cover-up, leaving her bikini-perfect body on full display. She bent in front of the cooler, reaching for a water bottle on the bottom rack, her shapely butt waving in the air. Kate couldn't see the man's face but even Johnny and Luke looked up from their phones.

However, the man didn't linger. He accepted the water, gave a polite incline of his head and strode from the pool enclosure.

Both Kate and Allie gaped until he disappeared beyond the gate.

"Wow, when did Mr. Hottie arrive?" Allie asked, theatrically fanning her face before slipping her cover-up back on. The boys hooted their disappointment, silencing only when Kate shot them a look.

"Guess he just came," Kate said, swinging the cooler door open.

"I figured you'd already met. The way you two were talking."

Kate blinked. They hadn't been talking. She didn't remember saying a word.

"Do you think he's here alone?" Allie asked, turning to help transfer a case to the cooler. "He wasn't wearing a ring. He seemed serious but sexy. And he moves like he'd be a great dancer."

Her gaze drifted to Kate's hair. "I'd just die if someone caught me wearing a hairnet. And sorry that I cut in like that, but I know you don't date." She paused to shout a warning at the boys who were spraying pop, sending a sticky dark shower over the pool chairs.

"That's why I love this place," Allie said, grimacing at Kate. "The bad kids always leave. Best of all, you never know what the next wave of guests will bring."

Kate shoved the last bottles into the cooler. Allie preferred dealing with grownups and more than once she'd rescued Kate from over-eager dancers, guys emboldened by a sense of freedom and a little too much alcohol. In exchange, Kate tried to help her out with the more difficult kids.

Allie wrinkled her nose in confusion. "But *he* didn't seem one bit interested. I even took my cover-up off. And that always works, with guys of every age."

"I don't understand why he didn't look," Kate said, totally sincere. Allie was a lovely person with a truly splendid body.

"Oh, he looked," Allie said. "But barely. I got the feeling he was evaluating me. Like he took three seconds to absorb everything about me, and then I was dismissed. Just like that." She gave a dramatic snap of her fingers.

"He's probably here with someone," Kate said.

Women often came to the ranch alone, drawn by their love of horses. Men, not so often. Unless they were here for a cattle working package or a fall hunting trip. But this guy didn't fit in either of those categories. He certainly didn't look like he needed an instructor, of any sort. In fact there was something about him that left her uneasy, like when she came across the track of a big grizzly and wasn't sure if the animal was behind or in front of her.

"Oh, well." Allie shrugged and closed the fridge door. "At least he knows I'm interested. And thanks for bringing the water. Glad it's stocked up for when you're gone."

Kate was already turning the empty trolley back toward the kitchen but stopped, her eyes shooting to Allie's face. "Gone?" she asked. "What do you mean?"

"I heard you're helping Monty with an important three-day ride tomorrow."

Relief swept Kate like a wave, but she kept her body relaxed, hiding the fact that she'd thought she might be laid off. Like the cook, Allie stayed on top of the news. The girl may not go out on rides, but working at the pool during the day and the dance hall at night gave her access to all the gossip. Everyone loved her bubbly personality.

"Are you all right about going with Monty?" Allie asked, her pretty face worried. "And doing an advanced ride? Maybe I can talk up your survival classes at the dance hall. Push some guests your way."

"I'm fine, thanks," Kate said, touched by the offer. "Anyway, it's not an advanced ride. Just a low-country trip, to see some wild horses."

"So that's where it's going. Monty wouldn't say, of course, and no one in the kitchen would talk either. Which is really strange because they usually tell me."

"Maybe I misunderstood," Kate said quickly.

"But the fact you're going means it's the Mustang River trail," Allie said. "We all know you don't like to ride in the mountains."

Kate's hand tightened around the trolley. Everyone knew that? No wonder guests weren't signing up for her classes. A search and rescue expert who couldn't rescue anyone wasn't much use.

"Maybe you should learn to dance better," Allie said. "I can teach you. In the winter, we cover the bar as well. And there are big tippers at Christmas, especially when they're getting a drink and a dance."

Kate appreciated Allie's support. However, she couldn't imagine forcing smiles for tips. On the other hand it was obvious she needed to prove she was an employee worth keeping. And that for the sake of steady employment, it would be wise to accept Allie's offer, even though the thought of spending more time in the dance hall left a sour taste in her mouth.

CHAPTER THREE

Music and laughter leaked from the wooden dance hall, following Kate as she skirted the building and veered toward the horse paddocks. She couldn't avoid the raucous hall for too much longer. But the sun hadn't set yet, and Monty might need help preparing for the trail ride.

A flashy palomino snorted, eyeing her suspiciously as she walked past the holding pen. None of the other horses even bothered to lift their heads. Most of the animals knew the ranch routine better than she did. Guests never rode at night and riders were brought back long before dusk. It was too dangerous to be riding trails in the dark. Even the overnighters stopped to make camp long before the sun dropped. The horses knew they wouldn't be saddled at this time of day and were more interested in gobbling up their hay than checking out a random human.

She scanned the two small paddocks and the animals that had been selected for tomorrow's trip. Two mules, two sets of distinctive ears. No, three mules. A wave of relief swept her. *Thank you, Monty.* Mules were smarter than horses, more cautious and unlikely to tumble off a trail. Or over a cliff.

"Evening," Monty said, his laconic greeting coming from the left side of the corral.

She walked over to join him.

"I had the wranglers round up Belle for you," Monty said after a moment. He was never one to rush his words, and Kate had learned to wait him out. "She'll question your judgment a bit. But she's a good girl."

"Thank you," Kate said, giving Monty a grateful smile. She hadn't wanted to inconvenience anyone by insisting on a mule, but Monty understood. Riding Belle also meant she'd be in back with the pack animals, where conversation with guests would be limited. And that suited her just fine.

At the sound of her voice, the palomino scooted sideways, ramming into the shoulder of a stocky sorrel who had been busy eating. The sorrel immediately flattened his ears, snaking his head and letting the palomino know of his displeasure.

"You teach him, Banjo," Monty said, scowling at the palomino.

"Is that a new horse?" Kate asked. The animal looked familiar, but he was acting like he'd just stepped off the trailer.

"No," Monty said. "We've had Slider a few years. He's popular in the arena. Just not my first pick for an overnighter."

Now Kate remembered. Slider was brilliant at all the reining maneuvers, and the wranglers loved to impress guests with his long slides and powerful spins. He was usually stabled in the barn though. Clearly he didn't appreciate his new sleeping quarters, or the fact that he'd been removed from his friends. He paced the far end of the corral, scooping up bites of hay and stretching his head over the top rail as he chewed. But he wasn't stupid. He now kept a respectful distance from Banjo.

Monty tilted his cowboy hat and swiped at his brow. "Guess he'll be okay," he said. "The two girls insisted on horses with color and both App mares are in heat."

They both stared in silence at the handsome palomino, neither Monty nor Kate saying anything more. Matching horses to riders was always a balancing act. Most guests were easygoing, letting the wranglers pick a suitable mount. But some people believed they were much better riders than they really were, or thought that experience at horse shows translated to the ranch. A different skill set was required on the trail and that applied to both horse and rider. As well, failure to win a blue ribbon didn't hurt anyone while mistakes on the trail could be painful, even deadly.

At least the ride would be relatively easy. In the summer, the wild horses grazed on the other side of the Mustang River where they were buffered from off-road vehicles and hikers. While it was an isolated area, far from roads and towns, the trail was relatively flat with the toughest obstacles being distance and water. All in all, the palomino was probably a better choice than either of the Appaloosa mares, that could quickly draw a feral stallion's aggressive attention.

Still, Kate couldn't stop a shiver of unease. The fact that riders wanted horses based on color revealed a disturbing lack of respect for the back country. And it was surprising Monty had even tolerated that sort of request.

But it wasn't her place to question him. Clearly, Sharon Barrett was prepared to go to great lengths to keep these particular visitors happy. And Monty knew it. Besides, Kate would be in the back with the mule train—a quiet attendant who merely set up camp, cooked meals and took photos of smiling guests upon request.

"I'm going to hang out here for a bit," Kate said, "and get to know Belle. And I can pack up the dry goods when they're delivered from the kitchen."

"That's all happening in the morning," Monty said. "Under supervision. We won't be touching anything."

Kate's gaze shot to the orange panniers lying in the open shed. Nothing had been packed yet, not even the tents. She remembered the cook's watchful gaze when she'd prepared the gluten-free wraps. So these people were paranoid. However, there was no point in asking questions. Monty wasn't prone to talking at the best of times, unless it was about the animals.

Besides, morning would come quick enough. She already knew there'd be five guests just by counting the horses in the holding pen. "I'll come early tomorrow," she promised, "to help with the animals. Is there anything else I should know?"

Monty fingered the brim of his hat, as if weighing his words. "The list that Boss gave me was very specific," he said. "One hatchet only, to be stowed in the locked panniers. No firearms or weapons of any sort are to be carried...at least not by us."

Kate shifted, her hand automatically reaching for her hip. Her knife wasn't there of course. She was headed to the dance hall. But the idea of riding without it left her feeling unprepared. And unsafe. And dammit, she could feel her heart quickening.

"I know," Monty said morosely. "We all need a knife. I had a packhorse topple over once. Fool horse wasn't paying attention to the trail. Or maybe I had the pack a little uneven." He paused as if considering the possibility of such a rookie mistake, then shook his head in quick dismissal.

"Anyway," he added, "next thing I knew, the horse was upside down, twenty feet below, feet waving in the air like a turtle. If I didn't have my knife to cut him loose, it would have been much worse. Luckily only his feelings were hurt. Most trail riders have had wrecks like that. I know you've seen worse."

Monty looked at her, as if expecting some sort of reply. But Kate's mouth felt bone dry. She'd been thoroughly grilled about the tragic mountain accident, by investigators, by the media and again in her exit interview. And she didn't want to talk about it ever again.

"We'll be riding the river trail," she said. "As long as the animals can cross the water, I...we, won't have any trouble."

"I know," Monty said. "You'll be fine. I'm just saying it's natural for anyone to want their knife. Especially you."

"Right," Kate said. However, the idea of riding without a knife to help in an emergency left her feeling physically sick, and while she appreciated his tact, they both knew it wasn't natural.

She flattened her palms against her jeans, wondering if she really was the best person for this trip. She'd probably been a little too eager to please. Maybe it would be possible to back out. Maybe Sharon could find another wrangler, one of the guys...

"They asked for a woman," Monty said. "Someone to help with lady stuff, but who won't sell stories to the media. Donna's hurt, and you're the only other one I trust. So bring along whatever you feel you need. Just know that Boss is depending on you. So am I."

Kate jammed her fists in her pockets. Monty wasn't usually talkative but he certainly knew how to push her buttons. No one had needed her in a while. That knowledge left her torn. Then his words sunk in and the vise around her chest loosened a notch.

"Bring whatever I need," she said hopefully. "So you're saying it's okay to bring my knife?"

"I'm not saying that, not exactly." Monty extracted a crumpled piece of paper from his pocket and pressed it into her hand. "Boss gave me this list, and we have to follow directions. Still, our most important job is to keep everyone safe. Animals included. And it's reassuring to know I have a partner who can untangle a pack string.

"Guess I'm just saying it's up to you." He yanked his hat lower over his forehead but not before she caught the conspiratorial twinkle in his eye. "And I don't suppose they'll check your boot."

CHAPTER FOUR

Kate stepped through the door of the lively dance hall, still absorbing Monty's words. He'd actually suggested she pack her knife, expressly against Sharon Barrett's wishes. If it were discovered in the morning, not only would she be replaced with another wrangler but she'd probably lose her job.

The guest comes first. That had been drilled into every ranch employee...unless it was dangerous to human or animal. And in Kate's opinion, it was dangerous for any trail rider not to carry a knife. Obviously that was Monty's belief as well. And she was the one who'd be responsible for the pack train.

She eased to the back of the hall, weighing her dilemma, automatically avoiding eye contact with any single males. Her throat was parched so at some point she'd have to squeeze up to the bar and grab a water. But that would involve making conversation along with a considerable amount of smiling. And she needed to acclimatize first. To get used to this confining space, and air heavy with sweat and beer and music.

Thankfully, her services weren't required yet. Allie was centre stage, head back and laughing. She always liked to break the ice by starting with the chicken dance, and now Allie was ringed by at least twenty people trying to learn the basic moves. Some of the guests looked like old pros, singing and flapping their arms in perfect harmony. Others weren't quite in synch. But almost everyone in the room was grinning, admiring the dancers' attempts, even if they weren't motivated enough to get up on the dance floor themselves. Of course, given time, Allie would have the entire hall rocking. Her enthusiasm was infectious.

Sharon Barrett wanted Kate to be a crowd pleaser like that. To make sure everyone had a good time and felt included. A small thing really. But for a reserved person like Kate, public demonstrations didn't come easy.

She pulled in a fortifying breath and checked the room, searching for the singles. *Time to do this.* Generally guests arrived at the ranch in groups or couples, but there were always riders who were exhausted after a long day in the saddle, leaving their partner to come here solo. Often they just wanted someone to sit with and to chat a bit while they enjoyed the music. As long as Sharon saw Kate mingling, it should earn some needed brownie points.

But first, she needed some cool water to wet her throat, preferably a full bottle to carry in her hand. Holding a drink was always a good excuse to avoid a rowdy line dance.

"Thirsty?" a deep voice asked.

Kate twisted, automatically accepting the chilly water bottle pressed into her hand. Familiar brownish-gold eyes stared down at her. The man from the pool, every bit as good-looking as she remembered. His mouth was still a flat line, but she didn't get the impression he was grim, only that he didn't bother to indulge people. This man only smiled when he wanted. And she was okay with that. Respected it even.

"I am thirsty," she said. "Thank you."

"Just returning the favor." The sides of his mouth remained flat but his eyes had an unmistakable sparkle. He was long and lean, with the kind of muscle that was built from activity, not hours in an upscale gym. His T-shirt wasn't tight, but it didn't completely hide his toned chest. A tattoo edged below the left sleeve. She hadn't noticed that earlier, hadn't noticed much else but his striking eyes and fresh masculine smell. She pulled in an appreciative breath.

"Or maybe you'd like something stronger?" he asked.

She realized she was staring, but men like this didn't usually pop up in the dance hall. He might be young—she pegged him in his early thirties—but she doubted he had a frivolous bone in his body. It was like walking out to your corral and finding a wild stallion had inexplicably jumped the fence and joined a placid group of trail horses.

And he wasn't shy. He was returning her scrutiny with an intensity that made her body buzz.

"No," she said. "Water is perfect." She twisted off the cap and took a long sip, guessing by the way her skin tingled that he was still watching her. However, when she lowered the bottle his gaze was on the dance floor.

"Some of those dancers look like they just arrived," he said.

His choice of subject was rather disappointing. She'd expected more from such a man. But in here, it was all about humoring the guest.

"Most of them have been here for a week," she said, following his gaze to the dance floor. "Only a few are new."

"Which ones?"

"The lady in the beige boots and cowboy hat. And the woman in the silver top."

"What about the guy in the black shirt?" he asked. "The one the lifeguard just pulled from his chair."

"He's been here for at least ten days," she said, hiding her surprise. Most men only noticed the female dancers. And the blond in the silver top was very attractive, rivaling Allie with her sheer physical perfection. Obviously he hadn't forgotten Allie and her bikini from earlier today, something Allie would be delighted to hear.

Kate took another sip of water. She didn't enjoy being here and even hanging out at the back was a chore. But judging by the way this man was watching the floor, he was here to dance. Guests didn't pay big money to be wallflowers. The more reserved ones just needed some prodding. Kate's job was to get him up on the dance floor. Then turn him over to Allie and her genuine enthusiasm.

"Do you want to try this line dance?" Kate asked politely.

"Not one bit," he said. And this time the corners of his mouth lifted in an actual smile. "I'm not much into dancing. Judging by your expression, I don't think you are either." His smile extended to his eyes, leaving them a little more golden than brown, and he seemed amused rather than offended by her lack of enthusiasm.

"Honestly, I'm not," she admitted, surprised at her candidness as well as his awareness. "But no guest is supposed to be left alone. I need to hang out here in case someone needs a partner."

"You work long hours," he said. "From kitchen to the dance hall. You probably know every guest. Most people here seem like horse lovers. Are there many hunters?"

"None right now," she said, thinking of Luke and Johnny and their brash father, who thankfully had piled into their Lexus and checked out immediately after supper. "The hunters mainly come in the fall," she added. "But they're restricted to the west side, far away from the trail riders."

He gave an approving nod. "Seems like a professionally run ranch. I understand your head guide has been around for a while?"

"Yes, Monty Trask is a legend around here." Now this was a subject she could embrace and she spent almost twenty minutes talking enthusiastically about Monty and his well-earned reputation. This man was so interested she even recited the story about how Monty had tracked down a man with Alzheimer's twelve miles from a state campground, long after his frantic family had despaired of ever finding their grandfather alive.

"And Monty went back to look for the man's horse," she added. "He delivered him safe and sound as well."

That prompted a series of questions about wranglers and dude ranches and the popularity of overnight rides. She waved a hand in animation, enjoying this line of conversation. But the music changed to a foot-stomping polka, with chairs emptying as dancers rushed to snag partners.

There weren't many single women left and a blond man with hopeful eyes was already barreling her way. He was with some investment bankers from Seattle, and his first evening it had taken her and Allie a half hour to coax him onto the dance floor. He and his friends had been stiff and reserved, but by the end of the night they'd been tossing their hats in the air and racing each other to find dance partners. Clearly, they were ready for a repeat.

She squeezed her water bottle, knowing she had to leave and put in her time on the floor, even though it was more fun chatting with this man about guides and guests and ranch horses. Perhaps dancing could be postponed a bit by pleading that she needed to finish her water. After that though, she'd have to move to the front and join Allie. That was unfortunate because this new guy was totally appealing.

She rarely felt comfortable in crowds, but tonight she didn't mind it so much. Just looking into this man's eyes—hazel she supposed, although that seemed a boring description for such a striking color—was a treat. And then she realized she was staring at him, her reluctance to leave a little too obvious.

"My name's Jack, Jack Becker," he said, and something in that deep voice made her skin go all tingly again. "What's yours?"

"Kate Miller," she said, glancing behind him. The blond man and two of his investor friends were only a few feet away pushing and shoving at each other in their eagerness.

There was no way Jack could possibly see them. But he shifted, raising his arm against the wall, blocking their approach, and creating a cone of intimacy that was impossible for them to ignore.

"How long do you have to be on that dance floor, Kate?" Jack asked.

"Until midnight," she said. "It's part of my job to dance with the singles."

"Well, I'm single and I need a partner." He snagged her water bottle, easing it from her hand. "We can do this. And keep everyone happy."

He placed the bottle on a nearby table and tugged her toward the dance floor, not giving her time to argue, or even a chance to psych herself up.

Less than a minute later, she was in his arms, moving to the catchy song without a shred of reluctance. And she didn't feel stiff or out of place either. In fact, she felt completely natural, absorbed in the rhythm, the vibe, the joy.

One song morphed into another but she didn't reach for her list of ready-made excuses. Didn't plead a sore ankle, or the need for a bathroom break, or that she had to leave and wheel over another case of beer. Tonight was different. Everyone was having a marvelous time. And the tiny dance floor was packed, making it acceptable—even necessary—for Jack to pull her against his hard chest. There was no doubt he had a six-pack, maybe an eight, something Allie claimed she could judge after a two-minute dance.

Kate wasn't so good at evaluating men's bodies, only that with Jack it was like being pressed against an oak tree, even though his shirt wasn't especially tight. It was almost like he hid it, or took his physicality for granted. Either way, she noted they didn't get bumped once, not by the drunk investment guys or the clumsy car dealer who usually stepped on everyone's toes. Jack made sure they had enough room around them and that in itself was liberating because after spending much of her life outside, she appreciated personal space.

Except she didn't need quite so much space from Jack. In fact, at some point during a slow waltz he'd tucked her head between his shoulder and chest, where his sculpted ridges formed the perfect resting spot. She was actually disappointed when the waltz turned to a line dance. But she stayed up on the floor, not even thinking of bolting.

She even participated in a round of the chicken dance, flapping her arms and genuinely laughing. And though Jack's mouth remained level, she could see his eyes were laughing too. And when he looked deep into her eyes, the corners of his mouth lifted. Not much. Just enough.

The singer took a break to adjust his guitar and Allie paused beside her. "I've never seen the dance floor this busy," she said triumphantly.

Allie's voice lowered and she pressed her mouth closer to Kate's ear. "How did you get him to dance? I tried and he refused. But having a real cowboy up here set a good example for the other men. Except for the woman on crutches, not a single person is sitting. Boss will be so pleased."

She moved away, still grinning, encouraging everyone to stay up on the floor. The dance floor was packed but tonight the crowd of bodies didn't fill Kate with alarm.

In fact, when the music resumed, she moved with abandon, smiling at Allie, smiling at the other dancers, smiling at Jack. Everyone was singing and foot-stomping, and Kate had never had a better time. On many occasions she had to switch partners—cutting in was actively encouraged—but Jack always reclaimed her. She felt amazingly relaxed, even in the confined space, and it was because of him. He moved easily, comfortable in his skin, and his confidence was contagious.

She was shocked when they announced the last song and it was apparent she'd stayed well past midnight. But she couldn't worry about missing her self-imposed curfew because Jack was twirling her around, encouraging her to respond with moves she hadn't thought she knew. Then he dipped her low, holding her for a long moment as the music died.

"Thought you said you couldn't dance," she whispered, looking up at his handsome face and feeling impossibly light.

"Said I don't like to dance. Not that I can't." His gaze locked on her mouth. "But there's still a lot of other things I'd rather be doing with you."

She stared into those golden eyes that were looking at her as if she were the most desirable woman in the world. It was obvious he wanted her, and her heart did a little flip. She was tempted to slide her fingers beneath that shirt and feel his rippled abs. To accompany him back to his room and explore that hard body that no shirt could completely hide.

And have a pink slip handed to her in the morning.

"I work here," she said lightly. "Dancing is all I can do."

"No problem," he said. "I enjoyed the night." But his expression sobered. When his eyes weren't smiling, he definitely appeared less friendly.

"Regrettably," she said, squeezing his hand. Maybe he'd ask for her phone number and they could meet away from the ranch. There was a small town only twenty miles away. "I have this Monday off," she added.

"I'm leaving tomorrow."

"You're only here one night?" she asked, hit by a sense of loss. She'd expected to see him around the ranch. Thought they'd have a chance to get to know each other, maybe even ride together. Most guests stayed a minimum of a week, more often two. She didn't realize it was even possible to have a one-night stay during the prime summer months.

"I'm here on a job," he said, remaining close, so close she could feel the pulsing heat of his body. "But I'd like to see you again. Maybe I'll drop by the dining hall next week, see if you're around."

She tilted her head, confused. What did that mean? He was leaving, then he wasn't? Besides, she didn't even eat in the dining hall.

"What's your phone number?" he asked.

She recited her number, reassured that at least he'd have a way to contact her. "Texting is better though," she said, "in case I'm busy. And the reception is poor except by the pool."

She waited but he didn't add her number to his phone. He just looked at her, his warm fingers still pressed against the small of her back, as if—like her—he was reluctant to move.

"Hey, Kate," someone called.

She glanced toward the voice. Charlie, the fire pit guy and general handyman. He was very nice, often bringing her morning coffee. Normally she enjoyed his banter. But right now she didn't want the interruption.

"Surprised to see you up so late," Charlie said, shooting Jack a quizzical look. "Some of us are going down to the lake for beer and hot dogs. You should join us. And where did you leave those new roasting sticks you carved?"

"They're by the gazebo," she said. "On the side next to the horseshoe pit."

Jack's hand dropped, leaving her feeling oddly bereft. She swung around, but he'd already eased away. "Nice meeting you, Kate," he said softly. "See you next week."

Then he turned and walked away.

Seconds later, a grinning Allie rushed to her side. "Hey, girl. Look what happens when you take my advice. I've never seen you move like that. Thought you were headed for a hookup."

Kate blinked, hiding her bewilderment. She'd thought Jack would linger. Try to prolong the night. But he hadn't asked about the plans for the lake or offered to walk her back to the dorm. He hadn't even pretended to take her phone number. In fact he'd already vanished.

"Where's he from?" Allie asked.

"I don't know," Kate said, realizing that for all their talk, he hadn't shared much. He'd asked plenty about Monty and the staff and hunting, but every time she had a question, he'd tugged her closer to his hard body and frankly that had pushed conversation right out of her head. "I don't know," she repeated. "He's just here for one night."

"What about his friends? Are they staying longer?"

Kate shook her head. "He's here alone."

"No, he's not. There's a group of them. I saw them in the con-ference room. The housekeeper said they're booked in the Look-Off. A bunch of men and women."

Kate's smile froze. The Look-Off was the huge and luxurious chalet high at the back of the meadow, complete with its own he-li-pad. Very exclusive. Very private. Not the type of place a single cowboy would stay. "I thought he was alone," she said. "I must have misunderstood him. Guess that explains why he took off so quick."

"Maybe he came with a girlfriend and they had a little spat. That happens a lot on vacation. And men like to prove they can snap their fingers and other women will come running."

True. And Kate had just proven that. Rather publicly too. She crossed her arms, suddenly cold, feeling as if she'd been stripped on the dance floor and then thrust aside. Still, she couldn't resist checking the dance hall one last time. Just in case Jack had stepped into the washroom and was actually coming back.

"It's just as well," Allie went on. "You know how Boss feels about staff that get too close to the guests. You were great out there. Now that I know you don't need lessons, I'll expect more enthusiastic participation in the future."

Kate gave a tight smile. However, she couldn't imagine dancing like that, feeling like that, with any other man.

"Because tonight," Allie went on, "you had more moves than a stripper on a pole."

Kate recoiled in horror.

"Sorry." Allie gave an apologetic shrug. "I didn't mean to be crass. Guess I was just peeved that when I asked him to dance all he did was scowl. But he liked you right off, even back at the pool. I was surprised you opened up to him so quickly though. Everyone was. You're usually the ice princess."

Kate had felt freer, almost liberated, but surely it hadn't been *that* noticeable. She glanced across the hall but didn't see Jack, only Charlie, lingering by the doorway. He immediately gestured at a case of beer and gave an enthusiastic wave.

"See what I mean?" Allie giggled. "The guys all saw you, and after months of you shutting them down, now they think there's a little hope. There aren't enough single girls to go around. So they're thanking that guy for showing us your wild side."

Kate squeezed her eyes shut in dismay. She certainly didn't thank Jack. It was already exhausting filling in wherever there was the biggest need, from carving classes to cooking, and babysitting to dancing. She didn't have the time or interest for temporary relations or the mind games she'd watched Allie and the others play. She preferred her men up front and honest.

At least tomorrow she'd be escaping to the back country. Where life was simple and straight forward, and far removed from baffling men and superficial flirtations she could never pretend to understand.

CHAPTER FIVE

Kate's alarm chimed way too early, yanking her from a restless sleep punctuated by images of a pine-scented dance hall and a man with smiling gold-flecked eyes. She kicked off the sheets and scrambled from the narrow bed, reluctant to acknowledge that Jack had crept into her dreams. At least it hadn't been the usual nightmare of black holes, broken horses and the sound of a dying boy's last breath.

She grabbed a quick shower, knowing it would be several days before she enjoyed plentiful warm water again, then gathered her clothes and trail essentials. She moved quietly, on auto mode. Staff had single rooms but the dorm walls were paper thin, and she didn't want to wake anyone. All her friends worked long hours and sleep was generally in short supply.

She'd organized most of her pack the previous night, and it only took minutes to finish. Her hair was still damp when she zipped her waterproof bag shut, satisfied that it complied with the typed instructions Monty had provided. She'd removed her bear spray, phone, camera, flares. Brought nothing that could take pictures or record events. No weapons of any sort, except her pocket jackknife, complete with tweezers and toothpick, so tiny it wouldn't even count as a weapon.

Her backpack felt oddly light but that was no big deal. She was no longer a park ranger or a member of an elite search and rescue team. She was a camp attendant. Her biggest challenge would be to lead the mules, keep the girls happy and prepare their meals. Monty would be responsible for guiding the group over the bogs and streams and rough ground. Still, with all the restrictions, she felt unprepared.

She fingered her pack, reminding herself there was nothing to worry about. No cliffs with narrow ten-inch ledges. Just a leisurely ride to the base of the foothills, and she'd even be on a mule. They were more sure-footed than horses, less inclined to spook. But her boots felt glued to the floor, as if they knew she was forgetting something. Trail riding was unpredictable, especially with guests whose experience in the backwoods was limited.

Danny had only been twelve when he died. Sharon hadn't mentioned the ages of these girls but even though Kate was just a camp helper, their safety was still her concern. She certainly intended they ride out in one piece. And to do that, she needed to be prepared, no matter the ridiculous instructions.

She wheeled, yanked open the dresser drawer and scooped up her trusty knife. Then carefully switched it from the snap-on belt clip to her concealed boot sheath. Once it was attached to the inside of her boot, she felt much better. Because essential trail equipment should never be left behind. Besides, she used the big knife around guests during her survival classes. Obviously she could be trusted with it.

Freshly confident, she strode from the dorm, detouring toward the dining hall. The sun hadn't poked over the trees yet but she knew every foot of the beaten path and relished the morning peacefulness. The only sounds were the muted chatter of kitchen workers and the occasional clinking of dishes.

She slipped into the staff room, poured a black coffee then began filling her jacket pockets with granola bars.

The cook shuffled over, her eyes slightly puffy. "You won't need those," she said. "They took enough food to last normal folk a month. And you're not allowed to take anything except what was approved. It all has to be safe for celiacs."

Kate quickly put the bars back on the table. So the guest rider wasn't just gluten intolerant. Celiac meant a higher level of care was required as food could be tainted merely by proximity to gluten in the packs. Still, if everything that was brought in was gluten free, that made her job easier. It was liberating for anyone suffering from food intolerances if they didn't have to worry about cross contamination. It was never fun to have an intestinal episode. But on the trail—far from the comforts of a bed and bathroom—it was exponentially worse.

"That's great to know," she said cheerfully. "Can you tell me which bars were approved?"

"Just those ones." The cook jabbed her thumb at some protein bars with a circular GF logo on the purple wrapper. "And I've been cooking for guests for more than two decades. Can't believe they wouldn't let me deliver the food. We had to get up extra early and unlock the storeroom."

"What do you mean?" Kate asked, busy replacing her granola bars with the gluten-free ones. Having food in her pockets satisfied her ingrained need to be self-sufficient. Riding at the back with the slower mules meant she'd have an opportunity to nibble on a bar whenever she wanted a snack.

The cook gave a disapproving sniff. "Those men came by half an hour ago. Wouldn't let food leave the storeroom without supervision. Very insistent. Crazy if you ask me. Even Monty was surprised."

"Monty was here? You mean the food's already gone?" Kate froze, then turned and bolted toward the door. She wanted to be the first at the barn, liked to have a relaxing moment to greet each horse, pull in a breath and just enjoy the solitude. A chance to prepare the animals before dealing with the people. And Monty had admitted he was the same way. But he was already there, alone with the guests. He must be frazzled.

"Don't forget your coffee," the cook said.

"You drink it for me," Kate called over her shoulder. No way did she want to wander up with a coffee in hand, looking like a spectator unprepared to work. Monty's wranglers would have assembled the trail equipment, but it was risky to pack in with a load she hadn't personally checked. It was important to have equal weight on both sides of the animal and not to hurry the knots. An uneven or slipping pack could cause delays on the trail or blister a mule's back or even worse, cause a wreck...

Stop it, she told herself, as she sprinted toward the barn.

She slowed before rounding the corner, calling out a soft hello so as not to startle the animals. They were all tied to the hitching post: six horses, three mules. The palomino was fidgeting, his white mane and tail gleaming beneath the exterior barn lights. None of the horses had been saddled and the mules' backs were also bare.

She pulled in a relieved breath, glad she wasn't late. There was still time to greet the mules, run a brush over their backs and pick out their feet. Monty would insist the guests groom their own horses but she preferred to double check. Riders often complained about saddle sores, but for the animal it was much more agonizing. And losing the services of a horse or mule, deep in the isolated back country was always disastrous.

"Stop right there," a craggy-faced man snapped as he swooped from the shadows. "You must be the replacement."

"Yes, that's right. I'm Kate," she said, surprised by his aggressiveness. "In for Donna."

"Yeah, I know. The mule girl." He glanced down at his sheet, silent for a moment. When he spoke again, his voice was just as curt, his posture even more rigid. "Set your bag on the table. Unzip it."

"Pardon?" Her arms tightened around her pack. "These are my personal things. Less than ten pounds." Exactly nine and a half pounds. And this man's attitude rankled. *The mule girl?* Besides, he was out of line. No guest had the right to search her bag.

"I need to see what's in there." The man stepped closer, his gaze raking over her body, rather rude in its appraisal. "I don't care about the weight."

"Well, we should care about the weight," she said, trying to be diplomatic. "The animals aren't machines."

He just glowered. She gripped the pack tighter, determined not to raise it over her breasts, or to step back. The man was probably in his late thirties, clearly accustomed to snapping orders and using his size to intimidate. His boots and jeans appeared brand new. He looked like he'd been in good shape once, but she noted how his gut sagged over his belt, and how he kept trying to suck it in. A bully who cared about how he looked. Interesting.

"And some guests are heavier than what the animals are used to," she added, holding his stare with a pointed one of her own.

"Raise your arms," he said, and now there was a new edge to his voice, as if he wasn't used to being challenged. "I need to check you. All over."

"I've got this, Kessler," a familiar voice said.

She blinked in shock as Jack stepped in front of her. "Place your bag on the table, ma'am," he said, his voice every bit as authoritative, his stance no less menacing. But it was his eyes that showed the biggest change from last night. They were totally glacial.

She stared, unmoving. Despite the coolness of the air, heat warmed her face. Less than five hours earlier she'd danced with this man, had been wrapped in those strong arms, charmed by his slow smile. Admittedly, she'd even hoped to see him again. She'd accepted that it had been a pleasant but meaningless flirtation—at least on his part—but she couldn't accept that he would pretend not to know her. That his face could look like carved granite, with eyes so suspicious.

And that these two men intended to rifle through her underwear.

"I don't understand." Her gaze shot past them, searching for Monty, for Sharon, for anyone familiar.

"You don't need to understand," the man named Kessler growled. "Come on. We need to hurry this up. We have people to keep safe. And you still have a non-disclosure agreement to sign."

"This way, please," Jack said.

It was the word "please" that prompted her to walk woodenly to the table and lower her backpack.

"Unzip it," Jack ordered, his cool eyes on her face.

She fumbled to unzip her bag, then watched as his hands slid expertly and impersonally over her spare socks, her jeans, her panties. He even opened her waterproof box of matches, checked her toothpaste and gave her fire starter a suspicious sniff.

"What is this all about?" she asked, hiding her hurt.

"It's protocol," he said.

"Protocol? For what?"

"Raise your arms, please."

She shook her head in disbelief. This was not protocol. She'd been on countless rides and ranch events with wealthy and important guests. Some had even arrived on their own helicopters. Never had this happened. "You're going to frisk me now?" she asked.

"Only if you choose to go on the trail ride." Jack's voice sounded mechanical, every bit of emotion banked. "You may elect to walk away, thereby avoiding the search."

"And thereby get fired," she said, looking over her shoulder again, desperate to spot a familiar face.

"Maybe." Jack spoke a little too agreeably. "Your employer agreed to all our privacy and security conditions. But you have the option to request that another agent search you."

"Is there anyone else but him," she asked, glancing at the sullen Kessler.

"No," Jack said.

"You do it then." She pulled in a fortifying breath.

Jack's hands were quick but highly efficient. He found her tiny red pocket knife in less than five seconds. "I have to take this jackknife," he said. "You'll be provided with utensils at camp."

"Is everything all right here?" Sharon Barrett's exasperated voice sounded from the doorway of the barn. "Monty and Kate are my most trusted employees. Is this really necessary?"

Kate shot her boss a grateful look. She appreciated being labeled as one of the ranch's most trusted employees, even though she knew it wasn't true. She was a relatively new hire, still fighting for steady work.

Jack didn't seem to give Sharon Barrett's words much credence either. "Yes, it's necessary, ma'am," he said, busy pulling granola bars from Kate's pockets.

He studied the ingredient list then carefully scrutinized each end, checking that the seal was intact. "You can keep these," he said, after a moment.

"I have to insist my staff, not yours, pack the mules." Sharon had stepped from the barn and was addressing Kessler. "That's *our* protocol."

"No," Kessler said. "We'll do it."

"It's okay," Jack said, his attention momentarily shifting toward Kessler. "That's a valid request. I'll oversee them."

Kate peeked at Jack. So he was some sort of bodyguard. His hair *was* close cropped beneath that cowboy hat. Probably she should have picked up on the haircut, as well as his sheer confidence. Certainly he'd swung her around the dance floor like he owned the building, as if everyone should give them room. When she'd met him by the pool, she'd been hit by a moment of breathlessness, a sense of danger. And Allie had thought him aloof.

But he'd given no indication he was anything but a guest, even when she asked how long he was staying. It was clear he'd purposely duped them. And most especially her. She was the one who'd been dancing with him all night, clinging to those muscled shoulders. And now he was pretending they'd never met. While she'd been obsessing over him, enough that he'd crept into her dreams.

She averted her eyes when he resumed the body search, staring stoically over the table, hoping the barn lights didn't spotlight her flaming cheeks. But when he crouched down, his face close to the zipper of her jeans, it was impossible to ignore her rush of awareness. And when his thumbs brushed the juncture of her thighs, she gave an involuntary flinch, resenting the violation, resenting that she'd actually considered sleeping with this man. And that his impersonal touch still made her pulse kick.

He must have done this a lot. Obviously it wasn't his first search. His stony eyes probably made even the most hardened criminal throw up their hands in surrender. What would he do when he found the big knife in her boot? Maybe she should confess before it was discovered.

But she didn't like to imagine his displeasure. Or Kessler's. And her boss was standing only fifteen feet away. Sharon would be annoyed that her rules hadn't been followed. Kate might never be entrusted with any more trail rides, forever stuck in the kitchen and dance hall. Or worse, let go.

So she stood stock still, pretending to be composed while she agonized about what to do, just praying he wouldn't find her boot knife.

Jack's hands moved lower, skimming now over the sensitive spot at the back of her knees. Her skin itched; her muscles tightening beneath her jeans. It was hard not to wiggle, harder still to accept that her traitorous body was responding to his touch.

His hands slowed, lingered, feeling almost like a caress. Was it her imagination? Or perhaps he wasn't quite as cool as he pretended.

"Not even dinner before groping, Jack?" she whispered, trying to distract him. She made sure to lower her voice though. Because even though she resented this man, she didn't want to get him into any trouble with Kessler. And for some reason, Jack wanted to pretend they'd never met.

Jack's head lifted, a hint of emotion flaring in his eyes. He dropped his hands and straightened.

"We're finished here," he announced. "You're free to join Monty in the clearance area."

"The clearance area?" She gave an exaggerated sigh, concealing her relief. "You mean the barn?"

"Exactly," he said, and now there was definite amusement coloring those eyes. "The washroom in the barn is also cleared, should you wish to use it."

She nodded, repacking her bedroll and zipping her bag, conscious of her big knife burning a hole in her boot. And she hadn't escaped yet. She could still feel his watchful eyes. Seconds later though, her skin stopped tingling and she realized he was gone. It was as if both he and Kessler had faded into the dark, and only her boss remained.

"Sorry about that," Sharon said, shaking her head in apology. "I wasn't allowed to reveal any details. But it's over now. Monty is in charge once you hit the trail, except in matters of security. Just be patient with them. Make it a fun ride."

"Of course," Kate said. "I assume those are the bodyguards. But who are we taking? A pop star? A paranoid actress?"

"No, just two seventeen-year-old girls." Sharon gave a strained smile, one that looked torn between triumph and concern. "But one of them is the President's daughter."

CHAPTER SIX

Kate took another curious peek at the two girls. She'd seen pictures of Courtney, looking extremely polished, posing beside her father in front of the White House. But close up, the President's daughter seemed like any other teenager. At least she appeared genuinely excited about riding in to see the wild mustangs. Her friend, Tyra, wasn't quite as enthused. In fact, the last twenty minutes the girl had been sitting on her horse, doing nothing but complain.

"My stirrups are *still* too long," Tyra whined. "It's impossible for me to ride like this."

"I'll shorten them some more," Kate said, noting Monty's irritated expression. The three Secret Service men—Kessler, Jack and a stocky man named Logan—were more difficult to read. They were probably accustomed to constant demands, but surely they must be impatient as well.

It had been hours since Kate's bag had been searched. The horses had been saddled before dawn. Even so, the sun was far over the horizon when the girls finally arrived, giggling and unapologetic about their tardiness.

Kate stepped back up to the left shoulder of Tyra's horse. "A western saddle is going to feel different than riding English. But you'll appreciate the longer stirrups by the end of the day."

"I know what I'm doing," Tyra snapped. "I'm an experienced rider. So shorten them another inch. I didn't realize these horses would be so small." She wrinkled her nose, not even deigning to look down at Kate.

Kate kept a diplomatic smile. In fact, Slider, the palomino gelding Tyra rode, was one of the ranch's tallest horses, almost sixteen hands high. She'd overheard the girls talking about riding warmblood hunters over fences in Washington, and those sport horses were huge. And while most horse lovers naturally had a breed preference, by the end of the day guests were usually impressed with their mounts, grateful for the ranch horses' ability to carry them safely and willingly over challenging terrain.

"Smaller quarter horse types are handier on the trail," Kate said.

But Tyra didn't answer. Didn't seem to even be listening. She hadn't spoken directly to anyone but Courtney, not even to Sharon Barrett who was holding the mules and anxious to see them off. Usually obnoxious riders were asked to tone it down, or politely pointed toward alternate activities. But this was a different situation.

Monty was making no effort to hide his impatience, mounting and dismounting twice, and Kessler kept scowling at the dining hall where early rising guests were beginning to appear. It wouldn't be long before someone wandered down to the paddocks, potentially recognizing Courtney and sparking a media frenzy.

Kate tried to hurry. But Tyra's leg was clamped against Slider's ribs, making it impossible to reach underneath to adjust the stirrup. And the horse was fidgety, unaccustomed to the leg pressure or the unusual delay. Kate edged Tyra's boot a little further toward Slider's shoulder, then used both hands to work the thick leather from the buckle. This was the fifth time she'd adjusted

Tyra's stirrups—on three different saddles—and if the goal was to ride out before sunup they'd already blown it.

"Can't you hurry it up?" Kessler snapped. "The plan was for no one to see her."

"This saddle is worse than the second one," Tyra announced, looking at Courtney. "Don't you think I should switch again? We both know how awful it is to ride in cheap tack. Anyway I like the color of the first saddle better."

Courtney shrugged with indecision. She hadn't been nearly as hard to please, but the girls had already been at the barn an hour and it was obvious she deferred to her more vocal friend. Of the two, it was clear Tyra needed more coddling.

Kate felt Jack's presence seconds before he leaned over her shoulder. He grabbed the stirrup, his fingers brushing her hand. He jammed the buckle in, not even pretending to adjust the length.

"All set," he said, his voice implacable. "You're ready to ride now."

Tyra looked at him, then did a double take. It was as if she'd never seen the bodyguard before, although Kate couldn't understand how she hadn't noticed a man like Jack.

"Does it really look okay?" Tyra asked, but her pink cheeks made Kate realize the girl wasn't quite as confident as she pretended.

Jack nodded, the corners of his mouth actually lifting in a gorgeous smile. "Yes, that saddle is perfect. And the light color matches your horse's mane, along with your hair."

It was the same charm Kate had experienced last night, the same smile Jack had bestowed upon her—the one she thought so special. Obviously this man could turn it on and off at will.

Clearly he wasn't just a fake, he was color blind as well. Slider was a palomino with a white mane and tail. While Tyra was most definitely a brunette, with hair almost as dark as Kate's.

Kate turned and strode toward the mules. Tyra remained silent, apparently flattered by Jack's attention, not even questioning why he hadn't adjusted her stirrups. There was no more talk about her cheap saddle or the too-small horse. In fact, Tyra quietly fell into line beside Courtney, still darting peeks at Jack.

"Let's go," Monty called, guiding Banjo toward the trees.

Kate took the reins from Sharon, pausing to give her patient mule an apologetic pat. "Thanks for holding the mules so long," she said, placing her foot in Belle's stirrup and swinging her leg high to avoid hitting the bulky saddle bags.

"I wanted to see her off," Sharon said, her gaze following the riders who were already forty feet away. "I still can't believe someone from the First Family is riding here."

She shook her head and turned back to Kate. "Please help Monty as much as you can. Tyra might be difficult but the girls need to have a good time. This visit will put the ranch on an entirely new level. No matter their behavior, I know I can trust you to take care of them in a responsible and discreet way."

Kate fought a spike of discomfort. She definitely would be discreet but she also lacked any real authority. What if the girls were totally wild? Drugs weren't allowed on the trail, but these two were seventeen. Judging by the way they'd been giggling when they arrived, this ride represented freedom, an adventure far removed from the public eye. And from their friends, their teachers, their parents.

"Were the girls' bags checked as well?" Kate asked. "You know, for...drugs or alcohol?"

"Oh, I've been assured there won't be a problem like that." Sharon waved her hand in dismissal. "But you know how impatient Monty can be with frivolous demands. You're more diplomatic, and people respect you. Just keep them happy."

"Okay," Kate promised, giving Belle's neck another pat. The three mules had been standing for over an hour, fully packed and loaded. That was irritating and unnecessary. But Sharon owned these animals, not her, and if her boss didn't mind, she shouldn't either.

"Once we're away from the ranch," Kate said, "they can't get into much trouble. I'm sure Tyra will relax. And it must be hard, dealing with that many hovering agents."

"They've set up a command centre in the Look-Off," Sharon Barrett said wryly. "So we have six more agents there. I assured them no one else at the ranch would even know Courtney's identity. You and Monty were very composed through the search and everything. Sorry I had to keep everyone in the dark. That was one of their stipulations. You better leave now," she said, stepping back, "or you and the mules will never catch up."

Kate turned the ever-patient Belle toward the receding line of riders. She tugged on Gus's lead rope, checking that the two pack mules were following. Gus was directly behind Belle and the third mule, Bubba, was tied to Gus's tail with a breakaway knot. Both pack mules were moving but they didn't look happy about leaving. They stretched their necks out, keeping their steps as slow and unhurried as possible.

But that was all right. Staying a careful distance behind the string of riders was her preference anyway. She wouldn't have to make conversation, wouldn't have to hide her growing aversion to Kessler, and best of all she wouldn't have to see Jack. And be constantly reminded that he'd charmed her every bit as easily as he had a seventeen-year-old girl.

CHAPTER SEVEN

Kate relaxed in the saddle, savoring the fresh forest breeze. They'd only been on the trail for half an hour but already she felt more at peace, any lingering worries about misbehaving children, vulnerable animals and job security melting away. Riding at the back of the line also gave a delightful amount of privacy, something she rarely experienced at the ranch. Horses were always in more of a hurry than her mules, so sometimes she was so far back she lost sight of the other riders.

On those occasions, Belle's ears shot forward and the mule quickened her walk, reluctant to lose sight of her equine companions. Earlier she'd tried to trot to catch up, but Kate had quickly checked her. The two mules following Belle were heavily loaded and there was no sense banging the packs around and possibly chafing their backs. Besides, the three mules had each other for company, and Kate knew she'd have plenty of time to talk to the girls in camp.

The order of the ride was now established. Monty led the way on Banjo, followed by Courtney and Tyra, and then the three protective men. Earlier Kessler had ridden second in line. But Courtney had asked to ride closer to the front where there was a better chance of spotting wildlife. The girls' excited voices every time they flushed an animal—deer, rabbits and most recently, a noisy partridge—made Kate smile, and it was a relief to be around guests who didn't want to kill everything that moved.

She guided Belle around a protruding branch on the trail, checking over her shoulder to make sure the pack mules skirted the obstacle. It was impressive how fast they learned the size of their loads and the necessary clearance needed to avoid scraping. Mules were the perfect pack animal, strong and smart about not catching their packs or getting hung up on a tree branch. They weren't as flighty as horses either and didn't have such a tendency to bolt when scared. Belle certainly wouldn't shy at a slipping saddle and tumble off a cliff.

Kate stiffened, ever so slightly, but it was enough that Belle took it as a signal to trot. The two mules behind her immediately followed suit, their packs thumping with the increased speed. Kate let Belle trot for a moment, by way of an apology, sorry that she'd given her mount such mixed signals. She was usually a quiet rider...or at least she used to be.

Ahead of her, Jack turned his horse and waited on the trail. "Everything okay back there?"

"Yes," she called, hoping he'd turn and ride on.

He didn't. He kept his horse stopped in the middle of the trail, waiting for her to catch up.

"Mules can be hard to handle," he said, as she approached. His gaze flickered over the pack train and then back to her face. "But you look like a pro."

"All the ranch animals are well trained," she said.

"Yeah, everyone seems happy with their horses. And their saddles." His mouth didn't smile but something resembling mischief sparked in his eyes, making him look more like the man she'd been so entranced with last night. And completely removed from the granite-faced bodyguard who'd frisked her this morning.

He was definitely a good actor, an ability he'd no doubt honed with his job. But she wasn't fooled by this new attentiveness. They both knew it wasn't her well-being he was checking. It was the mules. Not only did they carry all the food, but the agents had also loaded their communication equipment into the panniers, apparently intending to make regular status reports.

"I appreciate you checking," Kate said, her voice cool. "But your food and supplies are quite safe. And you don't have to worry. I won't let Kessler know we met last night."

Jack turned silent. However his reins tightened and it was apparent he was holding his horse back, forcing Dusty to walk alongside Belle.

"I wasn't sure how to play it," he said. "That was my mistake. I thought you worked in the kitchen."

"I help out there sometimes. What does it matter?"

He didn't speak, and she glanced sideways again. His face was stiff, his expression almost apologetic. And she remembered how his questions had centered on Monty, the wranglers, and any new guests.

"Oh," she said, as understanding dawned. "You thought I'd know all the gossip. You wanted to find out if the ranch was safe. That's why you...chatted me up."

She tried not to wince. They both knew he'd done much more than chat her up. And that he had been wildly successful. According to Allie, it had been obvious to everyone in the dance hall that she'd been his for the taking. But she'd never been drawn so quickly to someone before, and by the way Jack had acted, she assumed he was similarly attracted. She'd been mistaken.

Allie thought Kate was still wary of men after how things had ended with her ex. But that wasn't true. Because another hour with Jack and she would have been happy—no, eager—to go home with him. And no doubt he knew it.

She pinned her gaze on the trail ahead, hating how her face felt impossibly hot, revealing her embarrassment.

"I had to make sure the ranch was safe," Jack said. "I was part of the site survey." His voice was level, certainly not apologetic. But his horse was prancing so maybe his body had tightened. Perhaps he felt a tiny bit of guilt. However, that didn't make her feel better. She rarely let anyone get too close and could count her sexual partners on one hand. For her to be smitten so quickly wasn't normal.

Luckily he didn't know that. Maybe he thought she danced like that with everyone.

"I had to ask questions," he went on. "I was just doing my job."

She'd been his job. She hid her ache behind a polite but dismissive smile, the kind she'd perfected on over-friendly guests.

"No problem," she said. "So was I."

⊷◉⊶

THE MULES' HOOF BEATS sounded behind Jack, their steady plodding occasionally punctuated by the thump of a pack. A few times he stole a glance back. Somehow Kate managed to stay out of sight, always rounding the corner just as his horse, Dusty, turned the next twisting bend. She was certainly out of talking range, and it was clear she intended to remain that way.

His attempt at conversation had lasted less than three minutes. But she was the lucky one, avoiding the mindless chitchat up front. He wished *he* had an excuse to ride in the back. Even her silence was more appealing than talking to agents Kessler and Logan. But it was clear she didn't welcome his company. She hadn't even asked any questions: about Courtney, or their security precautions, or what it was like to work for the First Family. And in his experience, women tended to harp on that stuff.

"I know you love this backwoods shit," Kessler said, continuing his litany of complaints, "but my ass is damn sore."

Jack made another non-committal grunt, continuing his careful scan of the trail and paying close attention to his horse's ears. Even though the Secret Service had closed off this section of the trail, his caution was ingrained, and his horse was an excellent early warning tool. Twice his mount had alerted him to the presence of deer long before they burst out in front of the excited girls.

"Why do girls like horses so much?" Kessler continued. "*She* could have taken a helicopter, instead of riding these long miles. And then we wouldn't have to sleep in a damn tent."

Jack's mouth tightened. It was hard to hear anything moving in the underbrush with Kessler bitching beside him, and if Dusty hadn't pricked his ears, Jack would have missed the weasel darting across the path.

"Guess she wants to see things like that," Jack said.

"Like what?" Kessler twisted in the saddle, his hand shooting toward the holster beneath his shirt. "Oh, just some animal." He visibly relaxed. "We'll have to tell Monty to make a stop soon. In case she wants a break."

It didn't look as if either Courtney or Tyra needed a break. They both sat their horses easily, their heads swiveling as they took in the sights. Jack didn't particularly like the nervous energy of the tall palomino but Tyra didn't appear to mind, and the Mustang River trail was level and undemanding. Both girls chattered non-stop, their comments mixed with giggles and questions for Monty. And though the quiet guide always answered in measured words, Logan was quick to chime in. Unlike Kate, the agent was obviously the type who needed to feel important.

"First check-in isn't for another fifty minutes. And Petal's having fun," Jack said, careful to use Courtney's code name. "She's relaxed, enjoying the ride."

"Yeah." Kessler glanced longingly at the bushes. "Guess I shouldn't have guzzled so much coffee."

Jack's mouth twitched. Kessler might be uncomfortable but he would never stop his horse and take a leak. Would never let Courtney move more than twenty yards away. Jack had worked with the Secret Service before and they were all well trained, almost over-zealous in their duties. Their site investigation and background checks were meticulous. Except that Jack hadn't been provided with Kate's name.

"I was told our guides would be Monty and Donna James. Not Kate." Jack glanced over his shoulder to where a mule's brown nose was just rounding the bend. It took an excellent rider to maintain that precise distance without any obvious commands. And while mules were safe and steady, they weren't generally as responsive as horses. With all the quality ranch horses available, it was odd that a good rider like Kate would prefer a mule. Actually there was a lot about her he found intriguing. And she was the one person in the group that he knew very little about.

"The girls needed a woman," Kessler said, clearing his throat. "For female issues. But Donna James was hurt falling off a horse and couldn't go. So the ranch recommended Kate as a last-minute replacement."

"But you checked her out?"

Kessler scowled as if the question was a personal affront to the Secret Service. "Of course," he said. "We know what we're doing. Remember, you're not part of the official detail. You're on a need-to-know basis."

Jack considered reminding the man that he'd been hired directly by the President. But that was already a sensitive issue. The Secret Service was a closed rank, and by necessity paranoid, following complex rules and guidelines only they understood. They hadn't wanted an outside contractor. The agents were resentful. But though Jack wasn't wearing a Secret Service pin he intended to keep Courtney safe, even if it went contrary to Kessler's precious protocols.

"Correct," Jack said, hardening his voice. "I am on a need-to-know basis. And I need to know how thoroughly you checked out Kate."

"We did the regular background check," Kessler muttered. "Then went deep."

"Deep" meant Kessler knew everything about her, including how old Kate had been when she cut her first tooth as well as the size and color of each item in her underwear drawer. Obviously she'd passed with flying colors or she wouldn't be on this ride.

"I just wonder why you gave her such a hard time this morning," Jack said, his tone changing. Antagonizing the agents wouldn't help. But it didn't make sense. Kessler had been much more polite with Monty, even exchanging a comment about the chilly morning before asking to check his pack.

Yet the man had been an asshole with Kate. It had been impossible to stand back and let Kessler rough ride her. He assumed

Kessler would have been even more aggressive if he knew Jack had spent time with her in the dance hall.

"It was just a typical search," Kessler muttered.

Jack just stared, letting the man know he needed an answer. If it was an agency other than the Secret Service, he'd have suspected Kessler was taking advantage of the opportunity to frisk a beautiful woman, but he'd worked with the Service before and the agents had always been professional.

"I just wanted to be prudent," Kessler said. "Make sure she didn't have any contraband."

"You worried about drugs? Alcohol?" That made sense. Courtney was impressionable. It was always a dilemma when underage members of the First Family indulged. Agents didn't want to be tattle tales, but they could be demoted or fired if they condoned illegal behavior. Kate had only been drinking water last night. And those beautiful eyes had been clear and candid. Certainly not the type to hole up in a teenagers' tent and think it cute to sneak them a joint.

"Kate may have done some stuff in the past," Jack said, watching Kessler's reaction. "Everyone has. But I talked to her last night. She doesn't appear the type to encourage wild behavior."

Tyra would be more likely to have something tucked in her bag. And Jack didn't usually stick his neck out, protecting people he hadn't personally vetted. But in a way he had checked out Kate. He hadn't planned to spend the entire evening with her. Certainly he hadn't intended to hit on her. But the delightful curve of that smiling mouth, the way her body felt pressed against his, even the smell of her skin...

She'd been hard to ignore. And once he'd pulled out all the information he needed about Monty, he'd turned off work mode and simply enjoyed her company.

He liked her. The way she listened, how everything she said was worthwhile, and the way her intelligent eyes flashed with passion. And he sure as hell liked the way she handled those mules.

"She obviously is good with animals," Jack said. "You people should appreciate that." His hands tightened around the reins because it still annoyed him the way Kessler had treated Kate. And he was finding that difficult to let go. "I still can't figure out why you gave her such a hard time?"

"She's undoubtedly brave," Kessler said, almost grudgingly. "Just not my kind of woman. Let's leave it at that."

Jack hadn't really expected to pull much from the man. Anything the Secret Service had found was confidential. Rightly so, if it wasn't related to this particular job. But for some reason Kessler was uncomfortable with Kate. And that made Jack even more curious about a woman he found so appealing.

CHAPTER EIGHT

Belle's stride quickened, not much, but enough to alert Kate they were approaching a spot the mule remembered with pleasure. Kate didn't know this area nearly as well as Monty but they'd been following the Mustang River for at least a mile so the lunch stop was probably close.

Five minutes later the trail widened into a vibrant meadow colored by lilies, buttercups and Indian paintbrush. To the left, lay a fallen stump that previous riders had dragged onto the knoll to serve as a rough table.

Monty had already dismounted and ground-tied his horse. "I'll look after the mules," he said, hurrying out to meet Kate. "Give you a break."

"That's okay," she said, stepping down from Belle's back.

"Please," he whispered. "All this talking is driving me nuts."

She laughed, completely understanding his plea. She'd been free to enjoy the ride, remaining some distance back, while all the entertaining had fallen to Monty. The guide was usually taciturn—and guests accepted that as it met their stereotype of the gruff cowboy. But it was impossible to brush off the President's daughter, no matter how mundane her questions. Monty needed time to recharge, and Kate was buoyant, refreshed and well able to take over the task.

Still smiling, she passed him the lead rope.

"Thanks, Kate." Monty's voice lowered. "And by the way I'm sorry about this morning. They took my boot knife. Shouldn't have tried to bring it. But I never expected a search like that."

"No problem," she said.

"They're sure a suspicious bunch." His gaze cut to the horses who were pulling at their bits, wondering why their riders didn't dismount and give them a chance to eat. "Thoughtless with their animals too," he added. "Looks like they intend to use their horses as chairs."

"It's okay," Kate said. "They just don't understand. They probably never rode this long before."

She turned and walked over to the girls.

"You can dismount now," she said, smiling up at them. "And give your horses a rest. Are you enjoying the ride?"

"Loving it." Courtney leaned forward and patted her horse's black-and-white neck. "Oreo didn't shy once. And Monty said he's great at crossing deep water too. I've never ridden a paint horse before. Glad I'm getting this chance."

"What about you, Tyra?" Kate turned, determined to include the second girl as much as possible. "How are you getting along with your horse?"

"He's okay, I guess. But I still hate these long stirrups." She dismounted and shoved her reins into Kate's hand. "I'm starving. When's lunch?"

"We'll eat after we unsaddle the horses," Kate said. "They've been working harder than any of us."

"But I want to stretch my legs," Courtney said. "Can you look after my horse too?"

Kate hesitated. Generally riders looked after their own horses, under supervision. If they didn't know the basics they quickly learned. But on this ride, etiquette was obviously different. Probably both these girls were used to having a groom or two for assistance. She certainly couldn't force them to look after their own animals if they didn't want to.

The trail horses wore halters beneath their bridles so it was a simple matter to slip the bits from their mouths. But removing the saddles while keeping the horses apart was a trickier matter, especially if none of the five guests planned to help. And Tyra's palomino was low horse on the totem pole, afraid of the other geldings. Slider wouldn't want to stand too close. If he did, the bossier horses would take it as a challenge to their authority. And it would be hugely inconvenient if a horse was kicked and left too lame to be ridden. Painful for the horse as well.

"I'll unsaddle your horse over here, Tyra," Kate said, making a quick decision and leading the palomino further into the meadow. "And I'll be right back to help you, Courtney."

"I'll help her," Jack said.

He dismounted, keeping his horse well back from Oreo, then showed Courtney how to slip off the western headstall and hang the bridle over her saddle horn.

The other two agents were off their horses as well, but made no move to untack. They were busy scanning the sides of the meadow, their expressions unreadable behind dark sunglasses. It seemed as though Kessler and Logan were the actual bodyguards while Jack was here to help the girls as required.

Kate had to admit he was a good hand with a horse. He had three animals unsaddled and grazing peacefully by the time she returned for Kessler's horse.

"Are any of the horses likely to run home?" Jack asked, his gaze flickering over the hobbles tied to Monty's saddle.

"Not while they're hungry." She paused, still resenting this man and how he'd played her for a fool last night. But he had been a big help too, demonstrating to the girls how to care for their horses instead of doing it for them. Letting them know it was their job, something she and Monty didn't feel they had the authority to do. Besides, trail rides were safer and more fun if people weren't squabbling. "Thanks for the help," she said. "It's appreciated. I'll get the saddle bags now."

"How about I grab the food," Jack said, glancing over her head, "and you help the girls?"

She turned, following his gaze. Courtney and Tyra were staring at the trees, shuffling their feet and looking confused, as well as anxious.

"Right," Kate said, realizing they were searching for a bathroom. Or the closest substitute.

"Just ignore Kessler and Logan," Jack said, his voice lowering. "They'll follow you into the woods, but they won't come too close. And they'll be looking outward."

Kate's eyes widened. There were no other humans within miles. Yet Courtney wasn't permitted to duck behind a tree on her own? That would be like living in a glass castle. And being watched like that would be horrible.

"Yeah," Jack said, his astute eyes on her face. "Tough way to live, especially when she didn't choose it herself. She doesn't have much space." His face was expressionless, as if he knew better than to show criticism, but the compassion in his voice was unmistakable.

"We'll have to make sure she has a really good time," Kate said, looking at Courtney with ever-increasing empathy.

"Yes, and a safe one."

She glanced sharply at Jack. Was that a warning? But there wasn't anyone around who could hurt the girl. The ranch wasn't allowing any other guests to ride in this area and nobody knew Courtney was here. No one was even aware of her destination. Even if whispers somehow leaked that she was riding in to see the wild horses, there were several herds. And the spot where they were headed was at the western tip, where access was restricted by the mountains.

"Yes," Kate said lightly. "A safe and fun trip. That's what I'm here for."

She joined the girls, then guided them into the woods, amused by the crunching of branches as the trailing agents tried to be quiet. They failed miserably. Courtney and Tyra didn't seem to notice the men's presence, other than seeming rather subdued.

However, once they returned from their bathroom break and were back in the sunlit meadow, everyone seemed more relaxed.

Kate unpacked the food, efficiently setting out sliced meat, cheese, pickles and freshly made buns and pita bread. The girls ate quickly, not praising the meal but not complaining either. They took a last drink of water then turned their attention to the colorful meadow.

"Can you tell me the names of those flowers?" Courtney asked Kate. "I've never seen them before."

"Be glad to," Kate said, following Courtney and Tyra into the meadow, delighted to share her knowledge. This was much better than entertaining children who'd been sent to her classes under protest. And Courtney said she was taking Environmental Science in the fall so was particularly interested.

"Those are Indian paintbrush and golden banner," Kate said. "And this pink and lavender one is a Shooting Star. That's its name because there's no place for bees to land so they cling to the cone and flap their wings. That makes the pollen shoot out in a shower."

Courtney listened avidly while Kate spoke about the local flora. But Tyra's interest faded quickly. She was far more enthusiastic about picking flowers and trying to stick them in her hair. Eventually she coaxed Courtney into weaving daisies in Slider's long mane. However, they were laughing and entertaining themselves, so Kate hurried back to clean up the food area, aware Monty would be impatient to leave.

Other than her, Logan was the only person who hadn't had time to eat. He seemed to be waiting for her to make it, so she grabbed a bun and assembled a sandwich.

"All gluten free, right?" the agent asked, accepting the sandwich and then adding an extra slice of meat and cheese to his already bulging bun. "Even the sandwich bread?"

"Yes, everything we brought is safe," Kate said. "Including the desserts. There's no sandwich bread. It doesn't pack well. But those buns are gluten free, along with the pita bread."

"Good," Logan said, giving an approving nod. "That makes it easier."

Other than quick introductions at dawn, she'd barely spoken to this particular agent. He hadn't been present during the morning search but had arrived later with the girls. And he rode his horse up front, directly behind Courtney and Tyra.

He was much friendlier than Kessler and both girls seemed comfortable with him. He didn't share Kessler's aggressive air or Jack's grim wariness. Short and stocky, he seemed the type who appreciated good food, bringing to mind an amiable Lab dog.

Still, there was no overlooking the bulky gun holster beneath his shirt, or the reason he was on this trip.

"I didn't realize there'd be so many trails," Logan said, slowing his chewing now that he wasn't quite so hungry. He gave Kate a grin that split his round face. "Hope we're taking an easy route. Hate to admit it but I'm already stiff."

She smiled back and pointed at the wooded path beyond the grazing mules. "I imagine we'll be taking that trail. It's a gentle climb, no steep hills."

"Good," he said, appraising the trail. "At least I'm a better rider than Kessler. He won't like anything steep. I gather you don't either, considering your experience in the mountains last year. And I understand you only ride mules?"

He took another bite of his sandwich, his gaze fixed on the girls who'd succeeded in braiding Slider's mane with bright flowers and were now taking pictures of their handiwork. Luckily Logan was more interested in monitoring the girls than Kate. Or he might have noticed the flush that warmed her cheeks.

She concentrated on rewrapping the sliced ham. It was obvious the agents knew everything about her. But Danny's death left a raw bruise on her heart, and she didn't like talking about the accident, not even with her therapist. She certainly didn't intend to talk about it with a government agent, no matter how well-meaning. But Logan glanced back, obviously expecting a reply.

"I do prefer mules," she said. "I trust them. They're more sensible."

"A spirited horse can be scary," Logan said. "Especially when they cause a wreck like the one you had to clean up. But accidents happen. I saw a rider killed while jumping. Turned me off horses for a while. It's understandable. But you'll get over it."

"Yes," she said. *Maybe.* She glanced at Monty who was checking each animal's feet and girth area, the signal that it was time to saddle up. She reached for the containers and began packing the rest of the food, deciding to settle for a granola bar for her lunch.

"Did you really make a spear?" Logan asked. "Fight off wolves? You look far too beautiful to do that."

Kate stiffened. These agents were privy to her file but surely that carried some sort of professional courtesy. Didn't matter. She'd learned how to handle them.

"And you look far too nice to ever use a gun," she said, with saccharine sweetness. "Did you ever shoot anyone?"

"Women ask me that all the time," Logan said. "Let me tell you, mine is the most exciting job in the world. And I've certainly had occasion to use my gun."

Kate's mouth twitched and she struggled to hold back her smile. This agent was certainly self-absorbed. She'd meant the question only as a simple shutdown but he was proceeding to tell her about every time he'd pulled his gun. And it sounded memorized, like pick-up lines he used in a bar.

"Wow," she said, when he slowed to take a breath.

His eyes narrowed so obviously she hadn't sounded suitably impressed.

"That's really something," she added, all the while hurrying to replace food in their containers.

Logan gave a self-important nod and patted his shoulder holster. "I can tell you more stories later," he said. "But right now it's time to check in. And that requires privacy." His voice turned formal, and he sounded almost like Kessler. "Please tell Monty we need another twenty minutes before riding out."

"Certainly," she said. "But phones won't work, not back here." She doubted even the walkie on Logan's hip would reach more than a few hundred feet.

"Our equipment works," Logan said, sounding almost smug. "You can wait by the horses with Monty. I'll make the call right here on the knoll."

Kate obligingly moved over to the horses as Logan gathered the girls around the tree stump. He fiddled with a gleaming black radio and reported in at exactly twelve-hundred hours. Moments later, his low words were replaced by Courtney's voice, higher and more distinguishable. Portions of her sentences drifted as she spoke animatedly about seeing rabbits and partridge, how she was being careful to protect the wilderness, and that she was even burying her own toilet paper.

"Not much of an escape," Monty muttered, "when you have to report how many times you wipe your ass." But he gave a reluctant smile when he spotted the flowers woven into Slider's mane.

"The girls are having fun," he said. "And they're smart. They remember everything you told them, even the Latin names of the flowers. I'm glad you're here, Kate."

He jabbed his thumb toward Slider's left hoof, his smile fading. "That front shoe's loose. I'll reset it tonight."

Kate sighed. This was typical with horses like Slider who didn't have good feet. His were white, dish-shaped and obviously brittle. Unlike the tough mules who didn't require shoes, the palomino wouldn't be able to cope barefoot for long. He came from a reining line, bought at an auction and bred primarily for looks and athletic ability. Not for hardiness.

"Will his shoe stay on another five hours?" she asked, turning and eyeing the orange pannier that contained their farrier tools.

Unfortunately the tools had been assigned to the agents—along with anything else that represented a potential weapon. And they were all packed alongside the satellite equipment, making it impossible to retrieve. Logan's directions had been polite but non-negotiable: She and Monty were to keep a prudent distance during all communication check-ins.

"Not much we can do about it," Monty said. "They might shoot us if we walk over there now. And they want to make camp by four o'clock."

"Is the horse okay?" Jack's deep voice surprised her. Only minutes ago, he'd entered the trees on the opposite side of the meadow. Few people could move that fast through the woods, or so silently. Certainly not something she'd expected from a Washington agent.

"Loose shoe," Monty said, succinct as ever when talking to people he didn't know.

"Can't you take care of it?" Jack frowned, obviously puzzled why a loose shoe was even an issue. A guide as experienced as Monty should have extensive shoeing experience. Kate had also taken several farrier courses.

"Our equipment was assigned to Logan," Kate said. "It was considered dangerous in our hands. And they want to ride out as soon as the call is finished."

"I'll collect your tools," Jack said, his gaze dropping over Slider's hoof and then back to Kate. "Take as much time as you need. To help the horse."

He headed toward the pannier, moving like a man who didn't expect to be challenged. He was lean and hard and undeniably lethal. She'd already felt the ridges of that muscled body and he obviously kept fit for a reason. But he didn't seem dangerous now, only helpful. And she couldn't help giving a little sigh because it was natural to appreciate such a good-looking male... Strictly from a distance of course.

"That agent isn't such a dick," Monty said.

Kate yanked her head away. "Logan isn't so bad either," she said. "They're a lot alike." And that was so blatantly untrue she half expected Monty to laugh.

However, Monty's gaze remained locked on the three men. Logan was looking at Jack, nodding permission, but Kessler appeared to argue before eventually jabbing his thumb at the pannier.

"Looks like we'll be able to fix Slider's shoe right now," she said, relieved Monty hadn't picked up on her reluctant interest in Jack. "At least all the agents want the same thing."

"Maybe," Monty said. "But there are strange undercurrents."

"What do you mean?"

"Not sure." Monty stroked the brim of his hat, his voice troubled. "Can't put a finger on it. But I get the feeling they're not just watching the girls. They're watching each other."

CHAPTER NINE

Kate took a last glance around the meadow before clucking at the mules and falling in at the rear of the other riders. Except for an occasional hoofprint, little evidence remained of their visit. As she'd anticipated, Monty chose the meandering trail past the old fir tree, the route skirting the base of Saddleback Ridge. It was a bit longer so the trail was less popular, but other than the river and a few rocky sections it was relatively easy riding.

Courtney and Tyra had already crossed several creeks, so the wider Mustang River shouldn't be too difficult. By now Monty had assessed all the riders and probably decided they were capable of squeezing around a few boulders. And with this route they'd be less likely to meet other people who might have entered to the north of the ranch. Even the most adrenaline-seeking four-wheelers couldn't come this way, and hikers preferred the scenic route with the glassy lakes and pastel mountain meadows.

Her relief that they were avoiding higher ground left her a little too relaxed. Belle had stepped out, eager to stay close to the departing horses. But the two pack mules weren't so keen. And when Gus balked, he jerked the lead line from Kate's hand. He looked momentarily surprised to be free, then both he and Bubba shoved their noses back down, snatching mouthfuls of grass and acting as if they hadn't been eating for the last hour.

Kate turned Belle, then leaned over her saddle, trying to snag Gus's lead line without dismounting. But Gus was crafty, inching his head away from her hand, just enough to stay out of reach.

She leaned further, stretching like a trick rider, her hand so low it brushed the grass. Finally she was able to grab the side of Gus's halter, pull his head up, and reclaim the dangling lead line.

Something flashed, a blur of white oddly out of place against the green and brown of the trees.

She straightened, keeping a tight hold of Gus's lead line and peered into the woods. But no matter how hard she searched, the pale shape had disappeared. It was probably nothing, perhaps the underbelly of an animal. Beneath her, Belle fidgeted, figuring they should either follow the other horses or be allowed to graze.

It was never wise to linger with a string of pack animals so Kate angled toward the trail, following the line of riders. But she studied the trees as she entered the shaded woods. She thought they'd been careful. Everyone had been reminded to respect the environment, and even the girls had scrupulously buried their toilet paper. Possibly a napkin had blown across the meadow and been caught up in the trees. It would have been easy to miss. She hadn't even noticed that flash of white until she leaned down to retrieve Gus's rope.

On impulse, she stretched low over her stirrup, scanning the base of the trees. And spotted the white blaze again. Not a napkin or an animal, but a fresh tree cut. The notch was low and unobtrusive, out of sight of a rider but clearly marking the trail. She wouldn't have noticed it if Gus hadn't grabbed the extra chance to graze.

The tree blaze might have been there earlier, serving as a trail marker for previous riders. However, most people preferred an environmentally friendly way of trail marking. Certainly Sharon Barrett stressed a "leave no trace" policy. And it was in an odd spot, poorly placed. Nobody would see it unless by accident.

Or if they knew where to look.

She peered over her shoulder. Both pack mules were following, keeping an optimal distance with no tension on their ropes. They didn't act spooked or curious about another presence. But a shiver of disquiet prickled her neck. She straightened, staring over Belle's long ears, then twisted, checking behind her again.

Nobody was there. Seconds later, the meadow disappeared, lost behind the mules' bulky packs and the flanking trees.

She squeezed Belle's sides, feeling isolated. She couldn't even hear the horses ahead. Gus's little escapade had only taken a minute, but with the winding trail, it was enough to put the other riders out of sight. And she suddenly craved company.

Belle's head lifted, her ears pricking. A horse and rider stood in the middle of the trail, waiting. Jack.

She gave him a grateful smile. Kessler and Logan may not have good trail manners, but Jack certainly did. He wasn't the type to leave anyone behind.

"Everything okay?" he asked, his gaze flickering over her face. "Want me to lead the mules for a bit? Your arm's probably sore. Or maybe your neck from looking over your shoulder."

She'd been about to mention the tree blaze but there was a strange note in his voice, almost of displeasure. Didn't he like that she was being watchful? Making sure no one was following? And he'd been alone in the trees for most of the lunch stop. Maybe he had left that blaze. He was the agent who moved like a ninja. Kessler and Logan rammed through the woods, arguing and snapping branches like bull moose.

"Are other agents riding in?" she asked. "Joining us at camp?"

"I think the five of us are enough to look after two girls," he said, not really answering her question. "They've learned a lot from you already. But they didn't give you a chance to eat. Let me take the mules for a while."

He moved his horse alongside Belle, his hand brushing her wrist as he reached for Gus's lead rope.

She fought the rush of awareness, the familiarity of his touch. But her body was on full alert, her skin tingling as it remembered how those fingers had held her hand, trailed over her hip, lifted her hair to cool her neck...and possibly slashed a tree so other riders could follow.

"I can wait until we make camp," she said.

"When the girls will be clamoring for your attention. It could be sundown before you have time for yourself."

He was probably right. Not only were Courtney and Tyra accustomed to a high level of service, they had no experience with camping or how to care for their horses, or even entertained the notion that they should think of their animals first. They seemed open to learning, but the process would be slow.

Even Monty hadn't realized that Kate missed her lunch. The fact that Jack noticed left her surprised. And softened. She let him pry Gus's lead rope from her fingers. Once her right hand was free, she reached in her pocket, searching for a granola bar.

"I am a bit hungry," she admitted.

"I filled some rolls and put them in the side compartment of my saddle bag," Jack said. "Didn't know if you'd prefer vegetarian or meat so I made both."

She pulled her hand from her pocket. "Thanks," she said, rather dumbfounded.

"Food's in the top compartment," Jack said.

She slowed Belle and reached into the bag behind Jack's saddle, pulling out the first sandwich roll she found.

"Which one do you have?" he asked.

She straightened in the saddle, peeled back the plastic wrap and peeked inside. "The meat one," she said. "Want a bite? Or would you rather I took the other one?"

"No." His eyes cut from her face back to the trail. "They're both for you."

"I'll eat fast," she said, already dipping her head for a bite. "Then I can take Gus and Bubba."

"No rush. I'm quite sure I can handle them."

If he were any other man, it might have sounded like bragging. But Jack was making a simple statement. And the mules were behaving perfectly. Gus had already switched his allegiance to Jack's horse, keeping his head two inches from Dusty's thick tail. And Belle was stepping out alongside Dusty, delighted to have equine company.

Jack remained beside her long after she finished eating. He was good company too, drawing her out with questions and actually talking about things that were of interest. He had a keen mind, able to discuss issues ranging from forest deterioration and hunting license reform, to lighter but equally debatable subjects. Like if Wranglers really were the best riding jeans and the reason why hinnies—similar to a mule but with a donkey mother and a horse sire—weren't as common as a mule sired by a donkey.

"In addition to chromosomes," Kate said, her voice firming, "I think the reason there aren't so many hinnies is because there are fewer female donkeys, and people that own them want to breed to donkeys."

"And I still think it's because the female donkeys are fussier," Jack said. "They prefer their own species. While a donkey stud is happy to overlook small differences." He reached over and gave a teasing tug at Belle's long ear. "Or even bigger ones."

Despite his straight face, his sparkling eyes revealed his sense of humor, something he seemed to maintain even when they held opposing views. And she was beginning to suspect he kept taking the opposite side just to keep her talking.

A strategy which was working. She'd talked more on this trail ride than on all the rides the week before. She'd certainly forgotten her earlier suspicion about a weird tree blaze.

And she probably needed to research this donkey subject a little more before taking on such an intelligent man. His knowledge of the back country rivaled her own. He didn't try to humor her either, seeming to respect her opinion. But she was competitive enough to want the last word.

"Maybe you're right," she said, giving a reluctant nod, "about stallions not being so fussy. Males of every species are less discriminating. Always more in the moment."

"I don't agree," he said. "Not with humans anyway."

She shook her head in frustration. He wasn't even going to give her that. Or maybe in his experience females *were* more forward. Someone who looked like he did never had to work very hard to get a woman. Despite his appearance, she knew there was a gentleness beneath that tough exterior. Even the mules were responding.

She tightened her hands around the reins, suddenly resenting how much she enjoyed his company. How he could charm her on the trail as effortlessly as he had on the dance floor, even after he'd called her "his job." But he was all-round gorgeous. He had the perfect amount of stubble on his hard jaw and his cowboy hat always seemed adjusted to the perfect angle.

However he wasn't going to coax her into talking any longer. Unlike Logan, Jack had avoided personal questions and she appreciated that. She knew, eventually, he'd ask about her past job. And the accident. Probably all three agents had seen her file. And for a private person like her, that just felt wrong.

"I'll take those mules back now," she said, reaching for the lead rope. "Thanks for the food, and the break."

"Any time." His gaze lingered on her face. And it was clear he intended to remain beside her, to keep talking.

She slowed Belle, easing her behind Jack's horse where conversation was more difficult. Gus rammed her leg, confused by the leader shift, and she spent an extra moment organizing the two pack mules. Jack was no fool and by the time she straightened in the saddle, he'd respected her wish and was back riding in the middle of the trail, ten feet in front.

Her heart gave a disappointed kick. However, this was perfect. A safe non-talking distance...and one she knew it was best to keep.

CHAPTER TEN

Kate was hiding something. Jack tugged his hat lower, simultaneously loosening the reins so his horse could scramble over a jumble of loose shale. Behind him, he could hear the mules' feet and their more deliberate steps as they crossed the section of rock.

He refrained from checking over his shoulder. She didn't want his company. No doubt she was accustomed to fending off the attention of every male guest, from the age of six to sixty. It was obvious from the cadence of the mules' hooves that everything was in order. The food and packs were safe. As was Kate. But there was something she was avoiding. He didn't know her background, hadn't been privy to her file, but he was certain she wasn't a threat to Courtney.

Almost certain.

He closed his eyes, trying to get a feel for the forest, the trail, the woman riding behind him. But he sensed no danger or discord. There was no prickling sensation between his shoulder blades, no feeling of ill will.

Ahead of him, Courtney and Tyra slumped in their saddles, their chatter more subdued than earlier in the day. Clearly they were tired. At the other end, Kate sat her mule as easily as when they'd started that morning. And the deeper they entered the wilderness, the happier and fresher she appeared. She hadn't even had a chance to sit down for lunch, not with the girls as well as the two agents treating her like she was their personal servant.

He scowled, impatient with his thoughts. This trip was about Courtney. He was a professional and it wasn't his habit to worry about anything but the job. He turned his attention back to the trail, feeling the moisture of the air long before Monty raised his hand, signaling everyone to stop by the rushing river.

"Wait for all the animals to drink," Monty said, gesturing at the sparkling water. "Then we'll cross in a tight line. Stay close to the horse in front of you, avoid the boulders. The water's deep but they won't have to swim if you stay in formation."

Jack studied the river while his horse sipped the water. White eddies marked a slew of treacherous rocks, and it was obvious motorized vehicles would never be able to handle the crossing. Kessler and Logan exchanged satisfied glances, clearly reaching the same conclusion.

Jack checked to see if Kate needed help but she'd already maneuvered the three mules a little further upstream where they could enjoy a clean and unhurried drink. It was apparent Monty trusted her implicitly. He never checked on her, something Jack found rather irritating. After all, the mules carried their tents, sleeping bags and food. It was only natural to want to help her out, to talk and keep her company.

"What are you staring at?" Kessler asked, turning his horse. "See something?"

Jack slid his gaze off Kate. "Nope. Just checking the lay of the land."

"Good idea." Kessler's voice rose as he turned to Monty. "Jack will ride over to the other side first. Make sure it's clear."

And then we'll have a gun on the other side, Jack thought, catching Monty's understanding nod. The old guide was sharp, needing little explanation and picking up on the agent's caution without alarming the girls.

"Best to enter the river here," Monty said to Jack. "Twenty feet in, dogleg around the boulders, than straight across. Your horse knows the way."

Jack pushed Dusty forward. The horse hesitated, as if surprised to be in the lead, but then stepped out boldly. Water splashed around Dusty's knees, then swirled against his chest. Jack shoved his stirrups forward, keeping his legs dry. The gravel footing felt solid, and from his vantage point high in the saddle the underwater rocks were easy to spot.

Dusty scrambled onto the bank on the other side and shook like a dog, invigorated by the frigid water.

Jack trotted him up the trail, studying the ground, analyzing the signs. Deer tracks, coyote scat, but no fresh sign of horses. There were probably other spots to ford the river upstream but at this crossing he spotted no tracks, shod or unshod.

He rode a quarter mile up the trail before circling back, coming out twenty feet upstream. "All clear," he called.

Monty nudged his horse into the water, obviously impatient with the delay. This was probably the strangest group the man had ever led. The two girls were smiling as they followed him into the river, clearly excited about crossing deep water and giggling when the cold water splashed their legs. Kessler and Logan followed, their expressions stoic. Kate brought up the rear, the mules walking less enthusiastically than the horses, but still obedient.

She was definitely handy to have around, Jack thought. From this angle, he could admire how she kept Gus and Bubba safely in line, the graceful way she sat in her saddle, the elegant curve of her cheekbone...the flare of her hips and breasts. She was a woman he'd like to trail ride with again, and as he'd whispered to her last night, do a lot of other things. More intimate things.

His kick of lust surprised him and he shifted uncomfortably, trying to create more room in the front of his jeans. This wasn't the place, or the time.

He pulled his eyes off Kate, monitoring the line of riders. Monty had almost reached the other side, with Courtney's steady paint close behind. But Tyra's palomino was jigging, clearly not used to the cold water bubbling beneath his tail. And Tyra was leaning forward, pulling at the bit and doing nothing to reassure him. Slider fought her hold, tossing his head so high he brushed Tyra's face and knocked her sunglasses off her nose.

Splash. Tyra squealed and leaned sideways, trying to grab the sunglasses before they sank. Slider shifted, obediently easing away from the left rein pressed against his neck...and moved off the safe gravel bottom.

Jack knew the instant Slider's front legs hit the boulders. The palomino lurched, the rims of his eyes flashing white. He jerked back on his haunches, his front legs flailing as he fought to find solid ground. Tyra, grasping one rein and already halfway out of the saddle, slipped to the right then disappeared beneath the flailing horse.

Jack kicked Dusty and charged down the bank. Tyra was caught up. He could see the top of her boot, still stuck in the stirrup. And Slider was panicking now. He had one leg wrapped over his rein, effectively holding his head beneath the water, making it impossible to breathe unless he was rearing.

Monty wheeled his horse to help. But Kessler and Logan shot forward, flanking Courtney, inadvertently blocking the guide's path as they rushed her out of harm's way. On the opposite side of the bank, Kate was pushing Belle, trying to speed up the mules. But Gus's ears were pinned back and he was obviously in no hurry to join the panic-stricken horse, and risk facing whatever perils lurked in the churning water.

Jack cursed, maneuvering Dusty over the rocky section of the river. He had to get alongside fast, free Tyra's boot from the stirrup, and just pray his horse wasn't hurt in the process. And he didn't have the luxury of going slow. The girl was still screaming which meant she was able to lift her head above the water.

But the palomino was having difficulty. Slider's nose was down by his knees, held by the rein caught around his front leg. His rears were turning increasingly desperate as he tried to raise his head high enough to breathe.

Dusty galloped into the water, all heart as he sent up a spray of white, scrambling over the underwater rocks until he was beside the floundering palomino. Jack leaned down and reached beneath the water. He grabbed Tyra's stirrup and twisted it inward. Her foot slipped free.

He scooped her onto the front of his saddle, safe from Slider's flailing legs, then reached down, trying to free the horse. But Tyra clung to his arms, completely hysterical.

"You're okay," Jack said, still trying to reach Slider. And quiet the girl. Tyra's screams were doing nothing to help the drowning horse. "Sit tight, Tyra. I have to untangle your horse."

But someone else had already splashed into the river between Dusty and Slider. Jack flattened Tyra's arms against her sides and glanced down. Kate stood beside Slider, chest deep in the swirling water. He swore under his breath. She could get hurt and the frantic girl in his arms was making it difficult to help.

However, Slider had quit struggling. In fact, his head was out of the water and he was able to breathe. His dripping forelock accentuated his white blaze. One sad, sodden daisy clung to his tangled mane. The horse eyed the bank, nostrils flaring pink as he gasped for breath. He looked ready to bolt for land with no way of knowing the path between him and the shore was littered with deadly rocks.

"Whoa," Kate said, one hand on Slider's shoulder, the other on his halter. The bridle had disappeared. Somehow, she must have managed to pull it off, letting Slider lift his head from the suffocating water. But the horse was shaking, too frightened to listen, his instincts screaming for him to run.

"Is he caught up?" Monty called, finally able to circle Banjo around Courtney and the two agents, and ride into the river.

"There are rocks all around him," Kate said quietly. "I can lead him out. But he needs to settle down first. And the bridle is wrapped around his feet." She looked at Jack. "Can you keep Dusty beside him? Give him some company. Everyone just talk calmly, please."

That was obviously a request to Tyra who was still wailing. At least Courtney had made it safely to the bank with Kessler and Logan. All three riders now gaped, as if astonished how quickly a simple river crossing could turn into chaos. They might still lose Slider, although it looked like the palomino had calmed enough to remain beside Kate.

Despite his fear, the horse appeared well-trained. Every time he made a move to lurch forward, Kate stilled him with a quiet whoa. And the horse listened.

Jack hated watching safe from Dusty's back while she assumed the riskier role, but Slider had locked onto Kate. Wanting and needing her leadership.

"I want to get off," Tyra pleaded. "Take me to shore now."

"Soon," Jack said soothingly. Naturally the girl was frightened but this rescue was only half complete. "Look at the mules," he added, trying to distract her. "They're delighted with the little break."

Tyra followed his gaze to where the three mules were contentedly munching grass. Their bellies were soaked, showing that at some point they'd been in the river. But once Kate had jumped off they'd turned back, prudently deciding to avoid whatever was attacking the palomino.

"They're not tied together anymore," Tyra said. "Did the rope break?"

"The third mule was tied to Gus's pack with a breakaway knot," Jack said, shooting Kate an approving look. Secrets or not, she was clearly competent. Courageous too. And very cold. He could see the paleness of her lips, the blue veins of her fine-boned hand...and how her taut nipples pressed against her shirt.

"Will our food get wet?" Tyra asked, sniffling again. She didn't seem concerned about Slider or Kate, or that Kate was now ducking beneath the swirling water, trying to work the bridle free from Slider's leg.

"No," Jack said, resisting the urge to clamp his hand over Tyra's mouth. It would be much more efficient than trying to distract her. "The panniers are waterproof."

And then he couldn't stand it any longer. He was trained for this. And though a human life always took precedent over an animal's, he couldn't just sit and watch Kate struggle.

"Monty," he called. "Ride your horse out here and take Tyra in. She's shivering."

It was a relief to plop the girl on the front of Monty's saddle and have his hands free again.

He unbuckled his gun holster, hung his Sig over the saddle horn and stepped down into the swirling water beside Kate. His balls shrunk in shock but it certainly wasn't the coldest water he'd faced.

Kate's head popped up, her dark hair slick against her white face. "I've w-worked the rein off his l-leg," she said, triumphantly waving a sodden bridle. "But his left leg is jammed between two r-rocks." Her hair was plastered to her cheeks, and she didn't seem to realize her teeth were chattering. "Next time I go under, can you push him sideways?"

He could only scowl at her fearlessness. No way was he letting her go back beneath that water, with her head so dangerously close to the horse's legs. Slider was quiet now, but at any second he could start flailing again.

Jack wordlessly picked up Kate and set her down in the water behind him.

"Hold my horse," he said, shoving Dusty's reins into her hand. "And keep talking to Slider. He wants to hear you, not me."

He drew in a practiced breath and ducked beneath the water, quickly locating the smooth rocks that imprisoned the horse's right front leg. He clamped his hands around Slider's fetlock, assessing how tightly it was trapped. He might have to twist it to free him, but time was critical now and it would be horrible if he broke the horse's bone. However, Slider's body suddenly shifted—resourceful Kate must be pushing against the horse's side. There was a slight release, almost imperceptible.

Jack moved his hands lower, cushioning the fetlock, then yanked. Slider sat back, helping his efforts and when Jack's head popped out of the water, the palomino was standing quietly.

He reached for the halter to lead Slider back onto safe ground. However, the horse pulled his head away, his eyes rolling as he searched for Kate, as if aware she'd saved him once and only trusted her commands.

Jack hesitated, not wanting her back in the danger zone. But she just passed him Dusty's reins, then squeezed past him to stand by Slider's shoulder. He kept a cautious hand on her hip, watching the palomino. If this went south, he'd pull her out of there and toss her on Dusty's back. No matter her objections.

But she managed to ease Slider forward a step. Said "whoa" through chattering teeth, then waited another patient moment and repeated the process. Slider stopped every time she asked, as if realizing she was searching for the best ground. Endless minutes later they were safely back on the gravel bottom, and Jack could breathe easy again.

They emerged onto the river bank, dripping a trail of water mixed with specks of red. However, Slider walked evenly, with no visible injury except for a scrape on his right heel. He still had four shoes too, so it was fortunate his loose shoe had been tightened during the lunch break.

Jack passed Monty who had deposited Tyra on land and was now heading back across the river to gather the mules. The guide tipped his hat to both Kate and Jack as he passed.

"We'll make camp here," Jack said. Kessler and Logan had wanted to ride another two miles but he didn't give a damn what they wanted. Kate and Tyra needed to dry out, and Slider as well. There was plenty of grass and a nice spot for the tents.

"Of course," Monty said, as if surprised there'd even be a debate.

However, neither Kessler nor Logan were happy with the decision.

"We were supposed to ride to the fishing camp by the lake," Kessler said, scowling at Jack. "And you don't have any say. Monty is the trail guide. Stopping here wasn't the plan."

"It wasn't the plan for riders to get soaked in the river either," Jack said. "And Slider needs time to recover. We don't have an extra horse."

"All right." But Kessler's mouth tightened with displeasure. "I'll check the perimeter. The guides can pitch the tents and start a fire."

Jack glanced over his shoulder. Tyra was standing by Logan, wearing a jacket someone had produced, still sniffing as she spoke about the river dunking. But Kate was already bent over Slider, running her hands down his legs, checking for further injury. She'd been in the water longer than anyone. And he damn well wasn't asking her to pitch any tent.

He opened his pack, pulled out his fleece-lined shirt and strode over.

"How's the horse?" he asked, draping his shirt over Kate's shoulders.

"S-seems fine," she said, giving him a beautiful smile. "Thanks for your help."

Her lashes were long and dark, accentuating her elegant cheekbones, and the way she smiled at him made his chest tighten. Water trickled down her cheek, but she didn't seem to notice. Her concern was for everyone else.

He reached out and brushed the drops away, his hand lingering on her skin. Something stirred inside him, an emotion he hadn't felt for a long time—tenderness.

"You need to get out of those clothes," he said, dropping his hand. "I'll get your pack and drop it behind that fir tree. We're not riding any further today."

"Oh, that's good." She shot a relieved look at the palomino. "I think Slider's okay. But I need to get him warm."

She pulled his shirt from her shoulders, rolled it in a tight ball and began blotting water from Slider's neck.

"Kate," Jack said, reaching out and giving her an exasperated hug. "My shirt's for you, not the horse. And I'll take care of Slider. Go and get out of your clothes."

"But you're wet too."

"I wasn't in the water as long. But I'll be changing as soon as you come back."

She looked at him for a moment, then gave an assenting nod and eased away. And though she hadn't remained in his arms very long, the fact that she trusted him to care for the horse made him feel better.

She didn't pull on his shirt though. Instead, she placed the fleece side over Slider's back, shooting Jack an apologetic smile before turning and heading toward the trees. And maybe it was okay that she'd sacrificed his best shirt for Slider. Because her wet clothes clung to her body, molding her curves like a bodysuit. Even the way she moved was sexy. He turned away, feeling like a voyeur.

Logan was seizing the chance to check her out too. The agent's eyes were hidden behind his dark sunglasses. But Jack understood body language and he knew what the man was doing.

He also knew he didn't like it.

CHAPTER ELEVEN

The late-afternoon sun warmed Kate's shoulders, leaving her relaxed and drowsy. Or maybe it was the effect of the crackling campfire. Certainly everyone seemed calm following the river mishap. Tyra sat on the opposite side of the fire, eyes closed and cocooned in a blanket. Slider was with the other horses, contentedly eating grass.

Kate stretched, delighting in the luxury of being able to sit down and grab a little break before making supper. All the men were being astonishingly helpful. Jack and Monty had looked after the animals and pitched the tents, and Logan and Kessler had made a lovely campfire.

Of course, it was Jack who'd set the tone. She couldn't quite figure out the Secret Service men. At first she'd thought Kessler was in charge, but in some areas he seemed to defer to Jack. Kessler was definitely the most uptight, at least with her. He'd already moved to stand back by the trees, ever watchful while Courtney and Logan gathered more wood.

Jack strode back, effortlessly carrying the heavy panniers. He set them on the ground then walked over and re-angled the three pairs of boots drying by the fire.

"Almost dry," he said. "I checked your clothes too. They're ready."

He'd rigged up a clothesline a discrete distance from camp, and the thought of his big hands touching her underwear made her pulse quicken. Something had changed between them, evidenced by the easy way he sat down beside her, and how he'd so swiftly reassigned her duties, insisting she couldn't do any chores in bare feet. Being idle was odd, especially when she wasn't hurt. But it was also rather nice for a change.

"If diving in the water earns this much payback," she joked, "maybe I'll do it every trail ride."

"We all know it wasn't just a dive," Jack said. "You saved the day."

There was an odd look in his eyes, almost of admiration. And he gave her knee a little squeeze, the intimacy so sweet and unexpected that he captured another piece of her heart. But she knew she hadn't really done anything.

He was the one who had saved Tyra and ultimately freed Slider's leg. He hadn't hesitated to dive under and help out either, even though the water had been numbingly cold, so frigid that when she'd first jumped off Belle she hadn't been able to think.

"You're obviously used to trail riding," she said. "Do you always carry extra boots?"

"When I'm working, yes."

She peeked at his face. Was he reminding her that this new attentiveness was just part of his job? He was an intuitive man. Maybe he sensed her interest. He'd already shown a well-developed ability to keep women at arm's length. Both Tyra and Courtney blushed whenever Jack spoke to them. And Tyra now viewed him as her savior, her infatuation obvious. But he had no trouble brushing off their attention.

He just walked away, as he had with Allie by the pool. And Kate had personally experienced how quickly he could ditch a dance partner. But when he looked at her as he was doing now—as if she were someone special—it only left her confused.

She leaned forward and picked up her boots. Ran her hand over the leather, pretending an absorption with checking the sole. Luckily she'd had the presence of mind to slip her boot knife and sheath into her pack before turning her clothes over to Jack for drying. The agents still controlled all weapons, and she and Monty couldn't even use the hatchet.

"My boots are dry," she said. "So I'll start supper now."

"Okay," Jack said. "But I think it's time to return this." He took her hand, pressed something against her palm, then closed her fingers. "In case you need to rescue someone again."

The tip of her red jackknife protruded from her fingers. It looked tiny compared to her boot knife. But its significance was enormous.

"Every rider should have a knife," he said, still clasping her wrist. He had a cowboy's hands, tanned, capable, marked with faded scars. His index finger traced the sensitive base of her thumb, his touch gentle but deliberate. Possessive.

Her pulse jumped as his finger circled her palm, branding her with his touch. It was evident in the dance hall that he was comfortable with women, his slow smile, the brush of his mouth over her hair, the way he'd kept their bodies perfectly aligned as he guided her around the floor. But the way he caressed her now was different. And they both knew it.

She looked at him, then back at their joined hands where she felt the heavy thud of his pulse, beating in time with hers. Returning her jackknife was a huge gesture of trust on his part, and one that Kessler surely hadn't approved. Jack was sticking his neck out for her. And she knew she needed to tell him about her other knife. To explain why she always felt the need to carry it.

"You're so brave," Jack said. "Jumping in that water to help Slider. With nothing but your quick thinking."

The approval in his voice left her feeling like a fraud. Because she'd gone into the river knowing she had her boot knife. In fact, she'd been planning to cut the reins, but Slider had been drowning and there hadn't been time to get it out. It had been quicker to pull off his bridle.

Tyra abruptly sat up. "I'm hungry," she said. Her eyes were wide open and she stared at Kate with an accusing expression. "When's supper?"

"In thirty minutes," Kate said, slipping the jackknife into her back pocket. "Would you like to help grill the steaks?"

"No," Tyra snapped. "That's your job. Where's Courtney?"

"Gathering wood with Logan," Jack said. He rose in a smooth athletic motion, his voice much harsher than it had been mere seconds ago. "And since your boots are dry, this is a good time to check Slider. That's *your* job. Not Kate's."

"But I don't want to ride that horse anymore." Tyra pushed the blanket off her shoulders, not brave enough to look at Jack but clearly agitated. "He's not safe."

Despite the girl's entitled attitude, it was obvious from her quavering voice that she was genuinely afraid.

"We can discuss that later with Monty," Kate said. "He makes all those decisions. Don't worry. He'll do what's best for you."

"Yeah, right." Tyra rolled her eyes. "Nobody cares about me. If Courtney had fallen in the river, you'd probably call in a helicopter." She crossed her arms, looking belligerent but for a second her voice cracked, revealing a vulnerable teenager.

Kate was in the middle of tugging on her boots but she stilled. She'd thought the girls were getting along well but clearly

Tyra resented Courtney's elevated status. And her words rang true. Logan and Kessler had bolted to Courtney's side, and though the two men tended to bicker, their allegiance to Courtney was obvious. Jack hadn't hesitated to gallop back into the river. But now that Tyra had seen him holding Kate's hand, the girl obviously felt even more alone.

Kate dropped her boot and moved to the girl's side. "I'll look out for you," she said gently. "That's why Monty and I are here. And you know Jack is always watching. He was the first one in the water."

"But you're not Secret Service." Tyra's voice rose. "And Kessler and Logan *left* me."

"What happened in the river was truly frightening," Kate said. "But it won't happen again. Next time we cross any water I'll walk beside you on Belle. Mules never go where it's dangerous, even when the rider asks them. That's why they're so safe."

"I'm not riding in the back with the stupid mules. And I'm not scared of horses. I've been around them all my life. I just don't want to drown on a stupid trail ride."

"Hey, Tyra, you're awake!" Courtney called. She hurried toward the campfire, two branches in her arm and a wide smile on her face. "Logan says the mustangs are in the next valley. We'll see them tomorrow. Isn't that great!"

"Yeah," Tyra said. "Super great." And though she gave a vigorous nod, it was obvious her enthusiasm was fake; her mouth formed more of a grimace than a smile.

Kate peeked at Jack. His face had returned to its usual forbidding expression, but she caught the concern in his eyes. He gave her a sympathetic look and walked away. Naturally.

It was tempting to follow, to slip into the woods and escape. But they both had jobs to do. His to protect and hers to make sure the girls had a good time. Judging by Tyra's mutinous expression, Kate's job would be more difficult.

CHAPTER TWELVE

Kate pulled the boiling water off the grill and washed the last of the supper plates. The camp was blessedly quiet. Monty was buckling hobbles on the mules, switching horses off the picket line and making sure they all had a chance to graze. Courtney and Tyra were with Logan, in the middle of one of their private security check-ins, while Jack and Kessler stood watch somewhere in the trees.

Kate packed all the food away in the panniers, then moved them downwind, a prudent distance from the tents. The animal resistant panniers were effective and even if the scent drew wildlife, they'd be far away from the sleeping area. She'd grain the horses later, when they were all tied to the picket line, and also lead them to the river for a final watering.

Monty wandered back carrying his tin cup, looking relaxed now that the guests were out of earshot. "So, how are you holding up? You did a helluva job earlier. That Tyra girl is sure demanding."

He took a pensive sip, his gaze drifting toward the two girls gathered around Logan. "Wonder what they're reporting about the river incident. Never saw two men split so fast. All they did was get in my way. And their hands were on their holsters. Not sure how they thought guns were going to help."

Kate dumped more soap in the sudsy water, still feeling sympathy for Tyra. It would have been a scary two minutes hung up in that saddle, helpless and unable to breathe. "At least we know they're good at watching out for someone," she said.

"Yeah," Monty said. "It appears the President's daughter is quite safe. It would be hard to take down three agents, unless they're split up. Or totally surprised."

Kate's head jerked up. The tone of Monty's voice had changed, turning thoughtful. He no longer seemed to be talking about the river, but something else. And they'd been warned never to refer to Courtney as the President's daughter. They weren't even supposed to call her by name in the unlikely event they met other riders.

"You mean Petal," Kate said, edging closer and checking the contents of Monty's cup. The cook always tucked in a bottle or two, and most riders enjoyed a campfire drink. But Kate had assumed they'd abstain from alcohol, given the age and importance of their guests.

The drink in Monty's cup was amber colored though. Definitely not coffee. And now that she was closer she could smell the whiskey on his breath. "Are *they* okay with drinking?" she whispered.

"We always have a drink at night," Monty said. "That's part of the ride. And guests are fed, tents are pitched. We're done for the day. Besides, we need one after the river crossing. That girl is probably going to be terrified tomorrow. Boss won't be happy."

He took another brooding sip and it was clear he felt responsible for Tyra, and for almost losing Slider.

"It wasn't your fault," Kate said. "How about I saddle up Belle? And lead Slider across the river before it gets dark. Help him get back his confidence."

Monty nodded. "Good idea. And if Tyra really doesn't want to ride him anymore, would you switch? Belle will take care of her. And Slider trusts you. Think you could ride him?"

"Sure, if that's what Tyra wants." Kate gave a nonchalant shrug and turned toward the horses. But her heart was thumping. Tomorrow's ride included a long winding section along the base of Saddleback Ridge, nothing like the mountain pass to the west. But there were spots with ten-foot drops. And just the thought of riding a horse over that type of terrain—a horse named Slider—sent fear worming through her belly. She comforted herself with the knowledge that Tyra would never lower herself to ride a mule. Like Logan, the girl scorned them, considering mules inferior.

Rather reassured, Kate saddled Belle and collected the palomino. But even his friendly nicker didn't make her feel much better. Now she obsessed about his name. *Slider?* How ominous was that? More than ever, she wished Tyra hadn't picked a horse based on color.

Slider shouldn't be expected to do anything but look handsome in his golden coat while galloping around a tractor-groomed arena, flashing that thick white mane and tail. He was a performance horse, bred for high scores in reining, not scrambling over rough trails and rocky river crossings. He'd probably be too terrified to step one foot into that river, and after such an experience she didn't blame him.

But when she led him down to the water, he didn't hesitate. He splashed right in beside Belle, acting like a veteran trail horse, proving he was much more resilient than Kate.

Sighing, she stopped both animals in the middle of the river. She patted the ever-patient Belle, then reached over to stroke

Slider's neck. The palomino stood stock still in the swirling water, not stepping off the gravel path, taking his cues from the confident mule and Kate's reassuring voice.

"You really are a brave horse," she whispered. "But I still don't want to ride you."

She looked back at Monty who watched from the river bank. She gave him a thumbs-up, relieved Slider had no mental scars. He'd be fine for tomorrow. They'd just have to convince Tyra of that.

It was then Kate spotted the tree notch. Fifty feet to the right of Monty, on a steep bank by the water, out of sight of camp but visible to anyone approaching from the other side. And it was exactly the same shape as the mark she'd spotted at their lunch stop.

She turned her head, pretending to pat Belle's neck but actually studying the trees on the opposite bank. Was someone standing there? Watching her? Watching Courtney?

Goosebumps chilled the back of her neck. But Belle nosed at the water, playfully plunging her dripping muzzle in and out of the swirling eddies, and even Slider relaxed enough to paw and splash with his front leg. Neither animal acted as if there were any strangers spying from the woods.

Perhaps marking the trail was something the Secret Service did? They seemed obsessed about following some sort of procedure. Maybe it was marked so a rider could find the river crossing, in case something happened to Monty. Or maybe Monty was marking the trail for future riders. He was helpful like that, always giving less experienced guides valuable tips. But then she remembered... Monty didn't even carry a knife. His gear had been confiscated by Kessler.

She turned the animals and waded back through the river, studiously not looking over her shoulder.

Monty set down his cup and stepped up to the water's edge. She passed him Slider's lead line and stepped down from Belle's back, relieved they were still alone.

"Someone is marking our trail," she whispered. "I've spotted two fresh tree blazes, and there could be a couple more I missed. You're not doing it, are you?"

"Of course not." His smile faded. "Are you sure?"

"Maybe not about the one at lunch. But I'm positive the mark by the bank wasn't there when we first crossed." Then she hesitated. Maybe she had missed it. She'd been focused on keeping the mule train in line, and then on rescuing Tyra and Slider.

But Monty nodded, his voice troubled. "No, you're right. I didn't see a blaze either. And none of the agents said anything. The only time they were out of sight was at lunch...and now here."

They both twisted, peering around but trying not to look obvious about it. At first glance, the camp seemed normal. Contented horses, comfortable tents, a friendly fire. But the elaborate communication equipment was far from normal. And the bulges beneath the men's shirts were a constant reminder of Courtney's importance.

"We have to tell one of the agents," Kate whispered.

"Yes," Monty said. "But which one?"

CHAPTER THIRTEEN

Kate pressed some chocolate on top of the melted marshmallow and cracker. "Would you like another one, Courtney?"

"No, thank you," the girl said. Night had fallen but the glow from the fire revealed her subdued expression. And her voice was definitely strained.

"Everything is gluten free," Kate said, "so you don't have to worry about anything." Other than the fact that someone with hostile intentions might be using the blazed trees to follow their trail.

Kate's eyes met Monty's and he gave an encouraging nod. All three agents were patrolling the perimeter, and Tyra was holed up in the tent, sulking. There'd be no better chance to speak to Courtney alone. Kate's instinct had been to tell Jack about the tree blazes but Monty had been more cautious, wary of all three agents.

"Do you feel like having a private call with your family?" Kate asked. "We'd like to contact our boss too. Let her know how the trip's going."

"My phone doesn't work here," Courtney said. "Besides, I'm only supposed to call at preset times. Unless it's an emergency."

"And if there's an emergency," Kate asked, "do you know how to use the equipment?"

"No, only Kessler and Logan do. I don't even know the safe word."

Monty leaned forward and poked at the fire. "Which one of those guys has been with you the longest?" he asked. He'd quit drinking two hours earlier, as soon as Kate told him about the slashed trees. The knowledge that he'd put away his nightly whiskey underscored the seriousness of the situation, and drove home the fact that they were very isolated.

"Kessler." Courtney's voice warmed with affection. "He's been on my protective detail for three years. And Logan nearly as long. Logan taught me how to drive and we also ride horses together."

"And how long has Jack been around?" Kate asked. "Does he ride horses back east with you too?"

"Jack?" Courtney's nose wrinkled with puzzlement. "But he's not Secret Service. I assumed he worked for your ranch."

Sparks spattered, lighting up the night as Monty abruptly dropped his stick into the flames. "Do Kessler and Logan think that too?" he asked.

Courtney shrugged. "I don't know. But Tyra knows he's not an agent. That's why she's upset. She wanted Kessler or Logan to save her, not Jack."

"Why does it matter?" Kate asked.

"Well, Jack's good-looking but he's kind of intimidating. Tyra already knows Logan and Kessler so they're easier for her to talk to. Besides, it's their job to protect us. Now she feels like nobody really cares, you know, and that if something happens again there might not be anyone to save her. I asked Kessler and Logan to leave me and go in the river and help, but when I told Tyra that, she was even more upset."

Kate stared blankly at the gooey cracker in her hand. Obviously Tyra had been hurt when the agents deserted her and charged to Courtney's side. At the time, Kate hadn't understood all the reasons. Tyra did appear to be very relaxed with Logan, talking more to him than any of the other men. And if Jack wasn't an agent, who was he? She looked over at Monty, both of them speechless.

"You're making a mess of that s'more," Courtney said. "I thought we were supposed to be careful not to spill food. So we don't attract animals. Guess I can eat one more if you really don't want it."

Kate made an agreeable sound and passed it over. Her appetite was gone anyway. Now it seemed likely that it was Jack who was marking the trail. But he was the one she trusted most. More than that, she liked him. A lot. But perhaps he'd been charming her for other reasons.

Courtney finished chewing, wiped her mouth and rose from the log. "I'm going to join Tyra in the tent," she said. "See if I can cheer her up. She didn't talk to me much tonight."

Tyra hadn't talked much to anyone. She'd been sulking, retreating to the tent almost immediately after supper. She hadn't said anything more about not wanting to ride Slider. But now that was the least of their worries.

"See you in the morning," Kate said, waiting until Courtney crossed the grassy clearing. The tents were pitched away from the fire and lingering food odors, and Monty didn't speak until Courtney unzipped the flap and disappeared inside.

"We need to find out if marking the trail is normal," he whispered. "Before we panic. Maybe some other agents are riding in to join them."

"But wouldn't Sharon have told you?"

"Maybe she didn't know. Too bad they wouldn't let me make a call." He poked at the fire again, his frustration obvious. Both Kessler and Logan had flatly denied Monty's request to call the ranch, citing security concerns.

"I'm not going to report our position," Monty had promised. But the agents hadn't budged.

Kate glanced around, checking for the radio canister. It must be in the orange pannier, the one with the ammunition—along with the hatchet and anything else that qualified as a weapon. "I bet I could figure out how to use it," she said. "I'll check it tonight, when they're sleeping."

"They won't all sleep at the same time. Besides," Monty added, his expression chillingly serious, "they'd probably shoot you if they thought we were tipping anyone off about Courtney's location. That's top secret."

But someone was trying to give out their location, Kate thought. And while the tree blazes could be innocent, what if they weren't? The idea of Courtney being snatched made her stomach heave. Would they hurt her? Maybe they wanted to use her to leverage the President and nothing that terrorists ever demanded was good.

"We have to get her back safely," Kate said, her hands fisting. "Both her and Tyra."

"You bet." Monty's voice was just as resolute. He'd won top regional guide, eleven years in a row, and it was clear he intended to hang on to that distinction. "If necessary, we'll leave the horses and walk the girls out. I'll make up a survival pack in case we have to bushwhack."

Kate nodded. Monty had lived here all his life, tramped every square mile of this wilderness. He could find deer trails no one else knew existed, and that no horse could possibly follow. With a ten-minute head start they could melt away. There was a manned fire tower fifteen miles due south. It would be a rough hike considering the bogs and dense brush, but with supplies, it was doable.

Just knowing they had a backup plan made her feel more in control. The girls might not like walking but if they understood the reason—

Her relief fizzled as quickly as it had come. Judging by Monty's heavy sigh, it was obvious he'd reached the same conclusion. It didn't matter that there was a fire tower to the south. That they might be able to hike cross country and shake their pursuers.

Because without any real evidence, there was little chance they could convince the girls to ditch their supplies and all the comforts of camp. It was even more unlikely they could persuade them to walk away from Courtney's trusted bodyguards.

CHAPTER FOURTEEN

Logan stepped into the light of the campfire, a hopeful smile outlining his broad face. "I saw on your ranch brochure that overnight rides include a nightcap," he said. "Well, this is definitely night time, and Petal is asleep."

"I already put away the bottle," Monty said, not moving from his seat on the log. "Would have offered but I didn't think you'd want one."

"I can get the whiskey," Kate said. "Do the other guys want a drink too?"

"No, Kessler drew the short straw. I'm the one off tonight."

Kate checked the clearing. The animals were settled for the evening, tied to the picket line, their darkened outlines barely visible. She couldn't spot Jack or Kessler within the trees. And if the men were looking at the bright fire, their vision would be affected and they wouldn't be able to see the panniers a stone's throw away. This was likely the best chance for Monty to assemble a survival kit.

"I can't remember which pack the whiskey's in," Kate said, kicking Monty's boot. "Would you check for me? And maybe grab some peanuts at the same time."

Monty inclined his head, rose and ambled toward the panniers. He looked utterly relaxed, as if the only thing on his mind was collecting the whiskey. However, once he was behind Logan he scooped up his backpack, hiding it behind his outer leg.

"I better go with him," Logan said. "I have a good flashlight and the panniers are restricted."

"Monty can do it." Kate patted the log beside her. "You deserve a rest after riding all day and then standing in the woods for hours."

"I am a little tired, just from slapping flies." He settled down beside her and stretched out his thick legs. "Besides, I'd rather talk with a beautiful woman than a grumpy old guide."

Kate's mouth tightened. She'd heard Logan make snide comments before, but this was the first one directed at Monty. She wasn't the type to sit back and let someone talk about a friend. However, she bit back her reply, knowing it was more important to humor the man, and just hope he wouldn't notice that Monty was gone a few extra minutes.

"It's a beautiful night," she said.

His leg brushed hers. She automatically inched away, then forced herself to remain still.

"Yes," Logan said. "Too beautiful to waste babysitting spoiled girls. Or checking sweaty mule packs."

She gave him a sharp glance, wondering if his comment about the packs was a warning about sneaking to the pannier. But his expression remained bland.

"All we need is a pool and a warm Jacuzzi," he said, "and we could pretend we're like *them*. Everyone catering to us for a change."

There it was again. Another dig. But as long as he was sitting beside her, and not supervising Monty, she should humor the man.

"I like the bubbling river," she said. "And the sound of fish jumping. It's as nice as any manmade pool."

Logan gave a disparaging snort. "But we're stuck sleeping on the hard ground. Don't pretend you wouldn't prefer a hotel bed with silk sheets and champagne."

"I'm not pretending anything," she said, blinking in surprise.

"Come on. I know what women want. At least my girlfriends are honest." His sneer changed to an irritated groan as giggles leaked from the middle tent. "Sounds like the girls are still awake," he said. "Let's hope they're talking about seeing the mustangs tomorrow. It'll be awkward if Tyra refuses to ride. Petal has been planning this for almost a year."

"I thought it was a last-minute booking?"

"The actual ranch was. But not the trip." He paused, studying Kate's face as if concerned about revealing state secrets. Then he seemed to decide she was harmless. "The less people know," he said, "the easier it is to keep her safe. But a trip like this has been in the works for a while now. That's why we upped our riding to three days a week."

He rubbed the inside of his thigh. "I should have ridden more though," he admitted. "My horse is wider than the ones in Washington. Do you have any liniment around?"

"I'll check the first aid kit later," she said, her irritation with the man fading. Not many riders admitted they were sore on the first day, and she certainly didn't expect it from an elite government agent. But if she left Logan alone by the fire, he'd notice the length of Monty's absence. She needed to keep him entertained a little bit longer.

Act interested, Allie always advised. Men love a woman who hangs on their every word. But Kate had never been good at pretending, and she'd already discovered that Logan tended to brag. She wished Monty would come back and fought her urge to check the shadows. If only it was Jack who was off tonight. He was easier to talk to. Easier to look at too.

She forced an empathetic smile. "The western saddles are bigger than you're used to," she said. "So it makes the horses seem wider. Your leg muscles probably had to stretch a bit."

"Yeah," Logan said. "Guess you don't have that problem anymore, now that you don't ride horses. Mules are narrower, aren't they?"

She peered at him, but he was busy pulling off his boots and examining a blister. She already knew he'd reviewed her background but he seemed to think she was afraid to ride horses. He was wrong. She rode them a lot. She just preferred not to ride them in the mountains.

"Belle is narrower," she said, steering the conversation to a more comfortable topic. "But some of our mules are draft crosses so they're bigger and wider than a quarter horse. Bubba's sire was half Belgian. His feet are the size of dinner plates. Makes me wonder how big his parents were...?"

Logan just grunted. Unlike Jack, he wasn't interested in mule breeding or the best trail saddles or even the soothing sound of the bubbling river. He just wanted to complain about his stiff muscles and now the tiny blister on his toe. She couldn't help but wrinkle her nose as the smell of his sweaty socks filled the air.

And then he quit inspecting the sole of his foot to peer impatiently into the shadows. "I better go help Monty," he said. "One drink and I'll be able to get some solid sleep. Tomorrow's going to be a busy day."

"Oh, do you like wild horses too?" She leaned forward again, desperate for some way to keep his attention. "No wonder you're *her* favorite."

"Petal's?" He gave a satisfied nod. "I was actually the one who taught her to drive."

"She told us. That was *so* nice of you." Kate batted her eyelashes, smiling up at him and feeling like a simpering idiot. If this was how she'd have to act all winter in the dance hall, she'd definitely need more lessons from Allie.

"Not so nice." Logan gave one of his smug laughs. "I was under orders. But I was there—not Kessler—when she jumped her first cross rail. She's way more comfortable with me than him."

Obviously there was some competition between the two agents, but at least she'd found a subject that interested him. "She certainly talks about you more than anyone else," Kate said. "And you'll be the one with her when she sees her first mustang." She paused, carefully watching his face. "Or will other agents be joining us?"

"Joining us?" He twisted, his eyes narrowing. "What do you mean?"

"Just that we have so much food." He still looked rather alarmed so she jokingly touched his arm. "Although I guess a strong guy like you needs a lot of calories...you know, to keep up your energy. How about I make you a s'more?"

"Yeah," he said, looking down at her fingers splayed over his forearm. "Maybe I'll stay up a bit. Keep you company. And maybe you'd like to help me rub on that liniment?" His voice lowered suggestively. "Which tent are you in?"

She yanked her hand back. "Monty and I sleep beneath the tarp. Open air. The tents are for guests."

"Well," Logan said, his eyes drifting over her breasts. "I'm suddenly not so tired. And I imagine you get bored doing all these trail rides for local hicks. So I'll sit up a while longer. And you're welcome to join me in my tent. You never know when it might rain."

He stopped talking as Monty emerged from the shadows carrying a bottle of whiskey and a bag of peanuts. Logan rose and took the bottle. He untwisted the cap, lined up three tin cups and enthusiastically began pouring.

"None for me," Monty said. His gaze found Kate's and he gave a little nod. It was reassuring that he'd had time to prepare a getaway pack but the fact that he declined a drink showed the level of his concern. And magnified her own.

She covertly studied Logan. It would be a relief to tell someone about the trail blazes. Get it off her shoulders and let the Secret Service worry about it. Logan had an inflated opinion of his appeal, seeming to think any woman would be honored to have sex with him. Boorish but probably dependable. Certainly the White House trusted him. Still, she had a vague uneasiness and the feeling was growing the longer she was around the man.

She raised a questioning eyebrow at Monty but he just gave a little shrug, as if leaving the decision to her. Monty had certainly talked more to Logan than she had.

He'd ridden with Logan at the front of the line while she'd spent more time with Jack. However, the more she thought about it, the more she realized she didn't know anything about Jack's background.

And it was far too simplistic to judge a man by the thoughtful way he treated his horse, or be swayed by the fact that he'd been the one to jump in the river and rescue Tyra. That might mean Jack didn't care so much about Courtney...and so was more susceptible to selling out her location.

She rubbed her forehead just as Logan pressed a full cup into her other hand. The amber liquid reached almost to the rim. "Should we save some for Kessler?" she asked, inhaling the pungent odor and pretending to take a sip.

"No, he never drinks." Logan gave a dismissive snort. "He's no fun at all. Orders coffee at the bars. It's a mystery how he landed three wives."

"So you've worked with both these guys before?" Monty asked.

"Only Kessler. Jack's not part of our team." Logan's mouth tightened and just like the other two men, it was obvious he didn't intend to reveal any details.

Kate took a real sip of whiskey this time, feeling the burn all the way down her throat. She needed to think. It seemed crazy not to trust the Secret Service men, and she certainly knew Logan better than Kessler. Kessler barely talked to her, other than to snap commands. And this might be her only chance to speak to Logan alone.

"Maybe I'll go find Jack," Monty said. "See if he wants a drink before the bottle's gone."

"He's on the other side of the horses," Logan said. "And Kessler is watching the path. Better call out though. Let them know you're coming."

"Do you expect trouble?" Kate asked, warmed by the whiskey. "It's hard to believe anyone could find us here."

The flickering firelight outlined Logan's face and his emphatic head shake. "Of course no one can find us," he said. "But Kessler is always suspicious. He only trusts fellow agents. It's probably making him twitchy having Jack floating around."

"But why is Jack here?" Kate asked. "What are his qualifications?"

"Ex-SEAL," Logan said. "Hired by the President. Waste of manpower if you ask me. We certainly don't need him."

So Jack was a mercenary. And he wasn't as tight with the other two agents as she'd assumed. Even Monty was quiet, as if absorbing this new information and struggling to decide who to trust.

An owl's hoot floated eerily beyond the river, mingling with the sound of the bubbling water. Kate angled her head away from the crackling fire, trying to regain her night vision.

The river was an inky ribbon of darkness, but if someone approached it would likely be from that direction. And they probably shouldn't be sitting so closely around the campfire, where anyone coming would be camouflaged by the night yet could easily pinpoint their positions.

She wiggled uneasily, squinting so hard at the river it seemed to be moving. Rising. Then a figure took shape, the outline of a cowboy hat silhouetted against the moon.

"Coming in," Jack's quiet voice announced.

Logan twisted, his hand jerking over his holster. "Hey," he said, immediately relaxing. "How did you get back there? Thought you were by the horses." He rose and rummaged for a spare cup. "Want a drink?"

"Sure," Jack said. "I'd appreciate one of those s'mores too." He stretched out on the log beside Kate, smoothly confiscating Logan's spot.

Logan scowled, then thrust Jack a cup and shuffled over to sit beside Monty. He might consider Jack an outsider but it seemed he wasn't up to challenging for the seat.

"The girls sound happy in the tent," Jack said, glancing at Kate. Unlike Logan, he didn't seem to resent the fact that they were still awake and having fun.

"Yes," Kate said, "they've been laughing. Courtney is excited about seeing the mustangs so maybe Tyra will get pumped up about riding tomorrow."

"I saw you in the river with the palomino. He looked quiet. Good job."

The approval in Jack's voice made her flush. And twisted up her feelings even more. How could she be so drawn to a man who might be placing their entire group in jeopardy? And the fact that he watched her schooling Slider in the river was rather disturbing.

Because she could have sworn he and Kessler were both on the other side of the clearing. A man who could move so stealthily and see so much would certainly have no trouble leaving secret tree blazes.

Yet when Jack's hard thigh brushed against hers, warm even through the fabric of her jeans, she didn't scoot away. She just savored the pleasure of his company, appreciating his keen intelligence along with his fresh smell and sexy voice, a voice that didn't snap orders or gripe about petty things and instead could converse about a range of topics.

They sat for hours, with Jack making s'mores, Logan pouring whiskey, and Monty passing peanuts, talking companionably about horses, politics and how much bacon they should cook for breakfast. With Jack's influence, even Logan seemed to appreciate the natural beauty of the constellations overhead. And she didn't want the night to end, even after Monty stretched out on his bedroll beneath the tarp and Logan shuffled off to his tent.

"We better get some sleep too," Jack said.

He wrapped her hand in his and tugged her up from the log, not mentioning where he was sleeping or making any suggestion that they extend the night. And she felt rather foolish for even thinking that he'd been paying her special attention, that he'd listened intently whenever she spoke and how he'd toasted her marshmallows more carefully than the ones for the others. Not burnt black but with that uniform toasty brown which only the most patient person could achieve.

But in a way it was good that he didn't make a move because clearly she didn't understand him. So she definitely shouldn't trust him. And then he was cupping her face with his hands, and his lips were over hers, his mouth firm and demanding, and she quit thinking. Could only feel.

Wow, what a kiss. All night long his presence had heightened her senses, but now his mouth became her focal point, and the hooting owl, the crackling of the fire, even the rustling of the horses disappeared. All she knew was Jack, his lips, his tongue, his mouth as it joined with hers.

Then he pressed her head against his chest and simply held her, soaking her up, and she could hear the pounding of his heart, his ragged breathing, could feel his iron control. She wasn't sure how long they stood there. One minute, five, maybe fifteen. She only knew her body was so boneless she could only cling to his broad shoulders.

He was the first to speak. "I know we're both working," he said, whispering against her hair. "But we'll figure out where we're going with this when we get back. Okay?"

"Okay," she said.

CHAPTER FIFTEEN

The horse was panting like a dog, reeking of wet hair and skunk and garbage. He definitely needed a bath before any guests climbed on his back. She should find some soap and lead him to the wash stall. Jack might help—

Kate's eyes jerked open. The sky was a dark mantle, dotted by a patchwork of twinkling stars.

So, just another dream, waking her early. At least it had been different this time, not one of bleeding horses and a dying boy and a helicopter that arrived too late. Unfortunately she always dreamed in technicolor, with vivid images as well as sounds that were impossible to forget. Her sense of smell was not usually this acute though.

She froze, her eyes still locked on the dark sky.

Because the panting was entirely real. So was the stink.

A bear!

She lay motionless, hardly daring to breathe. The bear wasn't by the food, enclosed in the panniers a hundred feet from camp. He wasn't sniffing around the fire either, or checking the roasting sticks she'd carefully rinsed.

He was snuffling between the tents.

The horses fussed and snorted, straining at their ropes. She slid her hand along the ground, groping for the knife in her boot, and at the same time shifted her weight. Grizzly or black bear? It was barely fifteen feet away now, sniffing at the side of the girls' tent. Maybe it was only curious and she could scare it away. There wasn't any food close by, nothing to make a black bear want to put up a fight.

"Griz," Monty whispered, prone in his bedroll.

Her limbs turned cold, leaden. For a helpless moment she just wanted to pull the sleeping bag over her head and pretend it was all a dream. Maybe the grizzly would wander off if unprovoked. The food was locked up. Even if he walked over by the cold fire pit, he'd find nothing to eat. But for some reason the bear was between the tents. He wasn't moving away. In fact, he was intensely interested in the side of the tent.

And the only thing standing between the President's daughter and his long deadly claws was a fragile film of nylon.

She gulped, the sound loud in her ears. She felt a boot and ran her fingers along the inner leather, groping for the snap-in sheath. She'd replaced the knife after her boots dried, but she couldn't feel the sheath. It must be the wrong boot.

"We'll stand up at the same time," Monty murmured, his voice reassuringly calm. "Then we'll back toward the fire...see what happens."

She grabbed her second boot as she stumbled to her feet, reassured by the weight. This was definitely the boot containing her knife. And then she was edging backward with Monty.

The bear's head swung.

He was looking at them, even rising on his hind legs, curious about their odd shape. And that, of course, was good. They wanted to distract him, draw him away from Courtney's tent. Besides, she had the knife in her boot and some of the fire logs might still be warm. She already knew that fire could keep away predators...for a time.

There was thirty feet between them now, a distance she knew the bear could cover amazingly fast. She needed to pull out her knife, and just hope she didn't fumble.

The grizzly swung back to the tent, dismissing them.

"I'm going to bang some pots," Monty said, his voice not so low now. "Pull him away from the tent. You'll have time to run for that maple tree."

"No," she said fiercely. "I'm not leaving you. Besides, the two of us will look bigger."

The familiar click of a shotgun sounded behind them, the noise filling her with relief.

"Stay behind me." Jack edged in front of them, at the same time leveling the gun. His voice rose, calm and commanding. "If anyone is awake in the tents, stay inside.

"I've got a clear shot," he added to Monty and Kate. "But hopefully we can scare him off. He's just an adolescent. Go ahead and make some noise."

The bear appeared more interested in the walls of the tent then the three people standing in front of the fire. Kate dropped her boot and picked up a pot and pan.

Clang.

The bear jerked at the noise, then rose halfway on his haunches. Puzzled, indecisive.

"What the fuck!" Kessler called, running out of the woods to join them. His eyes widened and he yanked his gun out.

"No." She and Jack spoke at the same time. But Kessler pulled the trigger.

The grizzly charged, seemingly impervious to Kessler's increasing rapid fire of shots. And he was blindingly fast, between the tents one second and the next, less than ten feet from them.

Jack's shotgun blast was deafening. The bear dropped, his momentum carrying him forward until he was lying at their feet.

"What the fuck!" Kessler said. "He almost had us. Why'd you wait to shoot?"

"Because I was hoping I wouldn't have to," Jack said.

They all stared at the downed bear. He looked much smaller than when he'd been looming in the shadows. Clearly an adolescent, with three-inch claws, a distinctive shoulder hump, and a dished and bloody face.

Logan scrambled from his tent and jogged over. He studied the bear, solemn and white-faced. "I heard a handgun wouldn't stop a grizzly," he said. "Now I know that's true."

Seconds later Courtney and Tyra crawled from their tent, wiping sleep from their eyes and looking confused. Their expressions quickly turned to disbelief, and then something else. *Guilt?*

Kate sighed. She'd worked with too many teens to ignore the signs. She strode past them, lifted the flap and checked their tent. Chocolate bar wrappers littered the floor, along with a half-empty bag of cheese sticks. She looked back at the girls but Courtney was scuffing her toes in the ground, refusing to meet her eyes. Even Tyra looked subdued.

"I'm going to calm the horses," Kate muttered. She yanked on her boots, tight-lipped with anger. This was unnecessary and it could have ended in a tragedy. As it was, it was definitely tragic for the bear.

She walked to the picket line, calling quietly. Most of the animals were wide-eyed and snorting, but no longer so panicky, well accustomed to hunters and gunshots and the smell of blood. Only Slider, shaky and sweaty, twisted at his tether, still anxiously peering at the musky bulk lying on the ground.

She stroked his neck, needing time to curb her anger, struggling to be grateful that no humans or horses had been hurt. But she'd warned the girls about taking food in the tent, several times. A grizzly, no matter how small, was incredibly dangerous. This was their habitat and it was foolish to force unnecessary interaction. It never ended well.

At least Courtney and Tyra were safe. For a moment, when the bear had been so close to their tent, all she could think about was the power in those curved claws. And Monty had been so brave, and Jack so calm, reluctant to shoot. She no longer cared if Jack was the one marking trees. If it were him, he must have good reason. Because he certainly wasn't a killer. Just like her and Monty, he respected life and had only wanted the bear to leave.

She wasn't surprised when his arms wrapped around her. It felt right that he'd come to her as quickly as he could.

"You okay?" he whispered.

She gave a wordless nod, appreciating their easy intimacy.

"No one feels like going back to sleep," Jack said. "It'll be light in less than an hour. Kessler and Logan are making coffee, rounding up breakfast. You and Monty... Well, that was heroic, but you scared the shit out of me." His voice tightened. So did his arms. "But if something else happens, you need to look after yourself first."

She twisted, looking up at him. His face was shadowed but she could feel the stiffness of his arms, the depth of emotion in his voice. He sounded almost afraid, and she doubted he was a man who feared much.

"I don't think the girls will take food in their tent again," she said, trying to read his expression. She'd been prepared to confide about the trail markers, but there was something going on with him. Something unsettling.

"Just look after yourself," he repeated. "If something else happens."

"What else do you think might happen?" she asked.

Jack had just stood alongside her, facing down a charging grizzly, risking his life to protect Courtney. He wouldn't have done that if he didn't care about her safety. On the other hand, if someone wanted Courtney as a way to manipulate the U.S. government, the girl wasn't worth anything dead.

"What else do you think might happen?" Kate repeated. "Are you expecting trouble?"

"I just want you safe," Jack said, his voice so low it sounded almost pained. "But I'm paid to do a job. So *she* has to come first, not you."

"Naturally. We're all putting her first. That's how it should be." Kate hesitated, knowing she wasn't supposed to ask questions. But no one else was around and it was hard to believe Jack wouldn't tell her the truth. Not when he was already being so honest. "Courtney and Logan both mentioned that you aren't with the Secret Service?"

"That's right. I'm private. Hired as insurance."

She nodded as if that made sense. But insurance for what? She trusted him far more than Kessler but was her attraction to Jack clouding her judgment? "The Secret Service guys seem competent," she said slowly. "Very devoted."

"Yes," Jack said. And though his voice remained agreeable, she could feel the muscles cording in his arms.

A twig snapped, announcing someone's approach. Someone clumsy. Jack lowered his arms, gently brushed her cheek with his knuckle, then walked to the other side of Slider.

"How are the horses?"

Kessler.

"Quiet enough," Jack said. "Once it's light, we can use one of the mules to move the carcass."

"I don't see how we could have avoided shooting," Kessler said, his voice defensive. "Guess I'm glad you grabbed the shotgun."

"Kate and Monty had nothing," Jack said. "They were unarmed. They had nothing but courage."

"Well, they're only here to lead us to the mustangs," Kessler said. "We provide the protection."

"But they're helpless—"

"We can't trust outsiders," Kessler snapped, obviously unaware that Kate was standing on the other side of Slider. "Quiet," he added. "Monty's coming with the grain. And I need you to join Logan and me so we can figure out our report."

Jack waited a moment, then reached over Slider's back and squeezed Kate's shoulder before following Kessler to the fire.

A horse nickered, then another as the animals realized Monty was arriving early with their breakfast. Even Slider twisted in anticipation, seeming to forget all about the bear.

"I was hoping to sneak the hatchet," Monty whispered, as she helped him attach the feed bags to the horses' halters. "But they'd notice if it was gone. Maybe if we ask, they'll let us carry weapons now."

"Don't count on it," Kate said. "Kessler still doesn't trust us. I think he's the rotten one."

"Or he's just an idiot," Monty said dryly. "Did you say anything to Jack? About how someone is marking our route?"

"I almost did," she admitted. "I trust him the most. But he is a consultant, maybe more open to private deals, so...I don't know."

Monty blew out a resigned sigh. They were both quiet. The only sounds were the horses gobbling their grain.

"If someone is coming for Courtney," Monty finally said, "I figure they'll arrive in the evening, after the agents make their last security call."

Kate squeezed the bridge of her nose, hoping the pressure would help her think. Monty spoke casually, as if an abduction was an everyday occurrence, while she still grappled with the fact that someone in their group was leaving a trail.

"That would give them ten hours," Monty went on, "to ride out of here before the morning security check. There's a trail three miles north that would take them to the secondary road on the other side of the park. It's rough but doable, and they'd avoid all the security back at the ranch. I can't imagine they'd try Eagle Pass."

"No." She shook her head, hating to think of anyone dragging Courtney over that treacherous route. But she and Monty couldn't walk the girls out of camp based on suspicions. Besides, if Jack were involved he'd easily track them down.

"Maybe it's just media following us," she said. "And one of the agents—or Jack—is making money for an invasive story about Courtney. It's still not enough reason to slip the security detail." However, the thought of nude pictures of Courtney splattered over the Internet made her ache for the girl, and she resolved to be more careful during bathroom breaks. She'd definitely take the time to rig a tarp around the trees.

"Media types wouldn't go to this much trouble," Monty said. "But I figure we'll know if it's time to scat. Watch for anyone slipping off alone. And just look after yourself."

She cut Monty a sharp look. Ironically both he and Jack seemed to be issuing the same warning. But it was all so vague. Pointless too. Because until the danger was more defined, Courtney and Tyra would never leave their protective detail.

"If you're that concerned," she said, "it's probably best to tell Jack."

"But what if he's the one marking the trail? He's the best woodsman of the three."

"Then let's tell all three men at the same time. Let them sort it out."

"All right," Monty said. "But if we do that, you and the girls should be well away from camp."

"You really think one of them is going to start killing us?"

Monty's mouth set in a grim line. "Not all of us," he said.

CHAPTER SIXTEEN

Kate cleaned up the last of the breakfast dishes, feeling jumpy and vulnerable, her eyes constantly sweeping the meadow. Everything seemed normal. Dark splotches marked the ground where the bear had fallen, but Jack and Monty had already left with the carcass, using Bubba to drag the dead grizzly deeper into the woods.

Kessler and Logan lingered with Courtney by the communication equipment, finishing up their morning security call. They looked alert but not up-tight. Certainly neither man showed an inclination to sneak away for a rendezvous, either with media or someone more sinister.

Tyra was subdued but surprisingly helpful, even carrying a bucket from the river and making sure there was plenty of boiling water. "I'm sorry about last night," she said, plunking the bucket on the ground beside Kate. "I thought you were being anal, telling us to change our clothes after supper, and the stuff about the food in the tent."

She fiddled with the handle of the bucket, still not meeting Kate's eyes. "Jack told us how you and Monty risked your lives to save us. So, thank you. And Jack said I could stay in camp with you today, and not ride in to see the wild horses. But I want to go. And I'm okay, you know, about riding Slider."

Kate gave Tyra an approving smile. That made it easier. She hadn't realized that she would have been the person assigned to stay behind. Had assumed one of the men would remain back.

But maybe all three needed to watch Courtney...or else Jack wanted Kate to stay behind for some other reason.

She dipped the tin mugs into the soapy water, her thoughts scrambled. Monty had warned her to be on the alert for someone trying to split up the group, thereby reducing Courtney's protection. But getting rid of a guide didn't make sense. She and Monty didn't even carry weapons.

"Jack suggested that you and I stay in camp?" she asked.

Tyra nodded. "Yes, he thought I wouldn't want to ride today. In case there are more water crossings that would probably make Slider freak."

Kate gripped the mugs more tightly. That didn't make sense. Jack knew Slider was fine. He'd seen her schooling the palomino. Had even commented on Slider's good behavior.

"But Monty said there are no more rivers," Tyra went on. "And I want to be with Courtney when she finally sees the mustangs. She's crazy about them. She did her term paper about some anti-fertility vaccine that could save their lives and protect the range. And she invited me on this trip even though her parents wanted her to take someone else... And that's what I want to talk to you about."

Tyra needlessly moved the bucket another inch, then quit playing with the handle and looked at Kate. "I know you and Monty know so much and that you risked your lives and I should have listened to you about not taking food in the tent. And I'm sorry." Her words came in a rush now. "But please don't tell."

"We have to report any bear incidents," Kate said. "And I have to be truthful about why he was attracted to the tent. It's a safety issue. Besides, I'm sure Kessler and Logan have already reported it."

"Yes, but could you say I didn't know about the danger? That you forgot to tell me about not taking food in the tent? Because if you don't, I won't get to hang out with Courtney ever again. I won't be allowed to take riding lessons with her either. And we're best friends." Her voice rose in panic.

Kate sighed. No doubt the White House was necessarily strict and the list of Courtney's approved friends limited. But good ranch jobs were also hard to find. Besides, both girls hadn't followed instructions. It wasn't only Tyra's fault.

"It wasn't just you," Kate said. "There were wrappers by each sleeping bag. You were both in the tent, eating that candy."

"But I already told Kessler and Logan it was only me. That Courtney was asleep and didn't know about it. If I didn't, she wouldn't be allowed to go on any more trips."

"Wait a sec." Kate's hands stilled over the washcloth. "You're taking all the blame?"

Tyra gave a determined nod. "Yes, because her father's job is really hard on her. I think that's why she's so fascinated with the mustangs. Because they're able to run free. But his term is up in two years. And then everything will be good again. She won't have people following her all the time, watching every move."

Soapy water dripped over Kate's shirt and she realized she was still squeezing the cloth. But she'd been wrong about Tyra, focusing on the girl's self-absorption when she was actually a surprisingly good friend.

"Kessler and Logan must be very upset with you right now," Kate said. "If you let them think you were the only one eating that food."

"They don't like me much anyway." Tyra gave a flippant shrug. "I thought Logan did because he talks to me all the time, but he didn't even help me in the river. But I don't care what they think." However, she glanced wistfully at the group of three, and it was clear it did matter. And the fact that she was still determined to protect Courtney was rather endearing.

Kate wasn't sure if she had even one friend like that. Certainly after the accident her friends and co-workers had said all the right things. They seemed to be supportive, far more than her ex-boyfriend. But Andrew had confided she really made them uncomfortable, convincing her it was kinder to sever contact.

Now Kate wondered if he'd been exaggerating. At the time, she'd just wanted to escape the media. And she'd already wanted to put some distance between her and Andrew.

"So, will you do it? Please?" Tyra tentatively touched Kate's arm. "If not for me, for Courtney?"

Kate's throat tightened as she stared into Tyra's beseeching eyes. She had to help the girls, both girls. And just hope Sharon Barrett wouldn't fire her ass for imperiling the President's daughter.

"All right," Kate said. "I don't remember warning you about not eating in the tent. It was my mistake."

Tyra whooped in delight. "You're the best!" She surprised Kate by wrapping her in an exuberant hug.

"But you have to do everything I say from now on," Kate said. "Without question. Will you promise me that?"

"Absolutely. I'll gather firewood, do the dishes. Even bury the toilet paper, whatever you want."

It wasn't camp chores Kate had in mind, but Tyra seemed to trust her now. And having the girl's promise of future cooperation might be helpful. Because Monty wasn't the type to jump at shadows and the fact that he was alarmed enough to gather an escape pack was definitely ominous.

———◦———

BUBBA SNORTED IN DISTASTE as Jack backed the mule closer to the pungent bear carcass, giving the rope more slack.

"Damn shame to leave him," Monty said, uncoiling his rope from the bear's hind legs. "Someone always wants the meat. Don't suppose I can make a call? Let the ranch know?"

"Kessler and Logan control all communication," Jack said, coaxing the mule to take another step backwards. They'd chosen Bubba because he was the strongest mule but he wasn't happy about being separated from Belle and Gus. Frankly, Jack wasn't happy about being away from camp either.

"Doesn't it make you a little uncomfortable," Monty said, "that *they* can communicate and we can't?"

Jack grunted his assent and made a show of scratching Bubba's neck, giving Monty plenty of talking space. The old guide was a respected woodsman, held in esteem by virtually every cowboy in Montana. And if the man had any misgivings, Jack wanted to hear them.

But Monty kept coiling his rope, and the only sound was Bubba's heavy breathing.

"You have issues with either of them?" Jack finally asked. Monty was okay at answering trail questions, but he seemed only truly comfortable with Kate. Not surprising. She was like a refreshing drink of pure spring-fed water. Once you tasted it, you craved more.

And she was alone at camp with nothing but her tiny jackknife. He'd already witnessed she wasn't the type to run from danger. Something he generally appreciated, but now it only left him edgy. At least he'd laid the groundwork to keep her in camp with Tyra, away from the target and possible danger. If he had to protect Courtney, he didn't want any distractions.

"Something bothering you?" Jack asked, fighting the urge to throw a leg over the mule's back and gallop back to camp.

Monty just shrugged, his sun-spotted hand stroking the brim of his hat. The guide's astute gaze lingered on Jack as he scratched Bubba's neck, and Jack had the feeling he was the one being evaluated.

"Guess I'm not sure how much I trust two men who won't even stop to pull a girl from the river," Monty finally said.

Jack felt the same way. But the Secret Service operated by a different code, and their sole job was to look after Courtney. As was his.

He re-adjusted Bubba's harness, pulling it lower around the mule's rump. "That's understandable," he said, avoiding Monty's gaze. "But they have their priorities. And they assumed I'd look after Tyra."

"But will you look after Kate, if she needs help?"

Jack's head shot up. And this time he had no trouble meeting Monty's gaze. "Yes," he said. *If helping Kate doesn't put Courtney at risk.*

He waited for more questions. However, Monty only nodded, gave the bear one last regretful look and took Bubba's lead rope.

They trudged back to camp, Bubba's unshod hooves making a muted but rhythmic sound. A squirrel scolded and Jack caught a flash of gray as an animal slunk along the top of the ridge. A coyote probably. Scavengers never waited long before moving in for a free meal. At least Bubba had made it possible to move the carcass a prudent distance from the river.

Jack studied the ground as they walked, checking for fresh tracks. A deer had crossed the trail over the last thirty minutes but that was the only new sign. Certainly there was no evidence of riders, or even wild horses. Like Bubba, the mustangs wore no shoes. Their hoofs had a more concave shape than domestic horses, with not as much distinction between the frog and sole. Obviously the mustangs didn't use this approach to their regular watering hole. Monty said the herd hung out a little further to the west, where grass was plentiful and predators easier to spot.

A two-hour ride, Monty had said, more or less guaranteeing they'd see the mustangs before noon. With a little luck, that would be all they'd see.

But the tree blazes he'd found were troubling. Jack debated the wisdom of slipping back to the east and notching his own tree, possibly luring pursuers on a wild-goose chase. But any idiot would be able to follow the bear's drag marks and realize it was a dead end. At least Monty was taking a different route back, either by luck or design, and now they approached camp from the northeast.

The horses heard their steps first. One of them gave a guttural whinny. Two more animals nickered a greeting. Kessler and Logan were doing a lousy job on watch. In fact, they huddled around the cooking grill like sitting ducks.

Jack sighed, wavering between dark suspicions and the nagging belief that both men were too clumsy to even consider a traitorous move. He scanned the camp, searching for Kate. The instant he saw her hurrying toward them, he knew something was wrong. Then he heard painful whimpers coming from the girls' tent.

"Courtney has a migraine," Kate explained. "I left their tent up so she could stay out of the sun. And I gave her a little painkiller from the first aid kit." Her troubled gaze met his, then lingered on Monty. "She says it feels like she ate gluten."

"Impossible," Monty said.

"Yes," Kate said, looking back at Jack. "Everything we packed from the ranch was gluten free. The crackers, the rolls, the pita wraps. The kitchen has a separate oven and cooking station. And the cook is careful about guarding against cross-contamination."

"What about the candy bars Tyra ate in the tent?" Jack asked.

"I checked the wrappers," Kate said, an odd expression on her face. "All the ingredients were fine."

And even if the bars weren't safe, Jack thought, only Tyra had eaten them. Unless the girl had wiped Courtney's lips while she was sleeping, the food wouldn't have had any effect. And Tyra wouldn't do that. It was obvious the girls shared a special bond. He'd observed how they looked after each other on the trail, taking care to hold back branches so they wouldn't whip each other in the face. And Jack had personally checked all the trail food. Everything was approved. So this had nothing to do with Kate's cooking.

However, Kessler stomped up, red-faced and glowering. "You weren't careful enough," he said, glaring at Kate. "The grill must have been contaminated. You should know celiacs need a higher standard of care. This is your fault."

Courtney's pitiful whimpers affected them all but that was no excuse for his belligerence, or for so quickly laying blame.

"We don't know the cause yet," Jack said, easing between them. "Let's help her get healthy. Then figure out what happened."

But Kate slipped around Jack to face Kessler again. "The grill is new," she said. "There was no cross contamination. And I didn't make her breakfast."

"You're accusing *me* now?" Kessler glared down, dwarfing Kate with his bulk.

"I'm saying we need to check what she ate," Kate said, clearly not the type to back down from a bully, even a man three times her size. "And how the food was served. Maybe someone made a mistake."

"I've kept her healthy for three years. But maybe you're used to hearing kids cry." Kessler sneered the words, his lower lip curling. "Horses too."

Originally Kate had been full of fight but now she wilted, her shattered expression so anguished it wrenched at Jack's chest. He shot forward, grabbed Kessler's arm and yanked him toward the campfire.

"What the fuck—"

"It happened," Jack snapped. "Cool it. The real question is how do you want it handled? Do we call in a helicopter?"

Kessler yanked his arm free as he tramped back to the campfire. "Not yet. She'd be devastated. Guess you and the guides can scout out the mustangs," he said. "Find out their location. Logan and I will stay here."

Jack picked up the coffee pot, his suspicions churning. This was too convenient. Courtney had been laughing when he and Monty left with the bear carcass, thrilled about seeing the mustangs. Now she was too sick to ride.

He glanced at Kate. She and Monty were discussing something, their voices low but measured. He trusted those two more than he trusted Kessler and Logan. On the other hand, Kate *had* been in charge of the food. Clearly Courtney had eaten something that had made her ill. Something that would keep her from riding. And now she was stuck in camp, with tree blazes pinpointing her position as effectively as a flashing neon sign.

He certainly didn't intend to leave Courtney alone, no matter Kessler's rationale.

"Now where's *she* going?" Kessler muttered. Jack twisted, just in time to glimpse Kate's willowy figure before she faded behind the trees.

"Probably just a bathroom break," Jack said, hiding his own consternation. Because someone had been leaving a trail. He'd spotted four marked trees. And there was no denying the easy way Kate moved in the woods or her obvious desire to ride at the back of the line.

Alone and out of sight...just as she was now.

CHAPTER SEVENTEEN

Kate squeezed into the tent, stepped over Tyra's sprawled legs and knelt beside Courtney. "Here," she said, pressing a handful of freshly picked leaves into the girl's hand. "Chew on these. They're feverfew leaves. Bitter, but they might help."

"Nothing helps a migraine," Courtney said, her voice reedy. She kept her eyes tightly shut, her hands clamped around the edge of her sleeping bag. Her forehead wrinkled in pain and her legs were drawn up to her chest.

"She's nauseous too," Tyra said, her stricken eyes holding Kate's. "This is all my fault. It must have been those chocolate bars last night."

"It's nobody's fault," Courtney mumbled. "Just leave me alone. Go and see the mustangs."

Tyra shook her head and loyally stretched back out on the tent floor beside Courtney. "I'm not leaving. I never was that excited about seeing them anyway. I just wanted to go on a trip with you."

"Some trip." Courtney twisted onto her side. "Feel like I want to die."

Kate dipped a cool cloth into the wash basin and wiped Courtney's brow. "I understand how awful it is to be sick in camp," she said gently. "But if we can help the nausea and headache, you'll feel much better. Maybe you can drink the feverfew if I mix it in a cup of tea?"

Courtney just groaned. Even though the tent was darkened, the sun seeped through the thin nylon, emphasizing the staleness of the air, the pallor of her face.

"These leaves have helped a lot of hikers," Kate said. "And I'm sure they'll help you too."

"Kate knows what she's doing," Tyra said. "Why don't you try them? Maybe then we both can see those horses."

"Nothing helps," Courtney said. "Not drugs. Certainly not herbs." But she cracked open an eyelid, fumbled for the leaves and pressed one into her mouth.

She wrinkled her nose at the bitter taste. But she swallowed, her throat convulsing as she accepted a sip of water from the cup Kate pressed against her lips.

"What are you giving her now?" Kessler's suspicious voice came from just outside the tent door.

Kate shifted, moving to the front of the tent so she didn't have to raise her voice close to Courtney's ear. "Just some water," she said. "And the leaves I already showed you."

Kessler said something and she could hear Jack's murmured reassurance. It was good Jack was around. All three men had inspected the leaves, but only he had recognized the plant. Other than Monty, Jack was the only one who thought a herbal remedy worth trying. It was almost as if the agents didn't want Courtney able to ride.

In fact, the agent was still grumbling. "You don't realize what she's capable of," Kessler said. "I thought it was a good thing to have her along. Now I'm not so sure."

"What do you mean?" Jack asked, his words fading as the men walked further from the tent.

"Just be glad she doesn't have a knife," Kessler muttered, his voice almost inaudible now. But Kate had heard enough.

She turned back to Courtney, feeling the blood drain from her face. Danny's death was a tragedy, and there'd been nothing she could have done to save him. Few people knew all the details. Kessler did though, and clearly he disapproved.

"You look awful," Tyra said, her puzzled gaze on Kate. "Are you feeling sick too?"

"I'm fine." Kate fumbled for the tent zipper. "I'm going to collect some more leaves. Be back soon."

There were several small meadows north of the river where she'd spotted feverfew growing, the white and yellow flower unmistakable. If the herb worked, it would be good to have some on hand. Besides, she had to get away. She could pretend Kessler's comments didn't hurt, but they did. And she needed breathing room.

She stepped from the tent. Kessler and Jack were still talking, voices low, heads bent. Jack turned, his eyes holding hers. She steeled herself for his reaction, telling herself it didn't matter. But his expression remained unreadable. Maybe Kessler hadn't spilled the entire contents of her file. After all, the agents did everything by the book, and Jack wasn't one of them.

Monty walked over, his eyes concerned. "How's she feeling?" he asked. "Will she be able to ride?"

"Not yet," Kate said "I'm going to pick some more leaves and just hope she can keep them down."

Monty's voice lowered. "Kessler wants me to leave and scout out the horse herd. But I'm not going anywhere. I told him the horses need more grazing time."

Kate nodded. Kessler might be in charge of Courtney, but Monty was responsible for the welfare of the animals. More grass was a good excuse to keep the horses in camp, and the group together. Clearly there was safety in numbers.

"I'll take my time gathering the leaves," she said. "Be back before lunch."

"Just do your magic," Monty said. "Because someone doesn't want that girl riding. And we need her mobile, just in case."

"I expect the feverfew will help. Seems the migraine really was triggered by something she ate."

"That's what worries me," Monty said. "Because *you* didn't make a mistake with her food. And you know your herbs. So I trust you'll get her feeling better soon. And I'm glad you're so resourceful."

She gave him a wobbly smile. Jack might be influenced by Kessler's whispers but Monty still believed in her. Although his faith was somewhat misplaced. He had no idea about her constant flashbacks. How hard it was to block the images of Danny and his dad, the bloody buckskin. She'd learned to control her panic attacks, but Kessler's derogatory comments left her raw.

"Don't worry about that Washington dude," Monty said. "You did what had to be done. You had some bad luck."

But despite her best efforts, she hadn't been able to save them. Not Danny or his dad or any of the horses.

She pressed her clammy hands against her jeans, feeling the perspiration beading on her forehead. Andrew had said no one wanted to work with her, including the search and rescue team. Kessler considered her a fuck-up. Maybe she did bring bad luck. Because now Courtney was writhing in a tent, too sick to ride, and Monty thought it might be necessary to hide the girl from the very men sent for protection.

Obviously Monty knew a bit about what Kate had done. The official report stated that two hunters, along with their horses, had died after falling off a mountain ledge. Monty wasn't the type to google anyone. But he and Sharon Barrett were very close and they obviously discussed all the employees.

"Why did you even want me on this ride?" Kate asked. "Some of the other girls have worked for the ranch much longer."

Monty didn't hesitate, not even for a second. "Because you're brave and gutsy and will do what's necessary. To help people as well as animals. I'm hoping we don't need that. But we might.

"Don't completely trust the agents," he went on. "And we need to know for certain if we're being followed. So take the field glasses and check our back trail. See if you can spot anyone."

Now that was a job she could handle. She nodded, somewhat fortified by his belief in her, even if she didn't have the same faith in herself. "How will I know if they're dangerous?" she asked.

"You'll know," he said.

CHAPTER EIGHTEEN

Kate slipped Monty's binoculars into her backpack and hurried across the clearing, relieved to escape the tension-filled camp. She generally tried not to worry about other people's opinions, and men like Kessler didn't usually intimidate her, but right now she felt fragile.

And spooked.

Monty was too experienced to imagine danger where it didn't exist. And the trail blazes and Courtney's untimely migraine couldn't be ignored. But the way Kessler and Jack were hunched together by the coffee pot also left her on edge, and not just because Kessler was probably spilling every juicy detail about the mountain wreck. There'd been friction between her and the agent before they even left the ranch.

But Jack was different. Even Monty liked Jack. However, now it seemed as if Kessler and Jack were buddies, confidants. Maybe even co-conspirators.

Snatching the daughter of the President was a daring plan, one that would require help as well as collateral damage. But she couldn't picture Jack willingly hurting anyone. Not after the way he'd jumped into that rushing river to rescue Tyra, or how he'd stood beside Kate and Monty against an unpredictable grizzly.

Of course, she'd been fooled by him before. Had thought he was interested in her only to learn he'd just been doing his job. On the other hand, he seemed genuinely attracted now. No one could fake the desire in last night's kiss. Or could they? Maybe he was still playing her. Perhaps he'd seen her talking to Logan last night and worried that she might be telling him about the tree blazes. Certainly once Jack had sauntered up to the campfire, she'd put aside her internal debate about confiding in the agent.

If Jack and Kessler were in collusion, the rest of them were in big trouble. Because two armed men with the element of surprise could easily overpower Logan. And she and Monty wouldn't be able to sneak the girls away unless the danger was obvious. Even then it might be hard to convince them to leave. At the moment that was rather pointless to worry about. Because right now, Courtney couldn't even ride, let alone run.

Kate detoured around the grazing animals, murmuring a distracted greeting. They were busy eating the sweet meadow grass, taking full advantage of their extra grazing time. Certainly judging by their behavior, no one would question Monty's claim that they needed more time to eat. Slider was the only horse to even raise his head. He eyed her with dismay, clearly anticipating she was here to saddle up.

"Maybe this afternoon," she said, pausing to give his shoulder an affectionate scratch. If the feverfew leaves worked as she hoped, Courtney would be able to ride out sooner than anyone expected. While it was comforting to be by the cooling river with its surrounding trees and multiple escape paths, the forest also reduced visibility of approaching riders. So it would be good to break camp and move on to the open grasslands of the valley.

Logan stepped out from his watchful post by the edge of the trees. "Where are you headed?" His gaze narrowed on her backpack. "Toward the valley? To look for the mustangs?"

"Yes. I'm hoping to spot the herd. In case we can still make the trip."

"How's she feeling?" Logan's eyes cut toward the tent. "Think she'll be okay to ride tomorrow?"

Kate nodded but didn't linger. She hoped Courtney would recover much quicker than that, but both Kessler and Logan had scoffed at the efficacy of a herbal remedy. And she wasn't about to admit she was looking for more of the flowers…or that she was doubling back to check their trail.

She waved goodbye to Logan and slipped into the thick woods, not changing direction until the trees concealed her movements. It was a pleasure to hike again and in the dense brush a horse would only have slowed her down. She squeezed beneath several low-hanging branches before swerving toward the morning sun, heading east and following a narrow animal trail marked by cloven hooves. Deer always found the best meadows and even better, knew the shortest way to reach them.

Animal sign was plentiful here: bent twigs where a doe had been feeding, the oblong print of a coyote and the long narrow track of a moose. She grimaced when she crossed the trail of Bubba and the dead grizzly. Monty and Jack had dragged the body northeast, away from the river, and she was relieved not to stumble upon the bear's pitiful carcass.

The wind was at her back so it was unlikely she'd surprise any animals. Even so she deliberately made some noise. She glimpsed a coyote moving in the same direction as her, away from the dead bear. He'd probably been one of the first to feed on the grizzly before being chased away by more powerful predators. Judging by his speed, he was keen to leave the area, so he was definitely spooked. Maybe another bear. Or wolves. Or possibly humans.

She paused to listen, comforted by the dense branches so close to the ground. No one would be able to ride a horse through this terrain. Even the most aggressive hiker would choose an easier route. However, the coyote had been disturbed, not bothering to hang around for leftovers. And that was unusual behavior.

She maneuvered over a tangle of deadfall before stopping to listen again, feeling with every one of her senses. Was it her imagination or did the wind carry the faint whiff of tobacco? It wasn't totally impossible. The Secret Service had closed off access from the ranch, but there were alternate trails from the little town to the north. There could be hikers in the area, although horseback was the preferred method since no one wanted to risk soaking their gear in the river. And few serious hikers smoked.

She felt her pack, searching for the hard bump of the binoculars. She wouldn't have to move very close. A quick visual was all she needed. And in this thick brush she could move faster than almost anyone, except maybe Jack.

She squeezed through a stand of yellow pine thickened with scrub trees and low brush. The air was heavy with rotting vegetation but it was the pungent smell of cigarettes that made her freeze.

"Put that out," someone growled. Her heart slammed against her ribs. If the man hadn't spoken, she would have barged into their camp.

She dropped to the ground, pressing against the dank soil, needing a moment to steady her thudding heart. Then she cautiously lifted her head, peering around a sparsely needled tree into the tiny clearing.

Three men sprawled in a semi-circle. One gulped from a thermos, another pulled on a cigarette, and the third man had a long rifle lying across his lap. Definitely not a standard hunting rifle. Unlike the thin-barreled shotgun Kessler kept by the panniers, the same one Jack had used to shoot the bear, this man's rifle had a thick barrel with spiraling grooves cut into the bore. And the scabbard was camo, not hunter orange.

"We're five fucking miles away," the man with the cigarette grumbled.

"By horse trail. We're a lot closer as the crow flies. And the old guide is sharp, probably has a nose like a bird dog."

"Doesn't matter. We already know he's unarmed. So there are only two guns we have to worry about." But the man obediently ground his cigarette into the dirt before slapping at his neck. "Let's go there now. Grab the girl and get back to civilization. Damn flies are sucking me dry."

"Not yet," the man with the rifle said. He sat motionless, unfazed by the cloud of black flies.

Kate's stunned gaze shot back to his sniper rifle and she pressed closer to the ground, wishing now she wasn't so close. Did the smell of her fire, their breakfast, linger on her clothes? Two of the men looked unaware but not the rifle man. He was watchful, patient, as if accustomed to being in the woods for long periods. And she bet his sense of smell was every bit as sharp as Monty's.

She inched her head to the right, painfully slow, checking out their animals and gear. Six tethered horses. Light, tall Thoroughbred types. No mules, no packs, only saddlebags. Three of the six saddles had rifle scabbards. *Six saddles?*

She squeezed her eyes in horror, hit by the realization there were three more men. And she had no idea of their location. Were they behind her? One of the horses twisted against his tether, staring in her direction with pricked ears. Dammit, he was going to give her away.

A squirrel scolded and the horse's attention shifted to the left. Seconds later, two men emerged only thirty feet to the left of Kate. They were dressed in full camo. Even their faces were blackened. And the fact she hadn't heard them scared her even more.

The man with the rifle unfolded from the ground, his movement fluid. "Any developments?"

"Piece of cake. It'll be down to one gun, an old man and three untrained females. He couldn't split the camp but having them together is better. Said to weigh down the bodies and dump them in the river. With luck, they'll think he's in the water too."

Kate's body locked in horror. Black flies crawled on her cheek but she didn't move a muscle. Couldn't brush them away even if it was safe to move her arm. Which it most certainly wasn't.

"What about the horses?" the man with the rifle asked, calmly sliding it into his scabbard.

"Shoot them. So they don't run back to the ranch."

"I might check them out first," the man with the cigarette piped up. "Swap with theirs. Or else ride our extra one. My idiot horse keeps slamming my knees into the trees."

"Means he doesn't like you," one of the camo men said, his ugly laugh sending goose bumps down Kate's back. "But you can take your pick of horses. He's got the communication equipment and the safety code. Figures that buys us enough time to get her to the plane."

The man on the ground reached into his pocket and pulled out another cigarette. "Then it doesn't matter if I smoke now," he said. "If their fire is going, we might even be able to grab some coffee. Probably no black flies there either." His voice turned hopeful. "Maybe we could linger a bit. Seems a waste to snuff two broads without having a little fun first."

Kate squeezed her eyes shut, afraid they'd hear the frenzied beating of her heart. Everything felt loud, even the fly buzzing around her face.

"Just don't hurt the target. They want her undamaged."

"How do we know her?"

"Dark hair, purple jacket. She'll be the one in the tent. He slipped her some flour this morning. Bet she'll crawl out when she hears the shots though."

The man on the ground sucked thoughtfully on his cigarette. "Don't know," he said. "My cousin is gluten free. Can't leave the shithouse if he's not careful."

The man with the ugly laugh snickered.

"Then we better take a change of clothes for her," the rifle man said. "She'll be in the air for a while. Better take some of their food too."

That started a heated discussion about what made food gluten free, why so many Americans had celiac disease, and how all fucking needed to be kept to a maximum of five minutes.

Kate fought her urge to bolt. For a frantic moment, she even considered creeping into the woods and hiding until the men rode out. Even if they spotted her, they wouldn't be able to waste much time chasing her down. They were here to kidnap Courtney, put her on a plane to some foreign country...and murder all the witnesses.

So she couldn't just hide. She had to race back and deliver a warning. But bile rose in her throat and her heart banged a terrified staccato. Because someone in her camp was a traitor, conspiring to rob, rape and kill alongside this vicious group of men.

And it was a horrifying gamble trying to guess which one.

CHAPTER NINETEEN

Jack swiped at his forehead as he stopped in front of a thicket, one so dense he doubted even a rabbit could squeeze through. It was useless trying to follow Kate's trail any longer. She'd switched her southern route to an easterly direction and it was rough slogging. She certainly didn't need his help if she could move through this mess. Besides, it wasn't critical to find her. He just wanted to let her know that Courtney was feeling a bit better.

He blew out a rueful sigh. That wasn't quite true. He actually craved Kate's company. The agents were bored and bickering, and he didn't want to be stuck in camp listening to Kessler gripe about alimony payments or hear Logan's bragging about his girl-friends. Both men resented his presence but they still seemed to prefer talking to him, rather than each other. And now that Courtney's migraine had settled, Tyra was also chattering non-stop. Monty wasn't a big talker, but the grizzled guide didn't have the same appeal as Kate.

Jack accepted he had little tolerance for annoying people. And he didn't give a damn if they knew it. That was one of the reasons he'd started his own security company. Working alone suited him. So did a woman like Kate. And Kessler's veiled warn-ings about keeping her away from knives and other sharp objects didn't dampen his interest. Not one bit.

He veered west, picking up the wider trail they'd used to drag the dead grizzly, and followed it back to camp. Twenty minutes later he emerged from the woods, close to the line of picketed horses.

"Where were you?" Kessler called, his voice impatient. "And where the hell is Kate? It's almost lunchtime."

"I'm hungry too," Logan said. But neither of the two agents made a move toward the food cache. Two days in the woods had left the men stiff and sulky, and in Jack's opinion, even more disagreeable.

He paused by the picket line, in no hurry to join the agents. Monty had tied the horses in a neat row, as if planning to tack up. A small pack lay to the left of the saddles, one Jack couldn't remember seeing. "You riding out somewhere?" he asked.

"Yeah," Monty said.

Jack stepped closer. He appreciated having the steady guide around. Knew the man could be trusted to take care of the animals. And Kate. He'd witnessed the proof of that last night. "Can you wait a bit?" he asked, his voice low.

"I'm not going anywhere without Kate. If that's your concern."

Jack studied Monty's candid eyes. He liked and respected the guide, and if he knew Kate was with Monty, it would simplify his assignment. Because his job was to protect Courtney. And if there was some sort of hostile encounter, the President's daughter had to be his only concern.

So far, there'd been nothing but some tree blazes. The federal control center back at the ranch remained unconcerned. So did Kessler and Logan. But Jack's instincts were screaming, and he trusted those far more than any radio reports.

"If it was decided we had to leave this area," Jack said slowly, "what would be the best route? If we wanted to avoid our back-trail?"

"Follow the river eight miles to the north, then swing east," Monty said. "South is too rough for the horses. Nothing there but a fire tower."

"What about west?" Jack glanced at the mountains with the pristine snow glistening on their peaks. He'd studied the maps, had loaded them into his phone, and knew there was a mountain pass.

"Tricky," Monty said, "even on foot. Narrow corridors and ledges make it slow going. No, if you want to get out fast, it's best to ride north." Judging from Monty's adamant tone, the man had already given Eagle Pass careful thought. "North is more open country though," Monty said. "Hunters like it because of the easy riding and clear shots."

Jack dragged a hand over his jaw. Open rifle range was too risky. Maybe they should abort this trip. Call in a helicopter right now. But that was Kessler's decision. And Courtney would be resistant if she came all this way and couldn't see the mustangs. They were so close.

"Is the girl's headache gone?" Monty asked, seeming to read Jack's mind.

"Mostly. Those feverfew leaves did the trick. But she's still nauseous."

"So she won't feel like moving too much today. Be interesting what Kate says when she comes back."

"Did you send her out to look around? Alone?" Jack's voice hardened with disapproval. That explained why she was choosing routes that most sane people would avoid.

"She'll be fine. She's plucky, resourceful."

That was similar to Kessler's comment but Monty spoke with much more admiration than the agent. Kessler had been close-lipped, other than hinting that Kate's abilities with a knife matched Jack the Ripper's.

"I imagine you've worked with her a long time," Jack said.

Monty shook his head. "Only about five months."

Jack hid his dismay. That was about the time the Mustang River Ranch had been selected from the short list. And the same time he'd been contacted regarding his availability. Kessler had assured him that both employees had been thoroughly vetted and were trusted ranch employees. But Kate had been a late addition. And Kessler had been unusually aggressive when he'd insisted on checking her bag, as if not quite comfortable with her presence.

She always rode at the back. And it was obvious she could move easily through the woods. While anyone could have blazed those trees, it would have been much easier for her. And this morning she'd been gone for hours, giving her the perfect chance to rendezvous with other riders.

Kessler said she was tough and could improvise. What exactly did he mean? And why had Kate been approved to come if she was such a new hire? On the other hand, she only had a jackknife, and Jack hadn't given that to her until after the river incident. So it would have been impossible for her to slash any trees.

Still, it left him wary. And when she returned from her little foray, he intended to ask some blunt questions. He could tell she didn't want to talk about her past, and he'd respected that. But he had a job, a kid and a nation to protect. And if something affected Courtney's well-being, he needed to know.

He'd tried prying information from Kessler and Logan, but the men were too well trained, and Washington agents always stuck by the book. Conversely, they were overly eager to talk about things that made his eyes glaze: Kessler's three divorces, Logan's fixation on why women preferred scruffy SEALs over well-dressed agents, and the best way to score free ball tickets to a Nationals game. None of that helped Jack with his commitment to bring Courtney home safely.

He hardened his gaze on Monty. "It's time I know what Kate did. Why Kessler is so ambivalent."

Monty waited a stubborn moment. "Guess her strength scares some men," he finally said.

Jack gave his most withering stare, letting the guide know he needed more. Kate carried no weapons except for a tiny jack-knife. While she was in great shape—and he certainly appreci-ated the way she filled out her jeans—she barely weighed a hundred and ten pounds dripping wet. Even if she were a martial arts expert, she couldn't take down three trained men. And it wasn't as if Kessler totally distrusted her. He seemed to hold a grudging respect. After all, the agent could have vetoed her involvement in the ride.

"She had a tough go last year," Monty added, his voice reluc-tant. "Came across an accident in the mountains. Not something anyone should have to experience."

Monty stooped over Banjo's front hoof and it was clear he considered it disloyal to say anything more. But Jack wasn't let-ting Monty off the hook that easy. "What kind of accident?"

"Father and son hunting sheep," Monty said. "Had their horses tied together. One horse slipped, pulled everyone over the cliff. Rescuers didn't arrive until the next morning. It was a real mess."

Jack didn't realize he'd been holding his breath until it leaked out in a harsh sigh. "Was she able to help?"

"Not much anyone could do. But she gave the boy comfort, along with the dying horses." Monty looked up at Jack with eyes that were suspiciously wet. "She only had her knife and the horses were all busted up. And the wolves were coming closer. So she did what had to be done. What I hope I'd do."

He twisted back to Banjo, his gnarled hand brushing at his eyes.

Jack placed his arm on the horse's back, similarly seeking comfort. He remembered that incident trending over the Internet: a wild tale of a beautiful woman fighting off wolves, mercifully slitting horses' throats, all the while comforting a dying boy. He'd written most of it off as sensationalism. Still, if only a small portion had been true, the experience would have been horrifying, even more so for someone gentle like Kate, who valued all lives. Little wonder she avoided talking about her past, just like many of Jack's SEAL brethren.

"Thank you, Monty," he said gruffly. "I'll treat that information with respect."

He'd been drawn not just by Kate's stunning appearance, but by her composure and sense of inner strength, ever since their first meeting by the pool. The ranch clearly was her place to heal. And the last thing she needed was a firestorm exploding around her.

He brushed away a horsefly hovering over Banjo's rump, all the while weighing his options. Kessler and Logan would never discuss strategy with Monty. Or with him. The Secret Service was a closed network, with their own rules and policy, rather arrogant in the belief that they were the ultimate in protection. But Monty was always riding in front, the only man to never leave camp, making him the only person who couldn't have blazed those trees.

"I spotted some fresh tree marks on our back trail," Jack said slowly, "as if someone's been marking our route."

"Kate and I saw them too," Monty said. "We didn't know what to make of them."

"Me neither," Jack admitted. "There's no real evidence that someone is following, but I haven't had much chance to look around. If we are being tracked, it could be...troublesome."

"My boss would be disappointed if the ride is called off," Monty said. "Especially if it's a false alarm. That wouldn't help the ranch."

Jack glanced at the tent containing the President's only daughter. Courtney would also be disappointed. This was her graduation gift, a special trip she'd apparently wanted for years. But that wasn't his concern. Nor was the Barrett ranch. He was being paid to keep the girl safe. And it didn't help that everyone on the ride had their own suspicions, their own agendas.

He didn't like leaving Courtney alone, but he needed to ride out and determine if anyone was following. And if so, why. It could be relatively innocent, some freelance photographer determined to make a year's salary with a couple money pictures. At this point, it was more disturbing to think that Kessler or Logan—maybe both—were helping an outsider. There could be considerable payoff, depending on the photo. But that was the bright side.

It would be a cluster fuck if Courtney were kidnapped and used to manipulate political decisions. Certainly the President's judgment would be severely impaired if his daughter fell into the hands of extremists.

"I'm going to saddle up and follow our back trail," Jack said. "See who's out there."

"Take my horse," Monty said. "Banjo is faster and has more stamina. He doesn't mind going off alone either."

Jack gave a nod of acknowledgement. Loaning one's favorite horse was no small thing. It seemed this new trust was working both ways. His gaze settled on the small pack. An experienced guide like Monty could disappear into the woods. Keep Courtney safe if necessary. But before he rode out, he had to make sure Monty would take Kate as well. "You have enough food?" Jack asked. "Not just for the two girls but Kate as well?"

Monty gave him a reproachful look, as if an answer was unnecessary.

"Guess we should collect the farrier's kit," Jack said. "So you can fix that loose shoe."

Monty tilted his head in confusion, and then it was his turn to nod. The hoof knife and clinch cutters were plenty sharp and would be useful tools in the woods. Kessler and Logan wouldn't even notice they were missing. Right now, the two men were fiddling around the panniers, arguing about the best place to set up the communication equipment.

Jack strode up to them. "I'm going for a little ride," he said. "See if I can spot the mustangs."

"What about our lunch?" Logan asked. "Can the old guy make something?"

The old guy. Not only did Logan not know his horse's name, he didn't even remember Monty's, seeming to think the ranch staff was around to wipe his butt. "Monty's busy shoeing," Jack said, his voice clipped. "But I'll get something together before I ride out."

That way he wouldn't have to worry about Courtney eating the wrong thing. And maybe Kate would return before he left. He was curious if she'd spotted any shod tracks. Besides, he needed to see her after her wilderness foray, and reassure himself that she was safe.

"We're heading to that little hill," Kessler said. "See if there's better reception. Don't leave until we get back. We need more coffee too. Maybe you can get the fire going. Boil some water."

The fire was reduced to ashes and there was barely an inch of water left in the pot. Not one stick of firewood remained. The two men might be good with their guns but they weren't very handy, wasting much of their morning debating who had the hottest date at the last golf tournament.

"I'll have lunch ready when you come back," Jack said, only because he didn't want Kate stuck doing it. She was bound to be tired after her strenuous hike. It was doubtful she'd have spotted any mustangs. Deer might be able to move through bogs and deadfall, but horses preferred open grasslands where they could spot predators and have a chance to flee. The only horses in that thick brush would be ones forced in by their riders.

He checked his watch. Almost noon. He watched Kessler and Logan trudge up the hill, lugging the orange panniers. They rounded the bend and disappeared. If they called in at twelve hundred hours, and talked as long as they had yesterday, they'd be gone for approximately twenty minutes.

He glanced across the clearing at Monty, then jabbed his thumb at the pannier holding the farrier kit. If the man needed to collect more items for his survival pack, this was the perfect time. The farrier tools weren't as good as a hatchet, but they were easy to carry and it never hurt to be prepared.

CHAPTER TWENTY

Kate bent over, clutching her aching side, gasping for breath. Her face stung from the whipping branches and her boots were drenched and muddy from the last bog. But this route was quicker than the winding deer trail, and she had to reach camp before the riders. Had to deliver a warning.

She sucked in another painful gulp of air and lurched forward. A downed tree caught her leg in a snarl of branches and she wasted precious seconds freeing her boot. She felt slow and awkward, still grappling to accept the danger they faced. And the undeniable fact that one of her group was a yellow-bellied traitor.

It couldn't be Jack. Even if he were low enough to sell out his country, he'd never condone leaving her and Tyra to die.

Would he?

He'd fooled her before. And he used his gun for money. Mercenaries generally worked for the highest bidder. What would someone pay to have control of the President's daughter? It must be plenty. Courtney would give terrorists the ultimate weapon.

She hated to imagine the girl in the hands of a group like ISIS. Dying would be preferable, even a slow death like Danny's. She gave her head a shake and told herself that no one was going to die. She hadn't been able to save the boy, but this was different. This time she wasn't alone. All she had to do was deliver the warning and this area would be swarming with helicopters. There were also two loyal men with guns who were staunchly on Courtney's side.

The question was, which two?

She'd overheard their pursuers talking about an old guide and two men that needed to be taken out. But they hadn't mentioned names. She wanted to trust Jack but she had to go with her head, not her heart. The stakes were too high. So she'd whisper to Monty first. He could slip the girls safely into the woods before she asked the bodyguards to call for help. Two of them would want to...one wouldn't.

She ducked beneath a low-hanging branch and sprinted up the last hill, fueled by the knowledge that camp was close. She could even hear voices, men's voices.

She jerked to a stop, her blood chilling. The pursuers couldn't be here yet, could they? Even if they'd saddled up and galloped their horses the entire way, she should still be at least twenty minutes ahead.

However, voices sounded from the side of the hill. Masculine, then familiar...and her breath whooshed out in relief. It was only Kessler and Logan, maybe even Courtney if she was feeling better. They were obviously making the noon check-in call.

She charged toward the sounds, tripped over an exposed tree root, regained her balance and continued running.

The hilltop was visible with two men outlined against the blue sky. Kessler was kneeling by the equipment, putting it back in the radio canister; Logan stood behind him. Logan's arm moved. Something in his hand gleamed, reflecting the sun's silver rays.

He abruptly stooped, his arm jerked...and he slit Kessler's throat.

Kate gaped, unable to move. Unable to step back into the woods or even drop to the ground. Her brain moved molasses slow, struggling to comprehend. This couldn't be happening. They must be playing at something. In fact, Logan was looking down, talking to Kessler, his round, good-natured face still affable.

But a bright stain bloomed over the front of Kessler's shirt. And Kessler was holding his throat, his hands turning darker as he stared in disbelief. Logan laughed and raised his leg. Pushed with his boot.

Kessler toppled over, almost in slow motion.

Kate pressed a shaking hand over her mouth, feeling her anguish building. Just as her soul had wept when she'd had to cut the buckskin's jugular and bright red blood had gushed over his chest.

Images transposed across her brain, and the green grass morphed into dark rock, colored with bone and blood and bodies. And even though she knew it was Logan's triumphant voice talking into a headset, advising that he'd successfully taken out Kessler, it was Danny's whimpers she heard, and the sound of tearing flesh as wolves ripped into a horse's underbelly.

Her hand fisted against her mouth and she squeezed her eyes shut. *Keep it together. You are not on that mountain.*

But a man was dead and she could feel her body shutting down as the flashbacks took over.

She was conscious of dropping and curling in a ball, eyes closed but still hearing voices. She tried to count. One, two, three...breathe. Didn't want to think. Wasn't sure if she'd see Danny again as he begged for his dad. When she'd lied and said help was on its way, and that everything would be all right. And how she'd sung to him until her throat was hoarse, soothing little nursery rhymes, the only songs she could remember.

All she could do was struggle to breathe. And try not to think about dark things. Danny was gone but Courtney still needed help. Urgently. That knowledge kept her breathing and counting and breathing again until she managed to pry open her eyes.

This time she didn't see Danny, or the body of his father or the dead horses. Only Logan as he calmly wiped his knife on Kessler's jeans, then shouldered the equipment, and walked away. He wasn't headed back to camp, but toward his ugly gang of murderers. And that should be a relief because it would have been impossible to hide if he walked her way. But she didn't feel relieved, didn't feel anything but terrified.

She rose. Stumbled toward Kessler's prone body, her legs feeling like slabs of ice. She didn't want to see him. Didn't want to see his bloody throat. But maybe there was a slim chance, somehow, that she could help.

His face was turned toward the blue sky, his eyes open. He looked almost peaceful in death, except for his surprised expression. And the gaping wound in his neck.

She knelt down and took his hand, automatically feeling for his pulse even though it was obvious he was dead.

"Everything's okay," she said, her voice trembling. "Go in peace."

His hand quivered and for a moment she thought he was still alive, no matter how improbable. Then she realized she was the one who was shaking, her body drenched with sweat as the coppery stench of blood slithered up her nose.

She sucked in several mouthfuls of air, hating the smell and knowing she couldn't afford a panic attack. She had to get to camp. It wasn't far, maybe an eighth of a mile. But she didn't want to leave Kessler. Knew from experience what animals could do to a body, especially one so freshly blooded.

"I'm sorry," she choked, rising to her feet. "I have to go now. Back to—" Her voice cracked. But Kessler might be listening somehow, and he'd worry if she didn't use Courtney's code name.

"Back to P-Petal," Kate said. "But we'll get her home safely. I promise."

She backed up on legs that felt awkward, stumbled twice then jerked around and lurched into a run.

CHAPTER TWENTY-ONE

Jack watched as Courtney followed Tyra from the tent, her face wan against the deep purple of her windbreaker. Despite the warmth of the noon sun, she kept her jacket zippered with both arms wrapped around her chest as if warding off the cold. At least she was moving.

He gave a polite smile as the girls seated themselves on the log beside Monty. "Do either of you want some lunch?" Jack asked, gesturing at the wraps he'd just made.

"No, thank you." Courtney sounded as gracious as ever, but she shot a dark look at the pita bread. "I plan to avoid anything that isn't separately wrapped. Kate said all the food she brought was gluten free but that's not what my body is saying."

"And if the food just touches wheat," Tyra piped in, "it's enough to damage her intestine. Maybe Kate doesn't know that. Not everyone does," she added, as if feeling the sudden need to defend Kate.

"She knows," Monty said. He paused to swallow the bite of sandwich in his mouth. "So do all the kitchen staff. They're used to guests with food intolerances."

Jack knew the labels of the pre-packaged food had been checked before it went into the panniers. He'd examined it himself, along with two other agents. However, he hadn't checked Logan and Kessler's saddlebags. Hadn't had the authority.

"Who made you breakfast this morning?" Jack asked, keeping his tone casual.

"Kessler, I think," Courtney said. "Or maybe Logan. But it was only rolls and jam. And they wouldn't make a mistake."

"Maybe it wasn't a mistake," Monty muttered.

"It's okay." Courtney lowered her arms, tugging her jacket zipper a bit lower. "My migraine's almost gone, and I feel a lot better. Kate was right about those leaves. But maybe we can get up early tomorrow and still have time to see the mustangs? I really want to. So does Logan. He was as excited as me about this trip." She glanced around, her brow furrowing. "Where is he? And Kessler?"

"On the hill making the noon call," Jack said. "And Kate is looking for more feverfew leaves."

He checked the trail again, then scanned the river crossing, something he'd been doing all morning. Time crawled when one was stuck in camp, waiting for something to happen. And Kate was taking much too long. For that matter, so were the agents. He looked at Monty, his gaze narrowing in silent communication.

Monty immediately rose from the log. "I'm going to take a little walk," he said to Courtney. "But you have a good idea. We'll get up early tomorrow, see the mustangs and still be able to get you home on schedule."

Courtney gave such a grateful smile that even Monty looked a little flushed. The old guide might be a little crusty but he appreciated a horse lover's passion. It was obvious he didn't want to disappoint Courtney. She was surprisingly down to earth, and this ride had been touted as a guaranteed chance to see mustangs in the wild.

Slider twisted, straining against the picket line. White rimmed his eyes as he stared toward the trees. Seconds later, Banjo and Dusty lifted their heads, looking in the same direction.

Jack turned, trying to see what the horses had already heard. But the trail was empty.

Seconds later he caught the sound of pounding feet.

Dammit. He slid his hand beneath his shirt, reaching for his gun. But it was only Kate who burst into the clearing, bounding like a frightened deer. Her jeans were muddied, her face scratched, and her hands gleamed with red.

He instinctively started toward her, then caught himself and stepped in front of Courtney. "Get down, girls," he snapped.

He leveled his gun, his gaze sweeping the perimeter. Kate had come from the hill but no one seemed to be following. And there was no movement around the trees. Or by the river. Even more reassuring, the horses had lowered their heads, relaxing once more beneath the warm sun. Even Slider had settled.

Courtney and Tyra remained kneeling behind him, following his instructions, not saying a word. Thank God for their training.

Kate was only ten feet away now. He could hear her ragged breathing, feel her panic. Monty reached out and grabbed her arm, but she looked past him, searching for Jack. "W-we have to get out of here! N-now."

She stooped over, clutching at her side, gasping for breath. "Riders are coming," she said. "With Logan. And we need to call for help."

Jack swung toward the girls. "Go to your tent," he said, his voice urgent. "Grab some warm clothes. Get ready to ride."

They remained on their knees, staring at Kate with wide eyes.

"Now!" he said.

Tyra was the first to move. She rose, grabbed Courtney's hand and tugged her toward the tent.

Jack holstered his gun and hurried to Kate.

"Are you hurt?" he asked, calming his voice.

She shook her head. But her eyes met his, and the anguish in those dark depths made his heart squeeze. "How many riders?" he asked, wishing he had time to comfort her.

"Five," she said.

"How far away?"

"About five miles northeast. But they might have already started riding."

"Where's Kessler? Logan?"

Her mouth opened but nothing came out. Her shoulders were shaking, her entire body wracked with tremors. Then she shook her head, her composure obviously paper thin. "Kessler's d-dead," she finally managed. "*He* killed him."

Jack's fists balled but he kept his face impassive, knowing more emotion was the last thing she needed. "Where's the communication equipment?" he asked. "On the hill?"

"No. L-Logan took it. And he's meeting them and they're coming and they're going to take Courtney and they want to kill us and all the horses."

She was saying more but her body was shaking so much it was hard to understand her words. He needed to extract the details, quickly and objectively, but despite his training it was impossible to stand and watch her struggle.

He couldn't remember wrapping his arms around her. Told himself it was only to calm her down, not because he couldn't stand to see her wracked by such fear. "It's okay, Kate," he said softly. "Take some deep breaths. I just need to ask a couple more questions."

He could feel her breath shudder and roll out, knew when her breathing steadied. He inched back, still holding her in his arms but able to study her face.

"Did you see their guns?" he asked.

She nodded and now when she spoke, her voice was clearer. "Handguns and rifles."

"What about their horses? Did you see them?"

"Yes. Built for speed. Thoroughbred types. And they had one extra horse and saddle for Logan."

He gave her shoulders an approving squeeze, hiding his dismay. They couldn't even make a run for it across the north field. Not if their pursuers had rifles and speedy horses.

He glanced at Monty. "We'll take the girls and head into the woods. Rifles and horses can't help them there. If they're anything like Logan, they'll have difficulty following."

"But they're not like Logan," Kate said. "One of the men looks like a tracker. He was dressed differently than the others. And two more look like woodsmen. Their clothes looked worn, not brand new. And they were used to the flies."

"I see," he said, impressed by her analytical mind but swept with a burgeoning dismay. They had fast horses and there was no way to call for help. The thick woods still offered the best chance of escape, but Courtney wasn't feeling a hundred percent and wouldn't be able to move very fast. He'd have to buy some time. And figure a way to whisk the girls away from the action.

He looked at Monty. "Can any of your animals handle the south trail?"

"The mules can," Monty said. "Not the horses."

"Then saddle the three mules and take the girls. Tyra and Kate can double up on Bubba. I'll take the six horses and head west."

Monty gave a curt nod, scooped up his emergency pack and jogged toward the mules. Jack couldn't fault the man for lack of speed. Or Kate either. She was already hurrying toward the tent, newly composed and calling for the girls to hurry up and mount.

Their speed and efficiency with the mules was also appreciated. Within three minutes, they had the animals saddled and ready to ride. The pack mules snorted, rather puzzled at their change of status, and not very enthused about the prospect of being ridden. But they had strong legs, good feet, and were the best ticket to safety.

Jack tossed Courtney on Gus's back, then Tyra on Bubba while Kate tied a pack behind Bubba's saddle.

"Bubba is the strongest," Jack said, reaching up and helping attach the pack. "Shouldn't he be the one to carry double? Or will he buck with two riders?"

"I'm going with you," Kate said. "You'll need help leading all the horses. And Logan needs to believe he's following Courtney."

Jack scowled. "No, I'm riding alone."

"She's right." Monty leaned over Belle's shoulder. "Kate and I already discussed it. Two of the horses have never been ponied. They'd be impossible for one rider to handle, especially at speed. Kate's good. She can help."

Of course Jack knew Kate was good. But he needed her safe. Away from danger. There was no way she was going with him.

"I heard them talking about Courtney's jacket," Kate said, tapping her chest. "So wearing this will make sure they follow."

Jack stared in dismay at the bright purple jacket Kate now wore. But she was right, even if he didn't want to admit it. Logan would expect him to follow protocol and remain with the target. Logan would also expect the girls to flee on horses, not sneak out the back way on slower pack mules. It was possible he'd be so focused on overtaking Courtney's colorful paint, he might miss the mule tracks heading in the opposite direction.

It made sense to have Kate ride with him. But Jack still wasn't sold on the idea. However, Monty had already turned Belle and was heading out. The other two mules obediently followed—with Tyra and Courtney on their backs.

"See you back at the ranch," Kate said, giving the girls a wave and a strained smile. "You'll love riding the mules."

They just stared, white-faced and silent. But judging by their expressions, it was clear they understood the risks. And appreciated that Kate was volunteering to serve as their decoy.

Kate turned back to Jack, her smile fading. "There's no time to hide their tracks," she said. "But Logan won't expect anyone to ride in that direction. And Monty won't speed up until they're deeper in the woods. The mules aren't shod so their feet won't cut up the ground."

She spoke so calmly he wondered if she understood the situation. She didn't seem at all daunted by galloping cross country, posing as Courtney, being chased by a desperate band of killers—men who'd be furious when they discovered they'd followed the wrong woman.

But the plan made sense. The only thing left was to ensure Logan and his group wouldn't realize they'd been duped until it was too late. Kate was making it easy for him to do his job. And he couldn't stand here dithering, worrying about putting her at risk. Besides, the mules had already disappeared. There was no turning back.

CHAPTER TWENTY-TWO

Kate's horse stumbled. She automatically tightened the reins, helping Oreo regain his footing. Jack was setting a scorching pace. Obviously he wanted to leave a clear trail, but also hoped to stay out of sight of their pursuers. She was hot and thirsty, and her arm ached from leading Slider, but the discomfort helped her focus on their escape.

And not the murder she'd witnessed on the knoll. Not Kessler's blank eyes, the gaping wound in his throat or the way blood had spilled over his shirt.

She gave a choke of disbelief. Kessler had been the man she'd distrusted most, not friendly Logan. And she'd certainly never imagined either agent capable of slitting the other's throat. Courtney must be shattered. Those two men had been on her detail for years, and Logan had been her riding companion.

Courtney's abduction must have been planned for a while. Once Logan discovered her passion for wild horses, he would have known he'd be the logical agent to accompany her. But such ruthlessness was outside Kate's experience. She'd dealt with incompetence, braggarts and fools. Had helped fishermen, hunters and hikers who were simply the victims of poor decisions or bad luck. But people who abducted for money—and were willing to slaughter anyone who stepped in their way—that was hard to absorb.

She tightened her sweaty grip on Slider's lead line and urged Oreo for more speed. There was no doubt they were being followed. Six shod horses left a lot of tracks. How much time would Monty need? A fit man could walk down a horse or mule, but Monty knew the terrain. And if they were able to give him enough of a head start, she had no doubt he could deliver the girls to safety.

She took a peek over her shoulder, trying not to imagine the feel of a bullet as it ripped into her back. But no deadly silhouettes appeared on the hill. Besides, they wouldn't shoot her. Not yet. Those men had made no secret that Courtney was the one of value. All other riders and horses were disposable.

Kate followed Jack into another cluster of trees and breathed a little easier, grateful for the shelter and aware they'd just provided Monty with another twenty minutes.

Jack slowed his horse, trotting in a half circle. The three horses he was leading turned with minimal fuss, accustomed to being ponied. "How are you doing?" he asked, his gaze intent as he stepped down from the saddle. "Is Slider pulling your arm off?"

"He's figuring it out," she said. "He's going to be a better ranch horse after all this. So will Courtney's paint."

"And you deserve a raise after this." Jack smiled but it didn't reach his eyes and she wondered if he still wished she'd gone with Monty. But he would never have been able to make such good time leading all six horses. And if Oreo or Slider had broken away and galloped back to camp, Logan would have been instantly suspicious.

"Can you dismount and hold the horses?" Jack asked. "Keep them hidden in the trees while I check our back trail?" It was clear he had the same concern about an animal getting loose.

"Sure," she said, slipping from the saddle and taking three more lead lines along with another set of reins.

He unzipped his saddlebags and pulled out a set of binoculars. "A kiss for luck," he said, surprising her by brushing his mouth over hers before turning and jogging toward the trees.

That little kiss was comforting. This was a scary situation but she trusted Jack and suddenly things didn't feel quite so grim. As long as all of Logan's men were following, Courtney would be safe. She didn't want to think past that, to worry about their own predicament.

The horses milled around her, their flanks heaving, thickening the warm air with the smell of their sweat. She pulled off her jacket, then adjusted the lead lines, keeping Slider and Oreo on her left and the other four on her right, almost afraid to look at their back trail. Six riders, she prayed. *Let all six riders be following.*

Jack lowered the binoculars and jogged back, a satisfied smile creasing his face. "They're coming," he called. "All of them."

"Thank you, Kate," he said, easing between the horses and giving her a congratulatory hug. "I couldn't have done this without you. Now we just have to stay ahead. Keep them believing they're chasing Courtney."

She squeezed his hand in relief. It was going to be okay. Logan's group rode faster horses, but she and Jack had four extra mounts. They could switch animals, give their horses a breather. By tomorrow morning, Monty would have reached the fire tower and be able to call for help.

They just had to keep riding along the foothills. There was plenty of cover, yet some decent ground for galloping. With a little luck, they'd be fine. And when Jack stood close, holding her like this, his confidence was contagious...and she was able to act much braver than she really felt.

KATE WAS A HELLUVA rider and an amazing woman. Jack glanced over his shoulder, noting how Slider now kept an easy pace beside Oreo, no longer yanking at his lead rope. The three horses he led were neither better nor worse than when they'd started. But they were used to following Banjo and only occasionally pulled at his arm.

Having his gun hand filled with lead lines wasn't ideal, but the danger was at their backs. The open spaces scared him though. According to Kate, the men with Logan had sniper rifles. A good marksman could make a long distance shot, bringing down a horse or rider. She'd be the first one in their sights.

He pulled the horses to a stop, surprising Banjo with his urgency. "I know you're hot," he said, his voice rough. "But you have to put Courtney's jacket back on."

He reached over and grabbed Slider's lead line, nervously eyeing the open meadow they'd just crossed. A shooter might be lining her up right now and dammit, he wouldn't be able to live with himself if she were hurt. "Hurry up," he muttered.

"I'm riding Courtney's horse," Kate said. But she obligingly removed the jacket from her pack and pulled it back on. "You're right. We better make sure they think I'm her."

She was so damn brave and didn't realize he wasn't worrying about Courtney. He just didn't want a bullet in her back. They'd never shoot Kate if they thought she was the President's daughter. But his gut churned and he hated that she was riding in the most vulnerable position.

If Logan suspected Kate was a decoy, he'd have no qualms about picking her off. Based on the man's sexual bragging, he viewed women as disposable. Called them job perks. A few times Jack had sensed something darker lurking behind Logan's genial smile, even when he joked with Courtney.

Jack twisted in the saddle. "You ride in front for a bit," he said to Kate. "Set the pace."

"But don't you want them to see Courtney's horse? Her jacket?"

"Not necessary. They're locked on us now." He busied himself with rearranging the lead ropes in his right hand. Didn't want to admit he was letting emotion affect his judgment. Of course, Courtney was still his number one priority. Always would be. "We just need to cover ground," he added. "Head for that ridge. We'll switch horses on the other side."

"I know this area," she said. "Trails crisscross from all directions. It's a favorite spot for elk hunters. Monty's horse has been here a lot."

Good, Jack thought, following her toward the ridge. They could ride most of the night. Let the horses pick their way home, nibbling grass as they walked. A hub of trails meant their trackers would have to wait for daylight.

"Listen!" She swiveled in the saddle, her face bright with hope. "I hear engines. Maybe its four-wheelers from town."

"I don't hear anything," he said. But Slider was staring toward the ridge and seconds later the throb of motors drifted over the valley.

"Let's go," she said, turning toward the sound. "They'll help us."

"Wait!" Jack said, his voice urgent. "Hold the horses. I want to check first, just in case."

The hope in her face turned to dismay, and he hated that he'd put it there. But he needed to make sure. Logan had clearly planned Courtney's abduction in great detail. It only made sense for the man to have ground support, and not rely solely on animals.

Jack passed Kate his reins and left her holding the horses as he jogged up the ridge. He dropped several feet from the top then inched forward and cautiously raised his binoculars.

He spotted three four-wheelers, big powerful machines all headed in the direction of their old camp. The lead driver stopped to study the ground, then spoke into a walkie, probably communicating with Logan. But what really gave Jack concern was the black sniper rifle strapped to the second driver's back, proving that though it wasn't hunting season, it was most certainly open season on humans.

If the men had been riding horses instead of machines, their animals would have alerted them to their presence. As it was, he and Kate had almost galloped into them.

He gripped the binoculars, his thoughts churning. The net was tightening. Clearly both groups of pursuers were in radio contact. And Monty and the mules could still be intercepted. If Logan discovered Courtney was actually headed south, he'd simply arrange for his four-wheelers to speed back to town, then circle around and nab her at the fire tower.

Jack twisted, eyeing the mountains. It was still possible to buy Monty enough time. He and Kate would simply go where horses and four-wheelers couldn't follow... Eagle Pass.

He headed back to Kate, replacing his binoculars in the leather case while he jogged.

"Those men are working for Logan," he said, taking Banjo's reins and forcing his voice to remain unruffled. "No problem. We'll just climb higher."

"Climb? No, I think we should try to outrun them."

He shot Kate a wry smile. A horse couldn't beat a four-wheeler but he was glad she was keeping her sense of humor.

"Yes, we should run," she went on, her voice strengthening. "And we'll look for a stream. Or bog. Something that four-wheelers can't cross."

"We have something they can't cross." He jabbed a thumb over his shoulder. "Those mountains. They can't maneuver around us up there."

"Maybe we should split up. You climb, I'll gallop. That way we have two chances to get help."

"No," he said. "If they catch you, they'll make you talk. That puts Courtney at risk." And the idea of Kate being tortured made his gut churn. There was no way he was leaving her to face those men alone. They'd run her down in minutes.

"We'll switch horses now," he said. "Make a hard run to the tree line on fresh animals. Then dismount and climb."

He pulled the bridle off Banjo, slipped it over the rope halter on Dusty, then waited for her to follow suit. But she struggled with switching her headstall from Oreo to Slider, obviously exhausted.

He reached over her shoulder, helping to adjust the bridle over Slider's ears. "A few more hours," he said gently, "and it will be dark. We can rest then."

She just stared at Slider's neck. He'd assumed she was exhausted but now he noted the paleness of her face, the tiny tremor around her mouth. Obviously she feared the searchers on the other side of the ridge. As did he.

"As long as their engines are going," he said, giving her shoulder a reassuring squeeze, "they won't hear our horses. Don't worry. Even if they pick up our tracks, no four-wheeler will be able to follow us for long."

The pallor of her skin emphasized the reddened scratches from her earlier run through the trees. "And since we'll be high above the tree line," he teased, "you won't have to worry about any more branches jabbing you in the face. We'll be way too high for much to live."

"Great," she said. "That eases my mind."

But she didn't crack a smile. She just squared her shoulders and swung onto Slider's back, her stoic expression reminding him of a soldier headed into battle...a battle she thought it highly unlikely to win.

CHAPTER TWENTY-THREE

Kate stared over Slider's neck as the horse lowered his head and trotted up the steep slope. His breath came in puffs, his white mane a contrast against his sweat-darkened neck. But his ears were pinned forward, as if eager to carry her wherever she asked. Slider's pricked ears looked small, almost deformed compared to a mule's. His gait felt different too, more energetic, more trusting, as if he were keen to go forward...even into danger.

Stop it. She tried to refocus on the elegant beauty of his graceful neck but her mind kept swerving back to the accident. It had been a horse—not a mule—who had pulled everyone off the ledge, leaving that pitiful tangle at the bottom of the cliff. And no matter how hard she fought, the memories bombarded her, filling her senses until she could no longer smell Slider's sweat, the mountain heather or even the plentiful elderberry. She couldn't smell anything but the metallic odor of blood, and the smell of singed flesh as she jammed at the wolves with the burning wood.

Her knuckles whitened around the lead rope, but she didn't dare look back. Didn't want to accept that she was leading another horse, Courtney's paint. So far, Oreo was behaving. Not pulling at the rope or crowding Slider. But neither of the two horses were used to mountain trails. Before today, they'd never even been ponied. The girls had insisted on riding them because of their color. What if Oreo was nervous and clipped Slider's heels?

She quickly slipped her feet from the stirrups, remembering how the man's boot had been caught. He'd been still hung up in the saddle when she found him and the horse had been thrashing, frantic to escape the limp body stuck to his belly. Of course, the horse had essentially been dead too. All three horses were. She'd just made sure they didn't suffer. And that the wolves didn't bother them while they were alive.

A groan escaped from deep in her throat. Slider flicked an ear, as if wondering what was wrong. He was much braver than her, even though he had little experience with this type of trail. He was used to a fenced riding ring with every inch of smooth dirt groomed by a tractor. But he seemed to think that since she had saved him from the river, she could keep him safe anywhere.

Foolish horse.

A mule wasn't like that. No one ever rode a mule to death. She'd never heard of a mule walking off a ledge either. They looked after themselves first, one of the reasons she preferred them to horses, especially when the going turned tough. And now she was riding a horse alongside a steep mountain, a place she'd promised herself she'd never walk again, let alone ride.

Fortunately Jack was behind her and couldn't see her sickened expression. Her gut was churning and, no doubt, her face was as white as Slider's mane. She wouldn't be surprised if her breakfast re-appeared.

"I figure we have another hour until sundown," Jack called. "Let's stop up ahead and give the horses a breather."

It was asking for trouble to stop on a narrow ledge with four riderless horses who might fuss and mill around. She opened her mouth to protest but her throat was too dry to push out the words. But Slider slowed on his own, as if understanding Jack's words. And then he wasn't moving at all. His head was down and he was snatching hungrily at the grass.

Grass, not rock.

She glanced around, her sluggish brain accepting the trail wasn't so narrow after all. In fact, they'd entered a high meadow dotted with pink mountain heather. A steep slope, to be sure, but she doubted any of the horses would be foolish enough to slide down.

She peered over Slider's right shoulder, tempted to dismount on the uphill side. Away from the slope. But he was used to riders mounting and dismounting from the left side, and she didn't want to startle him. She could turn him around, point him in the other direction, but Oreo was behind her. And both horses were tired and hungry. Fiddling with their position would only cause frustration.

Besides, now that she'd gathered enough nerve to peek down the slope, she could see it wasn't too bad. No steeper than a black diamond run on a ski mountain. She just had to step down from the saddle and hope that Slider didn't topple over on her. And that, like her, he wasn't terrified of heights.

Slider's head was down though, busy grazing. He was probably thirsty and at least there'd be some moisture in the grass. He needed every precious minute to recharge. But she didn't move, couldn't, felt shackled to the saddle.

This is for Courtney, she reminded herself. *And Tyra and Monty and Kessler. It's just a little step down.*

She sucked in a fortifying breath, flung her right leg over Slider's back and forced herself to step down from the saddle. Seconds later, she was standing on firm ground. From the downhill side, Slider seemed ten inches taller but he remained stock still, contentedly munching at the grass. She scooted around his head, moving to the other side, hating that Jack might pick up on her phobia.

But he'd already dismounted and stood beside his grazing horse, binoculars pinned to his eyes as he scanned the valley. He looked relaxed, assured, in control of the situation. And slowly her heart stopped its erratic thumping.

"You're a good boy," she whispered, reaching out and scratching Slider's sweaty neck. He continued grabbing at the grass. But his eye was on her, calm and respectful, attentive to her commands. She had no doubt he'd gallop down this steep mountainside if asked. He'd conquered his fear in the river...while hers was proving to be more stubborn.

"I'm going to take a look from the other side of the tree line," Jack said. "Watch the horses. Keep them ready to ride."

She nodded, deciding it was prudent not to loosen the horses' cinches. Luckily there were no bits in their mouths. She and Jack had stopped riding with bridles an hour earlier, using only halters so the horses could grab bites of grass whenever possible. The lack of water was worrisome though. Horses colicked much easier than mules, and they were pushing these animals hard.

Her thoughts jumped to the girls, wondering how they were making out with the mules and if Courtney's migraine was better. That horrible Logan had certainly known how to anchor them. He must have deliberately exposed Courtney to gluten at breakfast, anticipating she'd be too sick to leave the tent. But both girls were proving surprisingly resilient. Logan had underestimated them. He probably never dreamed the mules could make it over such a rough section, or that Courtney and Tyra would be game enough to ride them through the thick brush.

She stepped back to Oreo, knowing she needed to look after their own horses, their own situation.

She checked each horse's heaving flanks, calculating their rate of respiration. It was probably best to switch mounts again, although she much preferred riding Slider. So far, nothing bad had happened when she was on the palomino. And if Courtney and Tyra could navigate around bogs and deadfall, she could certainly ride along a mountain slope. This section wasn't even that steep.

Not like fifty feet above, where there was a rockslide and a confusion of animal trails, crisscrossing horizontally. Luckily Jack had been permitted to bring his phone and though there was no reception yet, he was able to access his downloaded maps. They could follow any of the trails rounding the base of the mountain. Monty's horse, Banjo, didn't even need a map. He'd been ridden in this area frequently, and the experienced horse would know the best routes.

Slider lifted his head, staring down at a cluster of crooked fir trees, stunted and warped by the wind. Seconds later, Jack emerged, jogging easily up the slope.

He was in remarkable shape. The men had always worn oversized shirts in Courtney's presence, preferring to keep their handguns concealed, but Jack had peeled down to a T-shirt hours ago. Now his leather holster was clearly visible, draped over that big shoulder, drawing attention to his pecs and abs, those same washboard abs she'd first noticed in the dance hall.

The physical attraction had certainly grown, at least from her perspective. That kiss last night had been unforgettable. Right now though, Jack's mouth looked as hard as his body, and it didn't appear as if kissing was on his mind. Of course it shouldn't be on hers either.

She gave a guilty start, yanking her gaze past him and checking their trail, wondering why he looked so grim. All she could see was the tree line.

"Are they still following?" she asked.

He gave a brief nod. His breathing wasn't labored but it was certainly louder than usual. Until one scaled a steep hill on foot, it was easy to ignore how hard the horses were working. And how gamely they were carrying their riders.

"They're gaining," Jack said. "But they're killing their horses to do it. They're down to five."

She grimaced. Logan had never shown much consideration for his horse, and clearly this was a life and death chase, for horses as well as humans.

"Our boys are recovering okay," she said brightly. "I just checked their vitals. As long as we can give them breaks and switch regularly, they'll be fine. This trail we're following isn't bad. It's just winding around the mountain, and the four-wheelers can't get up here. So all we have to do is stay in front of Logan."

Jack just looked at her, not bothering to veil his expression. And it was apparent escape wouldn't be so simple.

"I can't push Slider much harder," she said, gesturing at the tired palomino. "Because he'll go until he drops. Please, don't ask me to do that."

"I don't want to ride any horse into the ground," Jack said. "But we can't stay on this trail. The four-wheelers have split toward the ridge. They'll cut us off within the hour. And they won't hesitate to shoot our horses."

Kate felt the blood drain from her face. She'd thought they were home free. Hadn't realized how simple it would be for the four-wheelers to charge ahead and cut them off. But Jack had. He was always so calm and analytical, unaffected by emotion. Already he was scanning the shale above them with assessing eyes.

"We'll leave the horses and climb over that scree," Jack said. "At least give the animals their own chance to escape. Hopefully they'll run home and alert the ranch."

Kate glanced up at the rockslide, then yanked her head away. It was steep, marking the terrain above the tree line, and she didn't want to picture the narrow ledges. She definitely didn't want to abandon the horses. It didn't seem right to take all their energy and then desert them to fend for themselves.

"I don't think we should leave them," she said. "Banjo will just pick the shortest route, as the crow flies. There's too many bogs and thick brush. And his saddle might get caught up in the trees. They wouldn't have much of a chance."

"We'll unsaddle them," Jack said. "Keep the reins but hide the rest of the tack. With a little luck, Logan might even follow them for a bit." He jabbed his thumb, the motion swift and authoritative. "We'll stick the tack behind those boulders."

Kate's hand tightened around the lead ropes. She was already intimidated at this height. No way could she climb higher. But Jack was already re-sorting items in his saddlebags.

"Logan will shoot them as soon as he has a clear shot, with or without riders," Jack went on. "This way the horses have a chance. And they need water."

Kate placed a reluctant hand on Slider's shoulder. Everything Jack said was true. Slider raised his head and looked at her with trusting eyes. And she knew she had to do it. The horses had been so brave, so loyal. They deserved their own chance to live.

"We should take off their halters too," she said, surprised her voice was level. "Less chance of them being caught up in the brush."

Jack gave an approving nod. He already had the saddles whipped off and now began peeling halters.

Kate slowly unfastened Slider's halter. He waited politely then lowered his bare head and continued grazing. By now, Jack had four halters over his arm. He reached for Monty's horse.

"Turn Banjo to the southeast," she heard herself say. "Lead him forward a bit. Then slap him on the butt. That's what Monty does when he wants him to go home. The other horses will follow."

"Thanks, Kate," Jack said. He led Banjo forward and started clucking, trying to infect him with a new urgency. The horses Kessler and Logan had been riding lifted their heads from the grass, instantly suspicious. If Banjo was leaving, they didn't want to be left behind. They'd been trailed together for years and were accustomed to following.

They wheeled and trotted after Jack and Banjo, keen to stay close to the herd leader. Then Dusty fell into line, followed by Oreo, all five horses trotting in formation.

Slider, though, edged closer to Kate. He stared at the others, clearly anxious about the growing separation but waiting for her direction. "You're such a loyal boy," she whispered, her throat tight. "But this is your only chance. Go on. Be safe."

She looped her hand around the bottom of his jaw and began jogging, urging him on. His step quickened to a trot, his attention shifting forward.

Jack pulled off Banjo's halter, stepped back and swatted the horse's rump. Banjo leaped forward, kicked out once, then surged into a canter. The other horses followed, bucking and snorting, graceful in their freedom. Slider charged after them, showing an impressive turn of foot, overtaking Oreo and Dusty and already galloping in fourth.

Kate coiled the lead rope. It hurt to see them running away. As if they'd just chased off their only friends. Banjo would be picking a trail without the help of his rider. What if he led the other horses into a bog? Or tried to cross a dangerous section of the river, the part that even the whitewater rafters avoided?

Jack walked back to her side, but said nothing. He just looped his arms around her waist as they watched the six horses gallop down the slope. And the fact that he didn't try to sugarcoat it and openly shared her concern made her appreciate him even more.

They wasted another precious minute watching the animals. Banjo, the acknowledged leader, was in front. The horses didn't look tired now, running with their heads high, tails streaming. Luckily, the wind was right. They wouldn't smell Logan's horses and be drawn to their animals...where they'd be ruthlessly shot.

It felt strange to be on foot and daunting that Jack wanted to climb even higher. But though she'd prefer to be on Slider's back, making a reckless dash for the ranch, part of her was relieved Jack insisted she remain. With him beside her, she felt stronger, bolstered by his confidence and the knowledge that she was helping Courtney escape.

She almost believed it when she told herself that everything would be okay. That no one was going to die on a bleak mountain. Not Courtney, Tyra, Monty or the animals. And not Jack either. Not if she could help it.

CHAPTER TWENTY-FOUR

Jack lay on the rocky ledge, binoculars pressed to his eyes as he studied the five riders below. Any second now, they'd reach the spot where he and Kate had freed the horses. From this angle, he could see the saddles they'd hidden behind the boulders. Kate had taken precious moments trying to conceal their tack, and she'd done an excellent job. Maybe, just maybe, the riders would turn and follow the trail left by the loose horses.

He tilted his head and checked on Kate. She remained behind him, fifteen feet back.

"Stay away from the ledge," he warned, knowing they were within rifle range.

"Absolutely," she said, her voice muffled.

She hadn't spoken much in the last hour. All their oxygen had been required for climbing. No doubt, she was drained. But the sun hadn't set yet and if their pursuers kept coming, he had to keep pushing her.

He turned his attention back to the men. The front rider, obviously Logan's tracker, raised his arm, stopping the group. The man walked his horse up the trail, his eyes pinned on the ground, then wheeled and trotted back. He spoke with Logan, gesturing in both directions. Nobody dismounted. Their heads swiveled sideways, checking the mountain then swung toward the ridge.

"They haven't found the saddles," Jack murmured. "Good job, Kate."

He kept the glasses glued to his face, praying they'd follow the horses. But the tracker twisted in the saddle, still gesturing, as if realizing the party had split up.

Two riders wheeled and galloped over the ridge. The other three turned and followed the steep trail up the mountain, their horses gingerly picking their way over the rockslide.

"Damn," Jack said. "Logan and two others are still coming. But a couple have split off in the other direction. Following our horses."

"It'll be hard to catch them," Kate said quickly, as if reassuring herself. "Loose horses can move faster. And squeeze through thicker brush."

"True," Jack said, inching back off the ledge. But he didn't want to look at her hopeful face. Because the two pursuers believed they were following three riders, and clearly they'd push their horses hard to catch up. Even if they suspected the animals were riderless, they couldn't risk letting them return to the ranch and raise an alarm. And they wouldn't have to get very close to gun them down.

"Logan is staying on our trail," Jack said. "So obviously he thinks I have Courtney with me."

"Great. That's what we wanted."

"Yes," he said, fighting his ambivalence, hating the thought of those desperate men close to Kate. If Logan could slit a fellow agent's throat, what would he do to her? The man's frustration when he discovered Courtney wasn't here might make him even more vengeful.

Jack dragged a hand over his jaw, weighing his options. There was only one way he could keep Courtney safe, and Kate as well.

"This is where we split up," he said. "I'm staying here. You go on. Keep climbing. Just avoid them until help comes."

Her eyes widened, dark against her pale skin.

"It won't be long before help arrives," he said, wrapping her in his arms. "Sixteen hours, max. Just go hide, sweetheart. You're good at hiding tracks."

"No. I don't want to be alone, waiting. I want to stay with you."

He could feel the pounding of her heart, as if it was in danger of jumping out of her chest. She'd never felt so fragile, and it stirred every one of his protective instincts.

"You can't," he said. "I want you safe...and I can fight better without you."

"But staying here and trying to hold them off won't help. That will just make them think you're protecting Courtney. And Logan will radio those other men to circle around. You don't even have much ammunition. Maybe we should climb back down." Her voice turned hopeful. "Run for the tree line. They won't expect that."

He looked down the slope in barely veiled horror. What she suggested was suicide. They'd be cut down before they even reached the trees. And if by luck they made it, the riders would quickly surround them. It was obvious Logan had hired the services of an experienced tracker, and Logan still had five horses.

"We'll stay together a bit longer," he said slowly, realizing she was in no state to make critical decisions. And no wonder.

She'd witnessed a man's throat slit by the very agent assigned to protect them. Had been operating on raw courage for most of the day, her body pushed to the limit. Besides, this wasn't the best spot to make his stand. There were too many animal trails. Logan would just keep him pinned until they had him flanked. Higher ground was necessary, where there was only one approach.

The more he could stall, the better it was for Kate. And Courtney too, of course. But the fact that he was now obsessed with Kate's welfare left him riddled with guilt. Courtney was his job. It wasn't just the President but the entire country that needed her safe. And he couldn't forget that.

He turned Kate toward the ledge and pushed her forward. "Keep climbing," he said gruffly. "Until I tell you to stop."

⎯⎯⎯◉⎯⎯⎯

A HAWK SCREECHED A warning. Kate peeked at the bird floating effortlessly to her left then quickly straightened her head. She didn't want to look down and see the sheer drop, or see how the bighorn sheep clung to the rock at such an impossible angle. Almost the same angle as her.

Oh God. She pressed her hand against the cliff, determined to keep her eyes locked on the solid rock. But her legs shook from exhaustion, and she felt like dropping to her knees in despair.

Maybe this was just another nightmare and she wasn't really walking on a foot-wide ledge, on rock buffeted by winds and her own turbulent emotions. Maybe if she closed her eyes she could pretend she was in a green field with solid fences to keep people from falling. Perhaps then she could even believe that Courtney and Tyra were safe in Washington, and Monty and the animals were all back at the ranch.

She closed her eyes, imagining a flat field. It worked for a few steps. Then her legs wobbled, leaving her staggering once again. A relentless hand tightened around her hip, keeping her on the inside of the ledge, but at the same time shoving her forward. Jack was always pushing her higher. A part of her resented him for it, even if his hand served as a lifeline, keeping her from falling.

He talked non-stop too, trying to distract her. He spoke about his ranch in Idaho, and the service dogs he adopted, and how one horse named Suds kept climbing on his porch and drinking his beer. Throughout the range of tales, she'd locked on-to his words, forming distinct images of his ranch animals, from the feisty Jack Russell terrier to the loyal Shepherd left terrified by loud sounds. However, she couldn't quite envision a bay geld-ing named Suds, climbing wooden steps and actually opening a can of beer. And as her mind jumped from green fields to bomb-sniffing dogs and a horse with a can of Budweiser in his mouth, somehow her rubbery legs kept climbing.

"Here," Jack said. Previously his voice had been calm, reassur-ing. But now it sounded different, almost hopeful.

She dropped to her knees, unable to stay on her feet without his steadying hand. All she could hear now was their ragged breathing. She realized they were no longer on a narrow ledge but at the mouth of some sort of cavern where there was little danger of plunging hundreds of feet to the rocks below.

"Don't move," Jack said, but she was already prone on the ground, her head pressing against the hard rock, obviously not moving anywhere.

He knelt beside her, raising the zipper and adjusting the hood of her jacket. "You're cold and exhausted," he said "Stay here while I check out the cave."

She could feel the concern in his gentle hands, and if she had the energy she'd be marveling at his endurance. Of course, un-like her he wasn't drained by fear. He probably wished she wasn't around to slow him down. But he didn't act impatient. He just wrapped her in his arms, warming her with his incredible body heat. Slowly her chest felt like it was no longer going to explode and it seemed like maybe she was in that green field after all, with Jack the solid fence.

He smelled of grass and pine and horse, everything she loved, and she rested her face against his chest, just so grateful to be off that ledge. Content just to be held by this man who, at some point in the climb, had become the center of her existence.

He shifted her to his left, moving her away from the hard outline of his gun, keeping it within reach. Because after all, this was still about Courtney.

"I'm okay," she choked. "Just not in shape for climbing."

She twisted, gathering her breath and peering out into the murky light. The horizon still glowed pink but night had fallen. In fact, she was surprised they'd been able to climb under such conditions. "Think they're still following?" she asked.

"No. They'll have to stop and wait for morning. There are too many places where they could lose our trail."

She gave an involuntary shiver, remembering when he'd jumped to the other side of a ledge, deliberately disturbing some rocks. And how he'd asked her to hold his gun before he made the daring leap. At the time she'd assumed he didn't want the added weight. Now she figured he'd accepted there was a chance he might fall into the crevasse. And that he didn't want to risk having their only weapon fall with him. He was looking out for her as much as humanly possible, and the least she could do was hide her fear.

"So what's the plan," she asked, her breathing still ragged. "Make a stand here? This looks like a good spot."

She peered into the yawning cave, accepting the further she was from the ledge, the easier it would be to conceal her phobia. They might even be able to find another escape route. "I want to come with you," she said. "Check out the cave."

"A minute ago you were exhausted," he said with a chuckle. "You sure recover fast."

But he reached out his hand, pulled her to her feet and turned on his phone light. It was obvious he was just as eager to discover what lay within that dark cavern, and that he shared her hope they might find another way to evade Logan. One that she fervently prayed would involve considerably less climbing.

CHAPTER TWENTY-FIVE

The temperature dropped with each step Kate took into the cave. The air grew darker and damper too. But it was comforting to walk on solid bedrock rather than balance on an eroded ledge. She still gripped Jack's hand and she didn't intend to let go. This wasn't exactly a flat field. And a cave could be treacherous, with eroded limestone and bottomless holes just waiting to snatch unwary visitors.

Jack shared her caution. He felt his way, his steps slow and deliberate as he maneuvered around a stalactite, all the while panning the cave with his light. The sound of dripping water was relaxing, hinting of a larger network of caves. But they saw nothing except dried rodent dung, eerie mineral formations and a scatter of bleached bones.

"Nothing back here," he said, sighing in disappointment. "And it's warmer near the front. But at least there's water." He skimmed his light over a large crack at the back of the glistening walls. "Unless there's another chamber behind that fissure. The opening isn't very big though. Think you could fit?"

"I could try," she said. But she didn't really want to go in there alone. There might be a steep ledge on the other side. And rescuers never came when you needed them.

But Jack was already pressing his phone into her hand.

"I know you're cold," he said. "But we can warm up later. For now, you're going to take this light, squeeze through that hole and check it out. You can hold on to the end of my belt the whole time. I promise I won't let you go."

His voice was so calm, so confident, that she nodded her head, hiding her reluctance.

He removed his belt. Pressed the hard buckle against her palm, his warm fingers brushing her skin. Then he tugged her to the opening, passed her the light and turned her sideways. Gave a gentle but insistent nudge.

She inched into the crack, one hand gripping the light, the other clenching his belt. The opening tightened. Rock pressed against her ribs, squeezing like a vice. For a moment it seemed she was stuck. But Jack was holding the end of the belt and she knew he'd never leave her alone, pinned between the walls.

She blew out her breath, narrowing her chest. Gave a determined wiggle and push, took a small breath, then wiggled some more. Trying not to think or feel. To only move forward.

Now her ribs weren't so compressed. The crack seemed to be widening. She wiggled again and pushed, gasping in triumph as the rocky vice loosened, releasing her into another cavern.

"You're right!" she called triumphantly. "There is another cave."

She panned the light around her feet, checking the floor. Solid rock, no holes to plunge through. She inched forward, emboldened. The air was better here, fresher and not as cold and damp, the cavern not nearly as black. Pinpoints of her light reflected over the walls, bouncing back in a boomerang effect. But that didn't make sense. Jack's beam cast too narrow a light to illuminate the entire cave.

She switched off the light. The cave still twinkled. She strained to see where the light was coming from, but Jack's belt was too short.

"I feel fresh air," she said, turning the light back on and twisting toward him. "Light too. There might be an opening. I'm going to let go of the belt now."

"No, wait!" Jack called. "Don't go too far. Is it a cave? Or a tunnel?"

"A cave, I think."

She dropped the belt buckle and stepped forward, running her light over the walls. "This place has a nice feel," she said. "It's different. Wow, look at this."

Jack muttered something but she was too busy reading the proclamation on the wall. *Those who love here, will love forever.* Over a score of names followed and seeing evidence that other people had been here, even if it was graffiti, was absurdly comforting.

"What do you see?" Jack asked, his frustration obvious.

"It's a neat spot." She peered at the dates. "Like a love cave. But the last entry was made eight months ago."

She blew out a sigh. They certainly couldn't wait to be rescued by lovesick hikers. Still, if people had climbed in here, there must be a way out.

She followed the wall, her hand on the rock, heading toward the end of the cave with the most light. She walked twenty-one feet, counting carefully, then pulled in a hopeful breath and tilted her head. And there was the sky, dotted with twinkling stars and all the familiar constellations, shining down on her like old friends. They felt unusually close, as if she could reach out and touch them.

"Wow," she said, almost reverently.

"What do you see?" Jack called.

"It's beautiful here," she said. "Like a cathedral, with the most amazing skylight."

"Can you get any reception?"

She pulled her gaze away from the swathe of stars and checked his phone. "Still no bars," she said.

"Can you climb out of there?" he asked.

She edged around an outcrop of rock and stared up. The walls were rocky but steep and sharply angled. Her ex-boyfriend had been a world-class climber but even Andrew would have needed equipment to scale this wall. Someone like her could never manage.

"Can you climb out?" Jack repeated.

She shook her head, even though he couldn't see her. But there was no way she could climb that high. "No," she said.

"Is there anything in there? Anything we can use?"

She circled around the small cave, flicking the light back and forth over the rock. "Just a little wood and some charred logs" she said. Nothing of use. A fire would only serve as a beacon for Logan.

"It's a pretty cave though," she added. "Wish you could see it. Maybe you can fit."

She assessed the crack with hopeful eyes, shining the light from top to bottom. But the crack was too narrow. Barely eight inches. It seemed impossible she'd managed to wiggle through. And she was hit with the fear she'd never get back to Jack. That they'd be forever separated by a rock wall, with only their voices for company.

"I'm coming back now." She shoved her arm into the crevice and reached out. For a paralyzing second, she felt nothing but space. Then his strong grip encased her hand and her heart kicked with relief. She let out a deep breath, wiggled sideways and let him tug her safely to the other side.

Emotion propelled her forward and she landed against his chest, her arms reaching up and wrapping around his neck.

"I'm cold," she said, covering her reaction. "That other cave is much warmer."

His arms tightened, keeping her against him even though she had no desire to move any time soon. "It's probably fifty degrees here," he said. "Next time we come, it'll be in style. In the meantime, I'll share all my protein bars. Even the chocolate ones."

"Water too?"

"Absolutely," he said, his voice smiling.

He pried the light from her hands, but kept his arm around her waist as he guided her back to the front of the cave. He switched off the light a prudent distance from the opening. She wished it could stay on but knew they didn't want to announce their location. Besides, it was a positive sign he was trying to save the battery. As if he really believed they'd be able to climb high enough to find phone reception.

"Let's see what we have for supplies," he said.

She sat down and tugged off her boots, giving her toes a grateful wiggle. Then reached into her backpack and pulled out the contents: matches, fire starter, protein bars, jackknife, a ball of twine, wool socks, two full water bottles, three bandages, a garbage bag and a pink roll of vet wrap.

He was already opening the saddlebags but paused, his smile widening when he spotted the range of her offerings. "Perfect," he said, tossing her a rolled blanket. "Now we have a ground sheet as well as a blanket."

She sighed with pleasure, cradling the wool blanket against her chest. She'd spent many long nights in the woods, staying warm with only a thin survival blanket. A wool blanket and a garbage bag were total luxury. And then she spotted two pita sandwiches and couldn't stop grinning. She'd expected only a power bar for supper, maybe two if they splurged. But the prospect of real food sent her scrambling to her feet.

She dropped the blanket and scooped up a wrap, peering delightedly at the contents. "Oh, wow! Cheese and ham. My favorite."

She gave an ecstatic grin, then stilled. He was staring at her with the strangest expression. And then she realized her mistake—he'd only offered to share the protein bars. Not his pita wraps.

She quickly placed it back down. Obviously he needed more food than she did. Besides, Jack had been carrying the saddlebags and had pretty much pushed her halfway up a mountain. He was the important one.

"I just need a protein bar," she said, miserable that she was such a liability. He could have moved faster alone, would have been able to climb higher. Once, she might have been able to hold her own. Well, not compared to him because clearly he was a super stud. But before the accident, she could have contributed more. Would have been a bigger help in keeping Courtney safe.

"I'm not even that hungry," she added, scooping up a protein bar, but this time making sure it was one that had come from her own pocket.

She didn't see him move—still wasn't used to his uncanny quickness. But his arms banded around her. "You're so big-hearted," he muttered. "So kind. And so goddamn brave."

Her jaw dropped. She was so stunned she just stood there, staring. It wasn't only his words but the emotion in his voice. Then his head dipped, his mouth claiming hers, and she guessed maybe he'd intended to share his food after all. But right now it was obvious he had a different kind of hunger.

He'd kissed her last night but that had been a polite parlor kiss compared to this. She hadn't even realized the extent of his restraint. It was a good thing he hadn't done this with his mouth on the dance floor. She would have melted, and it wouldn't have mattered if her boss or Allie or any of her other co-workers had been watching. Right now, Jack was her focal point. The only person who mattered.

He'd tilted her back so he had full access to her mouth, his lips taking possession, taking control. His fingers splayed over her back, urging her closer. His big hand slid beneath her shirt, sliding over her rib cage and higher. He cupped her breast, the hard calluses on his palm igniting her nerve endings, sending shivers of delight shooting to her core.

She felt her bra release, her shirt tugged away. Cool air brushed her nipples, quickly replaced by a rasp of stubble, then his warm mouth. And she was no longer cold. She was burning up, heady with need. It felt like he had two mouths and four hands and he was using every one of them. And when he wedged his hard thigh between her legs, she arched against him, making a sound of suppressed need.

"Drop your jeans, Kate," he said, his voice a husky whisper.

But she was much more intent on *his* jeans, her hands already fumbling with his belt buckle. And then he jutted free, so big and rampantly male she shivered with arousal. Maybe it was his experience with strip searches or the fact that he was remarkably adept at everything he did, but he didn't wait for her to unzip her pants. He had her naked and flat on her back in less than a minute, no help required. His mouth slanted back down, his tongue dancing erotically with hers, even as his hand slipped between her bare thighs, a tease of finger and thumb that sent moisture pooling between her legs.

She arched against him, her sensitive breasts pressing against the wall of his chest, aching for fulfillment. He entered her quickly, not a slow tentative thrust, but hard and bold, pumping with powerful strokes, one hand tunneled through her hair, holding her in place, while the other cupped her breast.

She knew she wouldn't last long, not the way he was making her body clench and burn. But it didn't matter. Her only regret was that they only had this one night. And even that wasn't a regret. Not here. Not now.

CHAPTER TWENTY-SIX

Jack slid his hand along the curve of Kate's bare hip, keeping them skin to skin, their legs entwined. She felt relaxed after their lovemaking—so different from earlier today—and he didn't want to move. Wanted to banish that fear in her eyes that she tried so valiantly to hide. At least, for the moment, he could make her feel safe.

"Warm enough?" he whispered, tucking the wool blanket around her before pressing another kiss against her smooth cheek. He couldn't keep his hands off her. Or his mouth. They'd have to sit up sometime and eat supper, but he sure as hell wasn't going to be the first to move.

She gave a throaty sigh, the sound of a woman well satisfied. He liked hearing that, appreciated wordless sounds much more than uncomfortable pillow talk. Women were usually overly keen to talk after sex anyway. Asking questions about his feelings, their possible future, and whether he ever considered moving into town. That kind of talk always made him bolt.

He definitely shied away from women who wanted directions to his ranch. His home was his refuge, where only dogs, horses, and select friends were welcome. He saw enough people when he was working. His parents had felt the same way, finding peace with nature, not in random hordes of noisy people.

But he wanted Kate to see his ranch. Wanted her to laugh at Suds' trick with the beer, to meet his dogs and horses, to do more than visit. She'd love the trails, and they could hike and ride and climb. It was obvious she loved the outdoors as much as he did. She was definitely his kind of woman, and he wanted to share his space with her. Wanted to share everything.

Yet she was so quiet. Not saying a word. Perversely he wanted to talk. Wanted her to question his feelings, his intentions. To compare scars, both the superficial and the hidden, and maybe forget for a few hours that they were being pursued. But other than the scream of a distant mountain lion, the cave remained silent.

And that was okay. He could open up first. He pulled in a breath and propped on an elbow. "I wanted this from the first moment we met," he confided, tracing a finger over the swell of her breast.

She gave a little laugh. "You don't have to say that. Obviously you want to have sex with a lot of your dance partners. I understand the situation. We're stuck together. This sort of thing happens."

His finger stilled. Was she brushing him off?

"I've certainly been stuck with other people before," he said. "But I never felt like this. Never *did* this with them. And the dance hall wasn't where we first met."

She gave a little snort, almost of disbelief. "The first time we met I came from the kitchen. Wearing a very unattractive hairnet."

"But I was still attracted," he said, surprised she wasn't taking him seriously.

"You were probably hoping I could cook," she said lightly. "And let's not forget how easily you walked away at the dance hall. It was your job to scope everyone out. You don't have to pretend there was an instant attraction just because we had sex."

She gave him a playful jab in the arm. "Even though it was really great."

She was still naked in his arms, but her emotions were definitely leashed. Making it easy for them to both pull on their pants and move on. Normally he'd appreciate that type of reaction, be grateful even. But not this time. Possibly it was the gravity of their situation but it was important she understand how he felt. Now. While he had the chance to tell her.

"I didn't want to leave that night," he said, leaning over and studying her face. "But I was on a job. I couldn't afford to be distracted. I always intended to call when it was over."

Her laugh sounded brittle. "You didn't even put my number in your phone. If I hadn't been assigned to Courtney's trail ride, we never would have spoken again. And honestly, that's fine. We have more important things to worry about."

That was certainly true but he knew enough about women to realize that walking away from her in the dance hall *had* mattered. "Believe me," he said. "I was going to call."

"Super," she said. "But I'd rather talk about what we're going to do tomorrow. Everything else can wait."

The finality in her voice showed she was truly finished talking. Obviously she didn't open up or give her trust easily. Kessler hadn't revealed much about Kate, only that her last employer had provided glowing references and that they'd been devastated when she'd resigned. Monty had been the only one who'd mentioned the mountain wreck. Kate obviously preferred to avoid the subject. Understandable.

Besides, she was right. It was more important to talk about their escape strategy.

"Okay," he said slowly. "Tomorrow we're going to climb higher, keep them chasing us. And try to find a cell phone signal. Monty should reach the fire tower by mid-morning. Once the command centre receives his call for help, it won't take long for them to have helicopters all over the area."

"Do you think Logan is going to believe Courtney can climb like that?" she asked. "He doesn't seem to have much respect for women."

That was an understatement. The man had been fawning when the girls were around but rather contemptuous in private. Logan had constantly referred to Kate as the mule girl and, even more infuriating, the fuckable cook.

"He might suspect we split up," Jack admitted. "As long as he doesn't realize it was back at camp, we're good."

At least Courtney was good. He and Kate were still in danger.

Though he wished Kate was safe back at the ranch, the selfish part of him was glad she'd been a last-minute replacement. Kessler had been ambivalent about her inclusion, but the ranch owner had lauded her experience as well as her ability to be discreet. Kessler confided he'd been swayed after Kate's glowing background check, as well as the fact that they had two experienced agents and a former SEAL on the ride. They needed a woman, not another guard.

Now Kessler was dead and Courtney was on the run without a single bodyguard by her side. Strange how things worked out.

"I have contour maps loaded on my phone," Jack went on. "And I can use my belt and the reins to make a rope. But we have to climb higher. It's the only way." He realized he was squeezing her a little too hard and concentrated on loosening his arms. But he hated the thought of asking her to climb without proper equipment. She didn't seem to have much of a knack for it. And rifle fire always made things trickier.

"How much ammunition do you have?" she asked, wiggling out of his arms and fumbling for their clothes.

"Enough." *Not much.* Only the ten round mag in his gun and the single bullet in the chamber. Logan had planned every detail, ensuring he removed all the ammunition as well as the radio. And Kessler had unwittingly helped carry the gear while Jack had been distracted, making luncheon wraps and worrying about Kate.

Logan might not be certain of Jack's ammunition though. It would have been hard to carry the loaded panniers after he'd killed Kessler. He would have made sure he took the radio.

Jack sat up, watching Kate as she organized their scattered clothing. Admiring how the moonlight caressed her skin was preferable to analyzing Logan's actions. But while he didn't want to dredge up the horror of Kessler's death, it was critical to know if Logan had carried away both panniers.

He rose and helped fasten the clasp on her bra, then tugged on his jeans.

"You were hidden, waiting until Logan left Kessler, correct?" he asked.

"Yes." She pulled on her shirt. The hem barely covered the top of her thighs. Damn, she had beautiful legs. Sleek and toned and fit, and they'd fit around his hips like she'd been built to ride.

He yanked his eyes back to her face. "I need you to tell me everything Logan did...afterwards."

"Why? What does it matter?"

The ammunition was in both sides of the panniers. Logan might assume Jack had recovered it. If so, Logan might not be so keen to storm their position. That would buy valuable time. But

Jack didn't want to put false ideas in Kate's head. It was difficult for civilians to recall details, and often witnesses tried too hard to remember. But first impressions were usually correct, even if incomplete.

"Just tell me what Logan did," he said gently.

"He didn't do anything," Kate muttered. "He turned and walked into the woods."

"Did he pick up anything?" Jack kept his eyes locked on her face, searching for that flash of recollection. Some people remembered images vividly, others stored their memories in words. He was betting Kate was an image person.

But he couldn't see her face, not the way she kept her head bent while she buttoned her shirt. Not buttoning...fumbling. His attention locked on her fingers. She wasn't actually doing anything with her shirt; she was just playing with the buttons. Hiding her expression.

That was when he felt his first prick of unease.

They'd never discussed Kessler's murder. She'd been traumatized and figuring out how to whisk Courtney to safety had been his biggest concern. But it was odd how she refused to look at him now. As if she were hiding something. And she wasn't usually an evasive person.

"I just need to know what Logan took with him," Jack said, fighting his urge to reach out and help button her shirt. "Logan had the knife in one hand. What did he carry away? Did he take both packs?"

"I don't remember." Her head remained bent, her voice muffled.

"Did he have a sheath for his knife?" Jack asked. "Or did he take it from Kessler's pack?" Logan might have been able to carry two panniers, but not if he bolted with a knife in his hand. And he wouldn't have been stupid enough to leave the murder weapon.

"This is important," Jack went on. "Do you remember if he left a pack? Or did he combine the ammunition in the radio canister? Did he put the knife in there too?"

"He wiped the knife on Kessler's shirt," Kate said. She was silent for a moment. She still hadn't made any headway with her buttons, and her bra gleamed whitely in the night. "There was blood," she said. "Blood everywhere. It wouldn't come off. Spatter was stuck around the handle...everywhere."

"So you saw the knife? Logan left it?"

"No, I was hiding. I was sc-scared."

"Of course you were." He reached out and clasped her hands. He should have known it was too much to ask. She wasn't used to witnessing such brutality. Even hardened SEALs forgot details, the mind conveniently locking out the horrors.

"He put the knife in the pack," she said. "The hard pannier with the lock and orange nylon straps. Then he dumped the ammunition on top, along with Kessler's gun. It didn't all fit, but he put the pack over his shoulders and he carried the shotgun and panniers in his arms. He didn't leave anything for me."

Jack's fingers tightened over her hands. This was helpful. Not good news but still helpful. Kate had been in shock when she bolted into camp; he'd thought it would be difficult for her to remember. It was unfortunate Logan had taken all the ammunition but it reinforced how thoroughly the job had been planned. Everything had fallen into place, from Courtney's gluten attack to Kate leaving camp and Jack being stuck making lunch.

Kessler never stood a chance. Wouldn't have seen the knife coming. He'd been more watchful of Kate and Monty than a trusted fellow agent.

Jack gave Kate's hands a reassuring squeeze then turned and reached for her boots. "Let's eat," he said. "Then we'll figure out our route. And make a climbing rope." He snagged one of her boots, surprised by the weight. His thumb brushed something hard, something on the inside of the leather. He reached in and slowly pulled a knife from a leather sheath. He stared in disbelief, struggling to absorb its significance.

This wasn't a rider's standard pocket knife but a serious weapon: a three-inch long, combo edge blade with a balanced skeletonized handle. The sheath was unique, crafted from leather with a Velcro strap and a snap-in clip. Few knives fit nicely into cowboy boots. This one did.

Kate was busy pulling her jeans up over those shapely legs, unaware of his discovery. Jack turned his back. Didn't want to look at her, hit by the realization she might be involved in this.

She had been a last-minute replacement. Kessler confirmed she'd been thoroughly vetted but why the wicked-looking knife? And how had it been missed during the security check?

Aw, fuck me.

His jaw clenched when he remembered how unbalanced he'd been simply running his hands down those beautiful legs. Still lusting after dancing with her the night before. If someone had wanted to pick the perfect woman to distract him, they'd done a helluva job.

But he still couldn't believe she'd slit Kessler's throat. Maybe she only carried the knife? She'd definitely kept it secret though, removing both the sheath and the knife before passing her boots over for drying after the river drenching.

His mind whirled, automatically clicking over every possible scenario. Perhaps it wasn't even Kessler who was dead. Maybe it was Logan lying there and Kessler was the dirty one. That would explain why Kessler had maintained she was safe, even as the agent ostensibly kept a hostile distance.

No one else had seen a body. Kate had charged into camp, shocked and bloody, infecting everyone with the need to flee. And Jack had sent Courtney off, alone with Monty. A civilian, Kate's friend, and probably a collaborator.

His mind churned with a web of suspicions, each one darker and more tormented than the last. Damn, he'd been gullible. He wanted to yell and curse and pound his knuckles against the bedrock. Punish himself for his stupidity.

He sensed her behind him, stooping to pick up her socks, her movements graceful and composed. She was like that, gathering herself quickly when only minutes before she'd acted too upset to button her shirt. Yet she'd recited minute details of Kessler's death, even the color of the straps. The average person wouldn't remember that. And she'd talked about the blood specks on the knife. How Logan hadn't left anything for her.

So that probably *did* mean it was Kessler who was dead. And she was colluding with Logan and Monty. Jack couldn't remember whose idea it was to take Courtney and flee on the mules, but he'd fallen right in with the plan.

Escape and evade. Normally acceptable tactics. But where the hell was Courtney now? Was it still possible to save her? On the other hand, if Logan had Courtney, why was he still following?

Why wasn't he trying to whisk the girl out of the country before the alarm was raised?

His mind felt sluggish, struggling to make sense of the events, hating to accept the extent of his stupidity. He just stood there, unmoving, feeling like a dolt.

Until Kate reached for his shirt...and his gun.

He shot forward, his hand clamping around her wrist. "How much are they paying you?" he growled. "Is Monty dirty too?"

She just stared at him, blinking prettily.

"No need to pretend any longer." He raised her knife and tossed it on top of his shirt. Then he wrapped his hands tightly around her upper arms.

"Talk," he said. "Now!"

CHAPTER TWENTY-SEVEN

Kate yanked at his arms, trying to loosen his grip. He could hear her shallow gasps but it was the panic in her eyes that made him loosen his hands.

"Just tell me where Monty fits in this," he said. "And I promise I won't hurt you."

It was patently clear, at least to him, that he wasn't going to hurt her. Just seeing her panic had been enough to make him queasy. But it was good she was afraid. People talked quicker when they were frightened, and he'd always been very good at scaring—

Her fist slammed into his stomach, making his breath ooze in a surprised whoosh. She didn't try to run, just glared with defiant eyes.

He took a painful breath then snagged both her wrists and yanked her forward, this time taking care to keep both her arms shackled.

"You're going to tell me everything," he snapped, furious at his weakness. "Starting with Monty and what his plans are for Courtney."

She was shaking her head so he twisted her arms behind her back, pinning her wrists with one hand. "Is that a no?"

She just glared up at him. Obviously she knew he'd never hurt her, and his helplessness mingled with a rising panic. There might still be time to save Courtney if he could climb the mountain high enough to find cell phone coverage. But he needed in-formation. And he needed it fast.

He turned her around, releasing her hands and forcing her to look out over the ledge. "Tell me where Monty's headed."

He'd assumed she had a respectful fear of heights, simply from the painstaking way she'd handled the climb. But now he suspected she'd merely wanted their pursuers to catch up. Like a lovesick fool he'd let her set the pace, giving her time to feel com-fortable, hoping she'd trust that he had her back. And the knowl-edge that he'd been so completely suckered fueled his hot anger.

He pushed her closer to the edge. "Struggle and you'll fall," he said, raising his voice so she'd hear it over the howling wind. "Now tell me where Monty's headed. Where is he taking Court-ney?"

She didn't answer but he could feel a change in her body. From proud defiance to a sudden wilting. Good, he was getting to her.

"Where's Monty headed?" he asked, using his coldest voice.

"To the f-fire tower," she said, gripping his arms, as if afraid she really would tumble over.

He didn't give an inch, just kept her posed close to that yawn-ing edge. "Who's meeting them there? And who's paying you? Is it Kessler or Logan?"

One of her hands clutched at his bare chest, no longer fisted but merely struggling to hang on. Her nails were sharp but she wasn't using them as a weapon. She seemed more like a helpless kitten about to be tossed into a bucket of water and unable to do anything to stop it. Her obvious fear cooled his anger. He pulled her back a step. But kept his voice steely.

"Tell me who's dead. Kessler or Logan?"

"K-Kessler," she said. She kept running her hands over his chest, as if looking for a place to grip. Then she seemed to realize she was scratching his skin and simply fisted both her hands over the waistband of his jeans.

Even in her terrified state, she was trying not to hurt him. And that knowledge broke him. There was no way she could have killed a man, at least not with a knife. He moved back, drawing her another foot from the ledge. "Logan really did kill Kessler?"

She just looked at him, her face so mystified his confusion grew. She couldn't be acting. Not the way she was shrinking against him, her heart pounding. One couldn't fake fear like that. And he couldn't dismiss the fact that someone was still following. If Monty were involved in the abduction, the man would have just waited in the woods. Then ridden out on the mules and handed Courtney over. Job complete. There'd be no reason to waste time with a pointless pursuit.

He squeezed his eyes shut. When he opened them, Kate's face was still a mask of fear, her hands clenched around his jeans in a death grip. He eased her back toward the mouth of the cave, more bewildered than ever.

"Just take some big breaths," he said gruffly. "You know I'm not going to throw you over."

He kept his hands on her arms, waiting for her breathing to settle. Still needing answers.

"Did Logan pay you to bring that big knife?" he asked. "Maybe you didn't know his plans? You probably didn't expect him to take Courtney. Or kill anyone." He eyed her hopefully.

She just stared, a pulse pounding erratically in her beautiful neck.

"Dammit, Kate." He gave her a frustrated shake. "You have to tell me. I know some good lawyers. But I can't help you unless I know everything."

"Y-you already do," she said.

Her voice was ragged, her chest heaving, but at least she was talking. Logan had probably bribed her, maybe even threatened her. Threats would be better. Certainly the courts would be more sympathetic, especially if Kate helped Jack turn things around and save Courtney.

"So Logan *forced* you to bring the knife," he said, studying her face. "But you had no idea of his intentions. Do you even know where they're taking Courtney?"

She looked at him, her expression not evasive or fearful or furtive. She just seemed blank.

A sick feeling built in his gut. Smuggling in a knife was risky. She and Logan had no idea if her boots would be checked. And Logan hadn't even been present at the pre-dawn check. Surely he would have made sure he was the agent to frisk her. But it had been Kessler who'd initiated the search, and Kessler hadn't objected when Jack stepped in.

Jack jabbed his thumb at the lethal-looking knife lying on his shirt. "Who owns that weapon?"

"Me."

"No one told you to bring it? So you're saying Monty is really taking Courtney to safety?"

"Yes," she said.

He lowered his arms. Scrubbed his jaw with his fist. She was still shivering, still frightened, but she was clearly cold as well. He could see the tips of her toes, curled against the rock, vainly seeking shelter from the wind.

He walked back to the mound of clothes, grabbed her socks and his shirt, along with the offending knife. Tossed the socks at her feet. "Put on your socks," he said. "And your jacket."

She just stood there.

"Sit," he said, angling her to the ground. He kneeled down, stuck her arms in the sleeves and yanked on her jacket.

"Can you tell me why you hid a knife in your boot?" he asked, his resentment still swirling. He'd returned her little jackknife yesterday, had thought she'd earned carrying privileges. Yet the entire time she'd possessed a killer shank. She must have been snickering.

"I don't like to feel helpless," she said.

"What if I found it at the security check?" He pulled up the zipper of her jacket, so fast it almost clipped the skin on her throat.

She winced. "Then I wouldn't have been able to bring it."

Her grimace showed she was aware it wouldn't have been so simple. She would have been treated as a suspicious person and the ensuing treatment by government security wouldn't have been pleasant. Quite likely her employment would have been jeopardized as well.

It was apparent she loved her trail job. Enjoyed working with Monty. Just last night she'd stood beside the guide, facing down a charging grizzly. When she'd grabbed her boot, he'd assumed it had been in shock. Now he realized she'd been trying to get her knife to fight the bear. And who would take on a grizzly with just a knife?

He shook his head, recalling that in the river she'd also been clutching at her boot, probably reaching for her blade to cut Slider's reins. Clearly, a conditioned response.

More significantly, on both occasions she'd been willing to expose the knife. Not keep it hidden for any nefarious purpose.

Still, his resentment bubbled. Anyone would have jumped to the same conclusion. It just wasn't normal for a woman to carry a lethal boot knife in a specially handcrafted sheath. If he'd found it on Monty, he might have been more understanding. A grizzled trail veteran wouldn't want to hit the trail without his knife. But Kate was a beautiful young woman. Her big knife was...unexpected.

He blew out a sigh, accepting that he was guilty of gender profiling in the very worst way, despite his considerable training. Dammit though, she'd had plenty of time to tell him. That would have made all the difference.

She should have told me.

He straightened and stalked over to the knife, his chest painfully tight. Of course, she might still be lying.

He switched on his light, angling the beam over the knife blade. There'd been no time for a thorough cleaning and it was hard to rub off every speck of blood, especially close to the handle. A part of him, his most desperate chauvinistic side, even hoped he'd find telltale specks. Otherwise he'd made a colossal mistake.

One she might never be able to forgive.

CHAPTER TWENTY-EIGHT

Kate wrapped her arms around her chest, too numb and cold to move. *He* was still examining her knife, inspecting it from all angles. She had an irrational fear that maybe he would find a drop of blood, even though it had been months since she'd used it for anything except children's carving classes. And even then she always cleaned her tools. Certainly she'd scrubbed that knife hundreds of times since the mountain accident.

But if Jack truly believed she'd endangered Courtney, there was no doubt he'd go to any lengths to make her talk. His job took precedence. He was a professional warrior. Maybe he'd throw her off that ledge after all, especially when she had no answers to give.

Her arms tightened over her chest, clasping so tightly it hurt. She should have told him about her boot knife. There'd been several opportunities: yesterday, when he'd demonstrated his trust by returning her jackknife or last night, when he kissed her by the fire, or even this morning, when he'd worried about her hiking alone and unarmed. But then he would have asked questions she didn't want to answer. Kessler's snide comment about her ability with a knife had already left her bruised. And she'd been too enamored with Jack, hadn't wanted to see that tender look in his eyes turn to revulsion.

Well, neither she nor Jack were enamored now. Part of her wanted to explain. He was wasting time and energy worrying about her as a threat, rather than Logan. But the words were too difficult, her heart too broken. Because once again she was stuck on the side of a mountain, frightened and powerless.

She heard Jack's steps, but didn't look up. Just clasped her arms a little tighter, wondering if he'd come to drag her back to the edge of the cliff. He was far stronger than her. She'd already experienced the way he'd pinned her with one powerful hand. Clearly he'd been trained in the most effective way to subdue a suspect. And though she told herself former SEALs didn't just fling people willy-nilly over a cliff, her terror was too real.

Something touched her arms. She flinched. But Jack had only draped the blanket over her shoulders.

"You need to warm up," he said, his arm moving again. "And eat."

She stared at the pita wrap he'd dropped on her lap. Only an hour earlier it had looked delicious. Now, her throat and stomach were so tight it would be impossible to force down. On the positive side, he probably wouldn't waste food if he intended to dangle her over the cliff, looking for information she didn't have.

That rationale made her feel better, but her appetite seemed to have permanently disappeared, and she was unable to summon the desire or energy to pick up the wrap. Her arms were too heavy, her body drained, the way she felt after a particularly tortuous nightmare.

"I understand you're pissed," Jack said. "But you need food." He opened the plastic around the pita wrap and jammed it between her numb fingers. "Eat."

She pressed it to her mouth, too afraid to not follow his terse instructions. But the smell of ham and cheese was repugnant, and her stomach lurched in protest. He pressed a bottle of water to her mouth, the gentleness of his touch at odds with the rough-ness of his voice.

"I'm sorry, Kate," he said.

His thumb brushed her cheek and she realized a tear had leaked from the corner of her eye. She jerked her head away, hating that he saw.

He lowered his hand and placed the water bottle by her hip. "I should never have suspected you and Monty," he said. "You've both been utterly courageous."

She wasn't courageous at all, she thought, numbly gripping the sandwich. In fact, she felt gutted with fear. She wanted to slink back into the cave, squeeze through that narrow crack and just stay safe from everything and everyone. Including him.

⸻ ◆ ⸻

JACK FOUGHT A SPIKE of panic. Kate looked so detached, uninterested in anything he was saying. He'd been apologizing for the last half hour, but she hadn't moved, still hadn't looked at him. It was as if she'd checked out. Other than a single tear, and flinching when he'd tried to touch her, she sat like a statue.

She hadn't pulled on her woolen socks either, and her toes appeared shriveled in the biting wind. He placed a cautious hand on her foot. She cringed, so quickly and violently it left him feeling sick.

However, he kept his hand wrapped around her cold ankle. "I just want to warm them up. Then get on those socks."

He edged closer, lifted his shirt, then raised her feet and jammed them against his bare stomach. Two ice-like slabs hit his skin and he sucked in a fortifying breath. Kessler had called her a survival expert but she certainly wasn't taking good care of herself now. It must hurt too, having the blood rush through her feet like hundreds of prickling needles. Aside from that initial movement though, she remained still, just holding the pita wrap, her head angled toward the cave. It didn't look as if she'd taken a single bite.

It was difficult to grovel when she wouldn't talk to him, wouldn't even look at him. It was as if he didn't exist.

"I'll eat that food," he said, half-jokingly. "If you don't want it."

He didn't know what to expect. Maybe for her to curse or yell or cry, or even to chuck the sandwich at his head. He only wanted to goad her into talking. But she didn't move. Didn't react. He'd been so busy apologizing, trying to justify his suspicions, that he hadn't noticed her total lack of response.

It still rankled that she'd hidden a lethal weapon, and her explanation that she wanted to feel safe didn't hold much weight. But she was acting weird, like a terrified captive who couldn't speak English and fully expected to face a firing squad. Incommunicative, afraid, helpless.

On impulse, he rose, scooped up the knife and placed it on her lap. Then he sat down, tucked her feet back beneath his shirt and resumed rubbing. They no longer felt like blocks of ice, almost matching his own body temperature, but he didn't want to stop. Not while he had the horrible feeling she might never let him touch her again.

CHAPTER TWENTY-NINE

Kate stared down at her knife, its curved steel glistening beneath the moonlight. It must have passed Jack's inspection. There was no way he'd leave it within reach if he'd found a speck of what he believed to be Kessler's blood. Not only in reach but on her lap. She set down the pita wrap and tentatively placed her fingers around the familiar handle.

Jack didn't whip the knife away. In fact, he seemed totally absorbed with rubbing her feet. She wrapped her fingers more firmly around the handle, checking his reaction. But he made no move to grab it. Maybe he believed her? Which meant he wouldn't be dragging her back to the side of that ledge. And she was flooded with such a wave of relief, her body spasmed.

His hands stilled. "Does this hurt?"

She shook her head, her fingers tightening around the knife.

"You're not going to stick me with that thing, are you, Kate?" he asked, his voice wry.

"I don't want to." Her voice vibrated in her ears, the sound almost foreign as she struggled to push the words through her dry throat. "But I will. If you try to throw me over again, I will fight."

His entire body jolted. "Kate...you must have known I could never do that. Would never do that."

She raised her head, checking his face, even though it meant looking in the direction of that dark yawning chasm. He looked incredulous. Then his hands dropped to his sides.

"Were you really that scared?" he asked, his voice so low it was distorted by the wind.

Scared. She didn't like that word. Didn't like to be reminded of her shortcomings, or remember how scared she'd been trying to keep those wolves away from Danny's father. It always left a numb feeling in her chest.

Her feet felt cold without the warmth of Jack's hands. She twisted, fumbling for her socks. However, he retrieved them first so she just eyed him, still defiantly gripping her knife.

The wind swirled, reminding her how close she was to the ledge. How precariously close they both were. He didn't seem to notice.

"You must have known it was a bluff," he said, propping her foot on his thigh and trying to tug the wool sock over her foot. "We weren't even that close to the edge."

She faked a shrug. If he didn't realize she'd been petrified, she was never going to admit it. But she could feel his confusion, his unusual clumsiness as he kept snagging the sock over her big toe. He made two more failed attempts then sighed and rose, scooping up her boots along with the socks.

"Let's move further back into the cave," he said, extending his hand.

She'd like nothing better than to move away from the ledge. But the wind was whipping and her legs felt weak. Standing seemed risky.

"Let's go inside," he repeated. "Back where it's safe."

She eyed his hand then checked his expression. There was nothing menacing and he didn't look disappointed in her. If anything he looked...stricken. It was probably wise to hold on to him. He was far too solid to blow off the mountain and his balance was uncanny. But then she wouldn't be able to carry both her knife and her sandwich. And she didn't want to leave either one.

"I'll bring your food," he said. "You carry your knife."

That sounded like a good plan but she still didn't dare stand. The wind was too gusty. Best to wait until it settled, or at least established a firm direction. Jack shifted, moving between her and the ledge, his big body buffering her from the wind. His feet seemed solid, his legs not swaying at all. Still, she scooted backward several inches before daring to rise, not far enough that he'd notice but enough to make her feel a bit more secure.

Then she rose, one hand gripping her knife, the other clutching his fingers and they walked silently into the cave.

She released his hand the moment they were surrounded by the comforting rock walls. He walked another ten feet, past the point where he'd first dropped the backpack. Then he spread the plastic on the ground and carefully placed her boots and socks beside it.

"This is good, right?" he asked. "No wind but there's still some moonlight so we can see a bit. Is this far enough in?"

Dismay clogged her throat. It was obvious he realized now she had issues. In fact, he sounded like Andrew, just before he'd advised that she was a liability and he didn't feel safe hiking with her.

She gave a little nod, then smoothed the edge of the plastic and sank down, knowing Jack was going to ask a lot of painful questions. And she wouldn't be able to stop the memories, the vivid pictures, and oh, God, she just hoped she wouldn't have a panic attack. Not up here, not when they still had to elude Logan.

But he didn't say a word. He just slipped the sock on her right foot, then the left, and tucked the blanket around her shoulders. Then he sat down behind her, wrapping her in his arms and legs, his chest pressed against her back. She jerked forward, trying to pull away. However, he kept her enfolded, his arms unmoving.

"You had a scare, Kate," he said, his breath fanning her ear. "This is the fastest way to warm up."

He swept aside her protest and tucked her head beneath his chin. His heart seemed to be pounding as fast as hers, overpowering the sounds of the wind outside. He didn't seem inclined to talk either, didn't ask what bones Danny had broken or if Smitty could still see out of his crushed eye socket. Neither did he ask about the cliff or how many feet the horses had fallen. And for that she was grateful. She gave another half-hearted wiggle, just to show her reluctance, but they both knew she wasn't going anywhere. His body felt like a furnace, blasting off so much heat she felt surprisingly comfortable. Almost secure.

Which was ironic considering how quickly he'd turned into her biggest threat.

Now that she wasn't so incapacitated with fear, she began to feel other emotions. Resentment, hurt, hunger.

The pita wrap sat on the other side of his hip and she considered reaching for it. But moving out of his sheltering cocoon meant the end of his warmth. It would also end their tacit truce. He'd have to grill her about the knife. If someone had smuggled a weapon on one of her trail rides, she'd want to know the reason why too. And he worked for the government. He was paid to be suspicious.

But she didn't want to talk about the accident. She'd be content if they could sit silently until dawn. Maybe they could pretend the whole thing was a little misunderstanding. Then neither of them would have to justify their actions, or take the blame.

Besides, if Logan and his men caught them, it wouldn't even matter. So there was no need for talking. In fact, she could wait until morning to eat.

Her stomach rumbled.

Jack leaned sideways. A blast of cool air chilled her back. Then his arms were around her again and the pita wrap was lying on her lap. And he was being so thoughtful, so *silent,* and her eyes pricked with unshed tears because even if they were able to escape, it was unlikely he'd ever hold her like this again.

She fought back the sting, relieved it was still dark. She had no idea what he was thinking, or how much time they had before dawn. And while she didn't want to fight, or talk about anything contentious, it seemed a waste to just sit.

She wet her throat, trying for a tone that was neither hurt nor angry. "It feels late," she said. "What time is it?"

"Twenty-three hundred."

His arm didn't move to check his watch, so clearly he was staying alert to the time. Probably wondering when she'd be composed enough to push off his lap. And the fact that he answered in agent speak, instead of saying eleven o'clock, underscored their differences.

His objective was to ensure Courtney's safety, not waste time soothing her feelings. Now that he realized she was such a liability, no doubt he wished she hadn't volunteered to go with him. But she hadn't realized they'd be climbing a damn mountain.

Her frustration welled. She'd only wanted to help, had been trained to rescue people. Now she was just a hindrance. "Bet you wish I'd gone with the mules," she said, keeping her voice light.

"Yes," he said.

Plastic sounded and she realized he was unwrapping her food. As if he considered her helpless. And maybe she had been reduced to jelly when she'd been standing next to a thousand-foot drop, but she was perfectly fine in the cave.

"I can do that," she snapped.

His arms tightened to steel bands, the way they'd felt outside when he thought she'd been working with Logan. When he'd threatened to throw her off the mountain. And she instinctively shrank away.

She heard his intake of breath, knew he'd felt her recoil.

"I admit I'm terrified of heights," she said, calming her voice. "But I can open my own sandwich."

"I didn't know." His voice was gruff. "I'm sorry, Kate. I hate that I tried to scare you."

His arms tightened a fraction. But earlier their strength had been frightening. Now they felt comforting, protective. Even though she was a rock around his neck, he didn't sound disdainful. In fact, he sounded pained.

She swallowed, but there was no longer anything to hide. "It probably wasn't hard," she admitted. "To scare me."

"But I did. My actions were unforgiveable."

He didn't go on about protocols, or threats, or that he'd had no choice because the job came first. And even though his corded arms remained tight, they didn't feel threatening. They just felt like they were never letting go.

She waited a moment, but he seemed to have finished speaking. And she was hungry. She fumbled with the plastic, then tore it off. She picked up the sandwich, took a tiny bite, then a bigger one, surprised by her appetite. She held it toward his mouth, trying to share. Felt his head shake.

"That's yours," he said.

He spoke no more, remaining silent even when he passed her a bottle of water followed by a delicious protein bar with chocolate and nuts. He waited until she'd swallowed the last piece of food and had wiped her mouth.

Then he reached around, encasing both her hands. "You're not going to be able to climb any higher, are you?"

Her eyes jammed shut. She'd known this moment would come. Wished it hadn't. To a man like him, she must seem cowardly. As a former SEAL, he'd obviously handled much bigger terrors, rebounded from worse events.

"And I caused that fear," he added.

"It wasn't you," she said, unable to be less than honest. "I was afraid from the moment we started climbing. That's why I didn't want to free the horses."

"You're incredibly brave. To climb so high. To make it this far."

She winced. "No, I was terrified the entire way. Even when we were riding."

"That's what courage is," he said.

Her therapist had said the same thing, but it sounded genuine coming from someone like Jack. And he didn't seem disturbed by her admission or act like he wanted to put distance between them. In fact, his body moved closer, his fingers entwined with hers as his thumb stroked the inside of her wrist. And he wasn't asking her to talk, wasn't saying anything, he was just...there.

Countless minutes passed, the only sound the relentless dripping of water down the cave walls.

"It's probably best if I just hide in the little cave," she said. "I used to enjoy climbing. Not any more."

He didn't speak, his very silence comforting. Inviting.

"My ex-boyfriend and I were both park rangers," she said, her voice rusty. "We hiked a lot when we weren't working."

Jack's thumb kept strumming her wrist, calm and soothing. It helped that it was dark and he couldn't see her face.

"That's what we were doing last fall," she said, "when we came across an accident... Danny, just twelve, and his dad, Smitty. Danny said the pack slipped and the horse spooked, dragging down the other two." She gripped Jack's hand, surprised she could even say their names. "Danny hit a ledge and didn't fall all the way to the bottom. He'd been alone, upset. Forced to listen to the sounds from below.

"Andrew went for help once Danny was stable. I did what I could for Smitty then climbed up and sat with Danny. All he wanted was reassurance that his father would be okay. He kept asking who was moaning. It was a relief when the crows came, and their caws covered up the groans."

She swallowed. "The wolves arrived at dusk. I lit a fire but they kept getting bolder." Even the spear she'd carved hadn't helped. Every time she chased them away from Smitty, they'd slink in on the horses. And Danny kept calling from the ledge, asking what was happening and pleading for her to come back.

"By midnight Smitty and two of the horses had died from their injuries. I used the last of the wood to build up the fire around Smitty's body. I couldn't leave the other horse to be eaten alive so I used my knife. And that's why I brought it on the ride. Because I couldn't imagine not having it."

She blew out a shaky breath. "The knife was never meant to hurt Courtney. It was only to help, although I guess it's really a crutch...for me. I can't face the thought of riding without it. And I know you have to ask questions, but that's the truth."

"I just want to ask one thing," Jack said.

She squared her shoulders. No doubt he was suspicious about Monty, and why the experienced guide even wanted her on the trail. But she couldn't answer that. According to Andrew, everyone had been reluctant to partner with her.

"I need someone who can watch my back," he had said. "I can't trust you anymore. You're too scared of heights. And its messed up that you could slit a horse's throat."

She'd given notice at her job the next day even though her boss had offered a paid leave. He'd even offered to transfer Andrew if it would make her life any easier. But Kate knew Andrew wasn't the problem.

She shifted uneasily. Didn't like to talk about it, didn't want to let the bloody images creep back into her head. But if she and Jack made it out, there would be an inquiry with far stiffer questions, and similarly hostile interrogators.

Although Jack couldn't really be termed hostile. Not any longer. In fact he'd lifted her hand and was kissing her palm, his mouth lingering over her skin in such a reassuring way it smoothed away her reticence.

"If your question is about Monty," she said, "you don't need to worry. He's totally trustworthy. Courtney is in good hands. I don't know why Monty wanted me on such an important trail ride. I really don't."

"That's not my question," Jack said. "I just wonder why your boyfriend didn't stay."

"Our cell phones didn't have coverage. He had to hike out and find a spot where it would work."

"That doesn't really answer the question."

"I never thought about it," she said. "It was an ugly scene, and they needed urgent medical help. Guess Andrew thought he could travel faster than me."

"And he probably knew you were more capable than him," Jack said. "That you could handle the tougher job."

"No, that was just the way it worked out."

"But he was the one who left. He chose the easier route. He left you with the carnage, as well as the fall-out."

The fall-out. Jack's voice gentled when he said those words, making her suspect he knew more about the accident than she'd thought. Naturally it had made the news under a variety of head-lines, most of them sensationalized, the words imprinted in her brain. 'Park Ranger Risks Life to Hold Hand of Dying Boy,' 'Wonder Woman Fights Pack of Wolves...And Wins.' 'Survival Nut Slits Throats Of Horses.'

That last one had hurt, and poisonous rants from animal lovers had resulted in her closing all her social media accounts. Andrew had persisted in reading the comments aloud though, seeming to delight in any negative ones. "See," he'd said, tapping the screen, "these people feel the same way I do. Let's face it, what you did wasn't normal. And I have to tell you, it's not just me."

"I wish Andrew had stayed instead of me," she said, feeling a warm tear slide down her cheek. "But I don't think he would have been good with Danny. Or the horses. And they would have suffered horribly."

"Yes," Jack said wryly. "And I'm sure he knew that."

Maybe Andrew had. Ironically, he loved the limelight. Had reveled in the media attention until questions arose as to why he'd been so slow finding an area with phone reception. He hadn't liked that she'd been hailed as a hero, and not him. It hadn't mattered to her. The end result was still the same; she hadn't managed to save anyone. And she couldn't believe she was sitting in an inky cave, hiding from killers, talking this freely about a time she'd always kept buried.

Her tears were flowing freely now but she didn't try to hide them, or even wipe them away. Jack was doing an admirable job, using both of his hands, cradling her face while swiping her cheeks with his thumb.

"This is a bad time to talk about this," she said, between sniffs. "Here. On a mountain. On the run from hired killers."

"Always the perfect time to unload," he said. And there was a hint of wistfulness in his voice.

Of course, he probably had stuff going on too. And she didn't want to hog their last quiet hours, rehashing events in her life that no doubt seemed trivial to a former SEAL, a man who performed secretive jobs for the President and had experienced so much more death and destruction.

"Now it's your turn," she said. "You have way more important things. You can unload anything. I promise never to tell." But she hesitated, wondering if she'd be able to keep that promise. If Logan caught her and threatened to throw her over a cliff, would she be able to keep her mouth shut? Probably not. As her ex had delighted in pointing out, she was a tiger on flatland but a pussycat at altitude.

"Better not mention names or jobs though," she added, giving an apologetic shrug.

She tried to straighten, but Jack kept her tilted on his lap, cradling her face. His fingers were callused but gentle, cupping her face the way one would hold a delicate bird. Her eyes had grown accustomed to the dark, but it was impossible to read his expression, even sitting so close.

"I've killed a few people," he said. "Some, I've come to regret. They weren't good people but their deaths may have been politically expedient. But my biggest regret is scaring you."

"Oh," she breathed, so softly it barely came out as a word. He must still care for her, even though he knew her limitations. Maybe he didn't mind that she was such a liability, especially since he was capable enough for three or four people.

"And I sincerely regret that you're here with me now," he said.

She wished he wasn't holding her face, making it harder to hide her hurt as her insides deflated. Of course he wouldn't want her company. It had become clear with her old job that she no longer brought anything to the team. She could build a shelter or start a fire with two sticks, but she was terrified of heights and had an unusual fixation on her knife.

"Naturally you'd prefer more useful company." She managed a flippant shrug. "You don't have to keep repeating it."

"Kate," he said. "I just don't want you to get hurt. There's no one else I'd rather have at my back, man or woman. Although it would be great if you had some extra ammunition in your pockets."

He scooped her up, keeping the blanket around her shoulders but positioning her legs around his hips. "Do you have any ammo tucked away?" he asked, his voice hopeful. "Maybe some you secretly smuggled in your other boot?"

"Sorry. I only have a knife fetish."

"Regrettable," he murmured. But he didn't sound disappointed. In fact, his mouth was grazing the top of her throat, planting kisses along her jawline. He tugged her closer, adjusting her over his hard belt buckle. No, not his buckle. Clearly his ardor hadn't been reduced one bit.

Was it only a few hours since they had sex? It must have been longer.

She thought about twisting, to check the position of the moon and figure out the time. But his knowing hand was on her breast, his mouth working over her collarbone, leaving her tingling with such pleasure she quit thinking about anything but the wonderful things he did to her body.

CHAPTER THIRTY

Jack cradled Kate in his arms, listening to the gentle rise and fall of her chest. She was sleeping so peacefully, he hated to wake her. This was the kind of night one hoped would never end. The wind had died, and a white tranquil moon lit up the mouth of the cave, providing the ultimate backdrop. He'd always enjoyed sleeping beneath the stars but it didn't get better than this. Neither did the company.

He slid his hand along the curve of her hip, checking that she wasn't cold. The blanket gave plenty of warmth but he wanted to keep her close. Their socks were the only clothing they wore, a small concession to the chilly air. Kate sighed in her sleep and wiggled closer, her breasts pressing against his chest. He only wished he could stop the minutes from ticking away and somehow erase the danger she'd soon face. The predicament he had caused.

He had no doubt he could elude Logan and his men, at least long enough to buy Monty time to reach the fire tower. But fleeing involved climbing. And Kate was maxed out. If it hadn't been for his blunder last night, he might have been able to coax her higher. Combined with last year's traumatic experience though, it was surprising she could climb a mole hill. That she'd made it this far was a testament to her courage, along with her selfless determination to protect Courtney.

If only he'd sent Kate with Monty and the mules. But wrangling all six horses alone wouldn't have worked. If even one animal had broken away, it would have prompted his pursuers to study the tracks more closely. As well, glimpsing the purple jacket on the back of Courtney's black-and-white paint had drawn Logan like a magnet.

Kate's help had been essential for the deception to work. But Jack didn't need her now. And his job was to ensure the First Daughter's safety—no matter his personal feelings.

Kate's soft breath fanned his chest. She looked so small, curled against his shoulder. So trusting. And he didn't think she trusted many people. Her yellow-bellied boyfriend had certainly done a number, running off and leaving her alone to handle a mountain tragedy.

Just as he planned to do.

His arms tightened, even as he assured himself that this was a completely different scenario. And Kate would be safe in the second cave as long as she remained hidden... As long as one of Logan's hired guns wasn't a skinny-assed weasel. One slight enough to squeeze through that crack and drag her out. Or as long as Logan didn't stick his gun through the hole and shoot up the cave out of spite. Kate described it as an open air cathedral. She hadn't mentioned any stalagmites, or places to hide. It would be like shooting fish in a barrel. And ricocheting bullets could be deadly.

His heart thumped so loud with fear that Kate's eyes snapped open. She immediately twisted, checking the night sky and it was obvious that, like him, she woke to instant alertness.

"Not dawn yet," he whispered, reluctant to move, still fighting his gut-deep apprehension. "We have another forty minutes. Let's talk more about the layout of that second cave."

"Oh, it's beautiful," she said. "Apparently if you make love there—" she paused to press a kiss against his chest, followed by a sexy smile that sent heat shooting to his groin—"your love will be sealed forever."

"I'm not superstitious," he said, even as he silently cursed Logan for keeping them on the run. Because there was nothing more he'd like to do then rappel into a lovers' cave with Kate. Failing that, he wanted to lie here and enjoy the sunrise, unhurried. With her sleep-rumpled and naked in his arms. And him moving inside her, slowly, deeply, listening to her sighs of satisfaction.

"We need to talk about the structure," he said, twisting to hide his erection. "Are there any good spots to hide?"

"It's just a little cave. But if I stay on the side close to the crack, I'm sure Logan won't see me."

She sounded confident but Jack wasn't so convinced. Logan was clearly a sewer rat, with fewer morals. Anyone who could slit an unsuspecting agent's throat wouldn't hesitate to take pot shots out of pure meanness. "But are there any formations?" he asked. "Anything you can hide behind?"

She looked up, her vulnerable neck gleaming in the dark. Elegant and exposed. An easy target for a mediocre shooter and everyone in the Secret Service was an excellent shot. The mercenaries could be even better.

"I was thinking," he said slowly, "that maybe hiding in the cave isn't the best option. Probably best if we both keep climbing." He didn't know where that thought came from. It was a lousy idea. With her limitations, Logan would quickly overtake them. And then realize he'd been duped.

"What do you mean?" she asked. "That hiding isn't the best option? For who?"

"For Courtney of course," he said. He turned his head and stared at the moon. The sky wasn't as dark now, or the moon as bright. They'd have to get moving soon. And he couldn't lie to her.

"For you," he added.

She was quiet for a moment but when she spoke her voice was fierce. Like a bear protecting her cubs. "You can climb much faster without me. We both know that. So that's the best option. For Courtney. For Tyra. For you."

He shook his head, already locked on the new plan. "No. You're going to come with me. A little bit higher and we should get enough reception to call for help."

"But with me slowing you down, Logan is sure to catch up. He'll have time to send his people after Courtney. And you can't get all soft just because we had s-sex."

He heard the catch in her voice and slid his hand around the back of her neck, cradling her head. "Are you that afraid of climbing, my love?" he asked.

"Yes." Her voice cracked. "I'd do anything for you, really I would. But I can't climb. Please, don't ask me."

She jerked from his arms, shoved aside the blanket and reached for her clothes. "Just do your job, Jack." Her voice strengthened as she yanked on her shirt, then paused, realizing she'd forgotten her bra.

He scooped it up and passed it to her, guessing she was truly flustered. Probably just as well. There wasn't much time to linger, and having her close and naked stripped away his objectivity. He needed to do his job, stick to the original plan. If Kate thought the other cave was safe, he had to believe her. Although it was disturbing the way she avoided his gaze while she rambled on about all the good places to hide.

She was still talking as she pulled on her boots. "It's *so* protected," she said. "There's even a little chamber off the cathedral room. I didn't tell you about it before because I was so excited about the skylight, and, you know, being able to see the stars and stuff. But it's the perfect place to stash a non-climber. So you don't have to worry about me one bit."

She was lying like a lawyer, making it easier for him. But that only increased his turmoil. And her words niggled at him. "Stash a non-climber." What if Logan anticipated that? If he suspected it was Courtney hiding in the second cave, he and his men would certainly detour around. They'd find the sky opening. And Kate would be alone to face violent and desperate men. Disappointed men.

There was no way he could leave her. But as long as he held Logan off for a few hours, he'd be keeping Courtney safe too. Decision justified.

"You're right." He gave an agreeable nod. "I know you'll be safe. But take the backpack with the blanket and some food. I figure Monty will reach the tower within the next few hours. Just promise me you won't come back out of that cave."

"But your phone will work once you're on the other side of Eagle Pass," she said. "You can call for help too, tell them where I am. And I'll see you back at the ranch, right?"

He'd been reaching for his shoulder holster but turned, capturing her mouth in a passionate kiss, one he deliberately deepened until she was clinging to his arms. "Just stay quiet as a mouse," he said, whispering the words against her mouth.

"Promise me you won't come back through the crack. No matter what you hear."

"Of course." Her voice was breathy.

"Swear to me," he said, knowing she was still off balance from the kiss.

"Yes, I swear. But only if you promise to be careful climbing."

"I'll be very careful when I climb," he said. He lowered his head for one last kiss, but this time he lingered, memorizing her mouth, her tongue, her very essence. Then he squeezed his eyes shut and pressed his forehead against her hair. "You're an incredible woman. Courtney was lucky you were here. Me too. Bravest partner ever."

She winced and he hated that she didn't believe him.

"I mean it." His voice roughened. "You dove into a frigid river to save a horse, stood down a damn grizzly, volunteered to serve as Courtney's decoy then climbed half a mountain when you were scared spitless. That's real courage, Kate."

She was looking at him with open skepticism, so he continued.

"I knew you were special from that first night in the dance hall. And I just want you to know how I feel. 406-534-3729. That's your phone number. I was absolutely going to call. And that was before I knew you can handle mules and love the woods and have such a brave heart."

Her face brightened with the knowledge he'd memorized her number but her expression turned wooden before he even finished talking. She didn't like to be called brave. Considered it prattle, a gratuitous spiel she quickly discounted.

"The mules know they can trust you," he went on, aching with the need for her to believe. "And mules are never easily impressed. Neither are Slider or Monty. The way I scared you with the cliff put you on a little backslide." The spike in his chest twisted and he hated himself for how he'd frightened her. "I'd spend a lifetime making that up to you...if only I could."

"Maybe we can all ride back sometime and see the wild horses?" she asked. "I'd like that."

She wasn't asking much, but he hesitated a little too long, loath to make a promise he might not be able to keep.

"That's okay." Her voice sounded small. "I'm not sure about my future employment anyway. Besides, it's doubtful Courtney will ever be allowed back here."

"Hey." He grabbed her hand. "This isn't the time to make plans. Just remember, you and Monty are heroes. Never forget that."

"Right. And now I'm going to hide in the other cave so you can go for help."

She twisted and scooped up the blanket. "You take the food and water," she said. "You'll need the energy more than me. And please stay ahead of Logan. He doesn't care who he kills."

She was right about that, and it only reinforced his decision. "Stay hidden," he said, slipping a few more items into her backpack. "Don't move even if you hear a helicopter. They have infrared. They'll find you."

"But I'll come back to this cave and signal. Sometimes they take a very long time."

"No!" He forced his voice to remain calm. "You don't want to run into Logan climbing back down."

"But Monty might reach the tower before you're able to call for help. And the horses could make it back to the ranch." Her face clouded but she gave a tight smile. "At least Banjo might."

Jack gave a little nod. However, they couldn't depend on Banjo, no matter how trail-wise the horse was. There was a real possibility all the horses had been shot. Even if a couple animals escaped the four-wheelers, there was no telling how quickly they'd wander home. Once they reached the familiar grasslands of the ranch, they'd just join their buddies grazing. Even an alert wrangler wouldn't immediately notice a few extra horses in a herd of a hundred, not unless the animal somehow made it to the barn door.

"Does Monty grain Banjo every day?" Jack asked.

"No. Only when he's ridden. Horses work one week, are loose with the remuda the next."

Damn. That confirmed his fears, that Banjo wouldn't go to the barn even if he were smart enough, and lucky enough, to make it home. But Jack merely nodded as he zipped up Kate's jacket, carefully adjusting her collar before scooping up the backpack and looping it over his shoulder.

"Time for you to go," he said.

He guided her to the rear of the cave, where the air was damp and heavy and depressing.

She paused, looked up at him, but he urged her into the crack. She twisted, seemed stuck for a moment, then her rib cage moved as she blew out her breath. She was so resolute, so damn brave, and he didn't want to ever let her go. His hand tightened convulsively around her hip before giving one last push. Then he could no longer feel her.

"You through?" he asked.

"Yes," she called, her voice already distant. He jammed her backpack into the crevice, felt the weight leave his hand as she pulled it through to the other side. Then he was alone. He pressed his face against the crack, straining to feel her presence, already missing her.

"I can hear you breathing," he said. "Go sit somewhere else."

"I will," she said, "as soon as you leave."

"I'm going now." But he didn't move. And he could still hear her damn breathing.

"You'll have to be quieter than that," he growled, fear roughening his words. "When Logan and his men come."

"I know. And you need to start climbing. Please be careful."

"You too," he said. He stuck his arm into the crack, knowing it was a futile gesture but craving one last touch. Miraculously her hand slipped into his, gripping his fingers, squeezing back.

"Just be safe," he said gruffly, wanting to say more but knowing it was best not to.

He pulled his hand back and turned away.

Time to refocus. He'd always been honored to serve his country. During his early years as a SEAL he'd believed passionately in every mission. Then he'd started to question the political motivations, an insidious shift that left him weary and cynical. When one of his team had died on a questionable assignment, he'd quit to work on his own. He still loved the element of danger, the unmatched adrenaline rush. But now each job had to appeal to his patriotism before he'd even consider killing. Guarding the President's daughter fit his strict code. But somehow this mission had evolved into something different. Something bigger.

This was no longer a job. It was personal.

CHAPTER THIRTY-ONE

Kate sighed and pushed herself away from the crack in the wall. Jack was gone. It was critical he take advantage of every second of light, but still, she missed his solid presence. When he'd released her hand and strode off, her heart had plummeted. But the faster he could call for help, the quicker he could ensure Courtney's safety. At least he'd have a head start since Logan and his men also couldn't resume climbing until dawn.

She set down her backpack and edged around the cave, keeping her hand on the rough wall and reacquainting herself with its dimensions. Twenty-two feet long with a gentle dipping bed. The narrow skylight had probably been formed by melt water. Already the opening high above was lightening. The stars had disappeared and the sky had faded to a colorless gray. For now, it was safe to sit beneath the hole and savor the growing light. Maybe she'd even hear Jack's steps as he passed. Perhaps he'd look down and give a last wave.

She stared up, trying to spot his movement, but all she gained was a stiff neck. However, the fact that she hadn't seen him as he climbed past was a good thing. It meant the trail didn't wind too close to the top of the cave. Logan and his men might rush past without even noticing the opening.

Conversely, Logan was familiar with Courtney's athletic capabilities and her limited fitness. He must be questioning how she and Tyra were still climbing...and no doubt he'd be on the lookout for possible hiding spots.

Kate gulped, remembering the men's comments. Rape, murder, dumping bodies—discussed like they were routine events. Maybe they were. But at least they wouldn't catch Courtney and Tyra so the joke was on them. Although right now Kate didn't feel much like laughing. Contrary to what she'd told Jack, there was no place to hide here, and her heart was hammering from the adrenaline.

Earlier she'd been determined to conceal her dread but there was no reason to keep it buried now. Damn Logan and his awful men. Frustration fused with her fear because once again she was stuck alone on the side of a mountain, unable to do anything to control the course of events. The only thing left to do was wait.

Waiting was always the hard part. It was tempting to curl in a ball and shut down her sense of time. And just pray the chopper arrived before Logan. She didn't think she could last through an interminable delay, worrying if Jack could climb fast enough, if the mules could carry the girls to safety, if Logan would find her. At least where she was, wolves weren't a danger. Only humans.

She paced restless circles, knowing she should conserve her energy but unable to remain still. She needed something to occupy her time. Maybe she could carve something. Make a weapon. Even if she couldn't use it, making it would keep her hands busy.

She checked the fire pit, sorting through the remnants of the wood, holding pieces up to the skylight and analyzing each one. There wasn't anything thick enough for a spear but some of the longer branches would be suitable for a bow and some arrows, and she had twine in her backpack. The crafting would take longer as well.

She seated herself cross-legged beneath the skylight, calmer now that she had a purpose. Her fingers flew over the wood, the familiar weight of her knife comforting. She even caught herself smiling while she worked. And thinking of Jack, who was a much more appealing subject than the men who were hunting them.

By now, he should be close to Eagle Pass. He had contour maps that would help him pick the best route and avoid being trapped in a dead end where he'd be picked off by Logan's snipers. Maybe another hour and he'd be able to raise a cell phone signal.

Then she'd see him again.

Based on his reaction though, he didn't seem keen to ride in to view the mustangs. Maybe he had another job lined up and that's why he hadn't been enthused. They seemed to enjoy the same things, although possibly Jack preferred a more reliable partner, a woman who could climb Mount Everest if she were inclined. Maybe Jack was turned off by her fear.

Kate gave her head a shake. He hadn't acted turned off. Not at all. Their physical attraction was undeniable; the sex had been bone melting. And he had memorized her phone number. Although that was before he knew she was afraid of heights and prone to panic attacks at the worst possible time.

Her knife slipped, leaving a thin line of red on her palm. She pressed her hand over the cut, appalled by her inattention. Besides, she didn't want to be greedy, to hope for things she didn't deserve. Jack was a good man and the country was more secure because of him. She just prayed he stayed safe and out of reach of Logan's snipers.

Besides, it was futile to agonize about what he might want, or wouldn't want, in a woman. There was a real chance she'd be discovered. And clearly Logan was a twisted man. He'd be enraged by the realization he'd been duped, that Courtney was safely out of reach.

She paused for a moment, gripping her hands and taking a minute to compose herself. Imagining Logan's reaction was counter-productive. She didn't want to let a picture of the man's face even enter her head. She picked the knife up, determined to focus on the task at hand, the one thing she could control.

Twenty minutes later, she cut the ends of the twine and tested the bow for suppleness. Not bad. If a guest had made the bow in her survival class, they would have been delighted with the result. Satisfied, she opened the backpack and replaced the leftover twine.

She tilted her head back, assessing the sky. Clear blue now, except for the edge of a wispy cirrus cloud creeping onto the pristine blue.

Definitely time to shift to the dark side of the cave. But first she needed to check her food. If there were two bars, she'd eat one now. Save the other for later in the day. Or maybe she'd eat half now, half for lunch, and keep the second bar, just in case.

She shoved her hand deep into the pack, rummaging beneath the folded blanket. Her hand closed around a bar, then another and still another. She pulled the bars out, one at a time, staring in disbelief as she lined them up on the floor of the cave. Seven bars and four bottles of water. But that was their entire supply. That meant Jack hadn't taken a thing. What was he thinking? He needed the food, most certainly the water, far more than her.

Then she saw his phone was in the pack too. Her breath caught in dismay. He was climbing so high, desperately seeking cell phone reception, and he'd forgotten the phone. Wouldn't even be able to make a call.

Crack!

She jumped, dropping the phone, as the sound of a shot reverberated through the cave. Then an answering staccato of gunfire echoed over the mountain.

She bolted to the crack in the wall. Pressed her face against the rough opening, straining to see. All was dark, except for a glimmer of light marking the mouth of the outer cave. Certainly there was no movement, no men storming inside. That first shot had been close though. The last round of gunfire had sounded further away, as if Logan's men hadn't reached the cave yet. But why would they be shooting?

The answer hit with sickening dread. It was the same reason Jack hadn't taken the phone. And why he'd made her promise not to come back through the crack. Because he'd never left.

That first shot must have been his. The rifle shots had been answering fire. And now he was pinned in a cave, trying to hold off a group of desperate mercenaries. Her groan was deep and visceral.

She clamped her mouth shut and pressed against the wall, remembering what he'd made her promise.

Stay quiet. Don't come back through the crack. He must have planned to make his stand there. But why? Did he feel responsible for her? Maybe he thought she wasn't able to climb any further because he'd scared her by the cliff.

But that hadn't changed a thing. Her fear was constant and she'd been relieved to hide in the second cave. Had preferred the coward's way out. However, she certainly hadn't intended to risk his life because of *her* weakness.

Another barrage of rifle shots sounded, staccato sharp, but Jack didn't return fire. Of course, he only had one magazine. Each bullet had to count. That first shot was probably to let them know he was there, to keep them from approaching. Or maybe he'd picked off Logan and the remaining men were fleeing.

Yes, that could be it.

She pressed her face back against the crack, hopeful now, listening for telltale sounds. But it was silent in the adjoining cave, as if Jack had hunkered down. At least he had the advantage of high ground. Maybe Logan's men were fanning out, searching for a safer approach. That would take time...and that's probably what Jack was banking on.

He was trying to keep her safe, yet he was also giving Monty the necessary time to save Courtney. It was a win, win...except for Jack. Once those men were level with the cave, he wouldn't have a chance. And now it was too late for him to run.

Her nails bit into her palms. This was her fault. And there was nothing she could do to help him. But she couldn't remain quiet while the shooters stormed the cave. Couldn't just sit and listen while Jack sacrificed his life. If only she could get behind the shooters and help.

She turned so quickly she tripped over the uneven floor, smashing her knee against a jagged rock. She scrambled to her feet and rushed to the skylight. Stared up, studying the rough wall, barely aware of the pain in her leg. Light streamed through the hole in the cave roof. How high was it? Thirty, thirty-five feet? People climbed in and out all the time, as evidenced by the names carved on the wall.

But they had gear. And even before the accident, she'd never been able to climb sheer walls like that. Not without a rope and harness and proper climbing shoes. Just the thought of trying to scale it left her light-headed. As her job change had shown, she was a lesser person now, good only for sedate rides, not challenging life trails. And Jack would die because of her phobia.

She pressed her fists against her chest, trying to pull in air, but it felt like she was squeezed against an impenetrable wall. With no way to breathe. And the knowledge that she was having a panic attack, while Jack was calmly preparing to fight, magnified her sense of shame. All she could do was stand and quiver, just like the drowning palomino had stood in the river.

But Slider had recovered.

However her hands were tingling now, every inch of her skin buzzing as her breath sawed in and out. And she couldn't grab it. Her lungs seemed to be stuck closed. Her vision grayed and she knew she was hyperventilating.

She forced herself to count off frantic seconds: in for three, hold for three, out for three. Kept repeating the count, desperately fighting for control.

Slowly it felt like her head was no longer going to explode. She didn't know how long she stood there, weak and sweaty, her lungs ragged but working again.

She stumbled to the cave wall. Tilted her head and assessed the rock face with a new desperation. It wasn't *not* climbable. The first section would be the most challenging but there was a good handhold at ten feet and another slightly above. She just needed to gather her strength, her belief. To not only decide to climb but to commit to succeed. Because this day people needed her: Courtney, Tyra, Monty, and most especially Jack.

CHAPTER THIRTY-TWO

Jack lay flat on the ground only inches from the cave entrance, his gaze fixed on the lower trail. Granite boulders to his right provided some cover but he didn't want to risk raising his head very high. Those sniper rifles were too accurate.

Below an arm flashed, the first movement he'd seen in a while. It was tempting to snap off another shot but he'd already used six bullets, just to keep them back. He doubted it was Logan behind that rifle. The agent wasn't the type to step in harm's way if someone else would take the risk. Judging by the drifting voices, two men remained with Logan. The other two had back-tracked, no doubt intending to circle from the other side. But that maneuver would take at least another half hour, and Court-ney should be safely extracted by the time Logan discovered Jack was alone.

Only he wasn't alone.

He tried to ignore the sweat prickling his neck, the hollow-ness carving out his gut. Kate would be okay as long as she re-mained silent. Out of sight. Still, his heart pounded with fear and that wasn't the best way to go into a gunfight. But she was going to get out of this alive. He'd protected many people be-fore—thought he'd been committed to their safety—but never had he felt such primal desperation.

A rifle barrel moved. He instinctively flattened. Bullets sprayed the rock inches above his head, chipping bits of debris over his shoulders.

Logan's voice followed the echoing sound of the shots. "We just want the girl," he called. "Hand her over and we'll be on our way."

Yeah, right. They both knew there was no way Jack would turn over Courtney. But the fact that Logan was talking, trying to distract him, probably meant the other two men were moving into place on his flank.

He edged back from the boulders and rolled sideways, scanning the side of the slope with his binoculars. It looked benign except that the sheep were no longer placidly grazing. They'd climbed higher up the mountain, their cloven hooves clinging to the mountain face. Two of the bigger rams stared downward, their attention riveted to the southern slope.

He couldn't spot any humans but he had considerable respect for a prey animal's ability to detect predators long before any human. He kept the glasses pinned to his eyes, watching the slope.

Finally he spotted movement—two men, obviously comprising Logan's flanking attack. If they kept coming at that angle they'd be level with the cave in approximately twenty minutes. Not bad climbers either, he thought. They'd moved much faster than he'd anticipated. Worse, they looked lean and nimble, possibly wiry enough to squeeze through the passage to Kate's hideaway.

If he could only take out a couple men with his limited ammo, it would definitely be those two. But they were still too far away for a decent shot. Best to go along with Logan's fake negotiations. Chew up more precious time.

He belly-crawled back to his original spot between the rocks.

"So if I send out Courtney," Jack called, "you'll let the others go?"

"That's right," Logan said. "There's no need for anyone else to get hurt. We just want the girl."

The girl. It was odd Logan still avoided using Courtney's name. But obviously he thought the group was together—still believed there had been five riders fleeing to the west. A weight lifted from Jack's shoulders.

"You must be tired of babysitting," Logan went on. "I've done it for three years now. We both know that pampered bitch isn't worth dying for."

Clearly Logan was trying to bury any personal connection. But he must feel some sort of regret. Guilt.

"Your *friend*, Kessler," Jack called, "thought that she was."

"He wasn't my friend." Logan's voice rose. "Just another brainwashed agent. Thinking it's an honor to give his life for our country. You know how it works. You left the Special Forces so you could make some real money too."

"I prefer choosing my own clients," Jack said, listening intently, trying to get a bead on Logan's position... Behind the smooth granite boulder with the silica flecks that reflected the sun. Thirty-five feet, moderate wind, downhill fifty degree angle.

"Of course. Me too." Logan sounded all agreeable now. "We need to get paid what we're worth. This one job sets me up well. I could probably find something in it for you."

"What are they paying?" Jack asked, then twisted, checking the approaching men on his flank. They had a radio. If Logan believed him, the men would probably stop climbing.

"More than enough to cut you in," Logan called.

"We'd be on the run the rest of our lives."

"I've got a place lined up in Kazakhstan. Easy living. We could freelance, use it as our base. Think about it..." Logan's voice drifted, perhaps as he picked up his radio.

Jack trained his binoculars on the climbers. They were still moving purposefully, almost level with his position. Clearly Logan hadn't called them off. And there wasn't much time left. Once the two men crested the bluff, they'd have the advantage of high ground.

"How many men with you?" Jack called. "What's the split?"

"Ten million, three guys. Four with you."

Jack grimaced. Logan wasn't giving up his other two men. The coward obviously planned to take him by surprise, regardless of any so-called negotiations. Luckily Kate had seen their camp yesterday and knew their real numbers. But once Jack turned and took out the climbers, Logan's group would rush the cave.

By then, he'd be lucky to have a couple bullets left. It'd be impossible to keep them at bay. He needed to lay more groundwork, while he and Logan were still talking.

"Sounds like a good deal," Jack said. "Makes me wish I really did have Courtney with me."

Logan chuckled, magnanimous now that his shooters were almost in position. "I know she's there. My four-wheelers followed the hoofprints where your trail forked. They spotted six horses. All riderless."

Spotted. Did that mean the horses had escaped? Jack allowed himself a moment of satisfaction, knowing the relief that would give Kate. "Your men should have driven closer," he called. "They would have seen Monty and the three girls clinging to their necks."

"There were no riders," Logan said. "And those horses are bear food now."

Damn.

"Besides," Logan added, "the horses we shot had no saddles. And everyone knows those girls can't ride bareback. But that's okay. They're good for riding something. I call first dibs on the mule girl."

One of Logan's men laughed, the sound resembling that of a braying hyena.

Jack clamped down his growing hate and swung to the right, checking the slope again. He was almost out of time. The two climbers were dangerously high, almost level with his position. Once he started shooting, Logan would charge. But he needed to make them believe he was alone. Reduce the chance they'd search the second cave. He also had to release some of his white-hot anger before he started shooting. He couldn't afford to miss.

He rolled back to his side, determined to wipe the satisfaction off Logan's face. "You're dead wrong," he called. "Kate isn't scared of horses. But it's lucky she's good with mules too. That's why Monty and all three girls have reached the ranch by now. So you douche bags better run. Find some shithole country where you can hide the rest of your short miserable lives."

Silence thickened the air, punctuated only by the piercing scream of a hunting hawk.

Logan started yelling. "I don't believe you! I know Courtney's there, you fucker."

"That's no way to talk to a future partner," Jack said, satisfied by the ensuing confusion. There was second guessing now, as well as anger, with none of the three men bothering to lower their voice.

"We didn't check the camp for mule tracks," someone was saying. "Because *you* told us to follow the horses."

"Yeah," the man with the hyena laugh said. "She might not have been on that paint. Maybe *he* was wearing the purple jacket."

"Don't be so fucking gullible," Logan said, all the while cursing Monty, Kate, and every mule on earth.

"Where the fuck is she?" Now Logan's voice was a mixture of rage and frustration, along with a hint of panic. "I know she's close. We can smell the bitch. How about I shoot your balls off. Then you'll tell me."

Jack rolled to the other side of the boulders. Logan was in a fury, his mercenaries questioning his leadership. Hopefully they'd be too unbalanced for anything but a cursory sweep of the cave. As long as the other two climbers were taken out, nobody would be likely to scale higher...and possibly stumble upon the opening to Kate's hideout. The only danger now was that one of the men might be small enough to squeeze through the crack.

But it wouldn't be these two back shooters. He lined up the sights of his Sig on the second climber. A body shot gave the highest margin of error. An even less-than-perfect shot would take the man out of action. He preferred to avoid kill shots when not under direct attack, one of the reasons he hadn't enjoyed the sniper team.

In this situation though, he didn't have one shred of reluctance. These killers were a threat to Kate. He was reasonably certain neither of them wore body armor, considering how fast they'd climbed. But if necessary, he'd use all five bullets to take them out.

He steadied his breath, leading the target slightly, then squeezed. The man dropped like a stone. The first climber twisted, surprising Jack by turning toward the thudding sound and not scrambling for cover, leaving Jack's second shot a clean miss.

Jack caught the white of panicked eyes, the flare of comprehension, as he squeezed off his third shot. The man fell, the same instant bullets spattered the rocks behind him.

Logan and his two thugs were charging.

He rolled back behind the boulder as hollers and gunfire stained the air. The three men were dangerously close, spraying his position, keeping him pinned as they charged up the path. Logan was in the rear. Naturally.

Jack kept his head pressed against the rock, gun gripped in his hand. His shoulder itched, clipped by either a bullet or flying rock. Adrenaline dulled the pain, conversely sharpening his senses. He could smell male sweat along with fear and fury. Could hear the frustration in Logan's shrill command. "Don't kill the fucker! He needs to tell us where Courtney is. I know she's close."

There was murmured agreement then Logan's voice rose in triumph. "You're almost out of ammo. Surprised you needed three bullets for two men. Heard you were a crack shot. At least now our split is down to three."

One of the men gave that ugly hyena laugh—the same man who had laughed about their use for Kate—and Jack honed in his location. That would be his next target. He'd swing low, to the left of the boulders. Go for the hyena, then Logan. He didn't want to wait for their rush. Logan would make sure he was at the back and Jack only had two bullets left.

He crawled to the left side of the ledge. "There's nothing to split," he called, "since you don't have Courtney. And never will. I know that's hard for you to understand. Kessler said you were dumber than a doorknob…and your tiny dick was the reason he had to fuck all your girlfriends."

He rolled to the other side of the boulder before he finished speaking. Curses sounded, along with a flurry of bullets that sprayed the boulder, ricocheting over the spot where he'd been lying. However, the men didn't charge as he'd hoped. Clearly they didn't want him dead. Not until they learned Courtney's location. But he couldn't give them the chance to extract that information and potentially discover Kate was the one who'd helped trick them…or that she was still within reach.

He had to make it impossible for them *not* to go for the kill shot. He pulled in a resolute breath, rolled to the left of the rock and came up in the open with his gun level. Saw his first target, the hyena man, and squeezed the trigger. The man's head snapped back leaving Logan exposed. One bullet left, with Logan in his sights.

Whenever possible, shoot in order of rank.

If he had two bullets left, he could have taken out both remaining men. Logan was the leader, the logical target. But the man on Logan's right was small, wiry and weasel thin. The bigger danger.

Jack shifted his gun and shot the man in the center of the forehead. He pressed again, aiming at Logan.

Click.

The sound of the empty chamber wasn't surprising. He'd known there were no bullets left. Had hoped for a miracle.

Logan had been down on his knees, scrambling away like a coward. Now he stopped and rose, the fear on his face turning to triumph. "You're out," he sneered. "Who's the dumb fuck now?"

He swaggered up the path, his gun leveled on Jack. "Didn't expect a hotshot like you to miscount. But you're going to wish you'd taken me out instead of Peewee. Because I'm going to enjoy killing you."

His eyes swept over Jack, his mouth lifting in an ugly sneer. "Let's see. Gut or groin? The latter, I think. So you'll die alone, knowing you're half a man. Although I could make it quicker. Just tell me where Courtney is." His eyes narrowed on the mouth of the cave. "Or don't. Because I know she's in there. I really don't need you alive."

"The cave is empty," Jack said, wishing Logan would step a little closer. Five more feet and he might be able to kick the gun from his hands.

"Cut me in," Jack said, "and I'll take you back down the mountain. Show you where she's really hiding."

"Shut up. Don't fucking move." Logan's mouth remained curled in a triumphant snarl, and it was clear he wasn't moving one step closer. At least not while Jack was standing.

He leveled his gun at Jack's groin. "I know she's in there. All of them are. Soon they'll see who's really in charge. Bet the mule girl will do anything to keep me from turning Courtney over to ISIS. I saw her file. She's stupidly loyal, just like you.

"I'll spread her legs," he went on, a drop of spittle forming on the side of his mouth. "And be buried balls deep before you even bleed out. Right after I kill the guide and that whiny bitch. Hate to waste young pussy but I'm in a hurry. So say goodbye to your nuts—"

Chunk.

The solid sound of something hitting flesh replaced his taunts. Logan staggered back, the gun clattering to the rock. He gripped his neck, his eyes widening as he stared down at the crude arrow sticking from his throat.

Jack shot forward and scooped up Logan's gun. Then turned and scanned the cliff.

Kate stood on the ledge above, bow in hand, a second arrow already notched.

He glanced back at Logan. "Don't pull that arrow out," he said, eyeing the crimson smearing the man's fingers. "Leave it alone, you might live. Where's your radio?"

"What the fuck?" Logan whimpered, still clutching at his throat.

At least he was able to talk. A good sign. But Jack wasn't feeling too charitable. Not to Logan. Kate was another matter.

He walked closer to the ledge and stared up. She looked like an avenging angel, calm, resolute and twice as beautiful. "How did you get out?" he called.

"Climbed."

He nodded, absorbing that fact. "Must have been quite a climb. Helluva shot too."

"Not really," she said. "I was aiming for his chest. Didn't want to miss."

"No, I wouldn't have wanted that either." He shook his head, confused but feeling lucky. Very lucky. And rather lost for words. "Wow, babe," he managed.

She tilted her head, her eyes narrowing. "What did you call me?"

"Never mind." His grin deepened. "I won't call you that again. Want me to climb up? Help you down?"

"No." She shook her head, and the smile she gave him was almost stunning in its brilliance. "Pretty sure I can handle it."

CHAPTER THIRTY-THREE

The helicopter rotor whirred, leaving Kate's ears throbbing. There were headphones in the back but no one was using them, perhaps because this helicopter was much quieter than others she'd ridden. The blond agent seated beside her certainly didn't seem bothered. Nor did Jack. He was busy analyzing computer maps with two other agents, arguing over the most logical exit points for the terrorists.

Logan hadn't been able to provide much information. Only that the plan was to deliver Courtney to a water plane on Echo Lake at fourteen hundred hours. At which time, ten million dollars would have been transferred to a bank account in the Cayman Islands.

She didn't think Logan had lied. His questioning had been too efficient, too ruthless. The agent in charge had spoken softly, almost in whispers, but his hand had been on the wooden arrow sticking in Logan's throat. Not trying to calm him as she'd been but threatening to twist the arrow. Logan had stopped swearing at Kate, quit moaning that he hadn't done anything wrong. He even stopped referring to the girls as useless bitches. At that point a stony-faced agent had pulled Kate away, warning that she needed to wait in the cave until a second helicopter arrived.

She pressed the back of her head against the seat, unable to remember who was the medic and who was the agent who'd propelled her into the cave. All the men were physically impressive, almost interchangeable except for the color of their hair. Logan certainly hadn't fared as well in the genetics department. After hearing his taunts to Jack, it was clear he was twisted with envy. Hated his job, his co-workers, even the people he'd sworn to protect. Still, to betray an innocent girl, to slit an agent's throat, to threaten to shoot off Jack's testicles... It was far beyond the scope of anything Kate had ever experienced.

She slipped her hands beneath her arms and shivered.

The agent seated beside her reached out and adjusted the blanket higher over her shoulders. "No need to worry," he said. "Both girls have been extracted safely. Stay warm. We'll be landing at the hospital in thirty minutes. You'll be interviewed there. All your questions will be answered then as well."

She could feel his scrutiny and guessed maybe he was the one who'd escorted her away from Logan. She'd heard his mutters too, while she'd been waiting alone in the cave. "What kind of woman can carve a bow and arrow?" the man had said, once Logan has been airlifted away. "Scale a vertical rock wall? Then take out a trained agent?"

A freak, she thought. This agent certainly seemed to consider her an oddity. Staring at her when he thought she wasn't looking, monitoring her every move, remaining glued to her side rather than helping analyze the terrorists' exit route.

Or maybe his real purpose was to keep her and Jack apart, prior to any interviews. She wasn't sure how long the grilling would take, only that the last inquiry after the accident had been gut wrenching. Anything related to the White House would no doubt be much more intense. A ball of dread lodged deeper in her chest.

She averted her head. It had been almost a year since she'd ridden in a helicopter—not since the last accident—and she'd been avoiding looking out the window. However, staring down at the rolling foothills was easier than accepting that she was once again embroiled in tragedy. While it was a relief the rescuers had arrived so quickly, judging by their air of mistrust it was obvious there would be considerable blowback.

She knew the whispers weren't so bad. She could handle rooms that silenced whenever she walked in. Avoiding social media was easy on the ranch. But it was the images that plagued her. And looking at countless pictures, being forced to justify her actions, only branded the trauma on her brain, making everything harder to forget. It was tough on her friends and co-workers as well.

"I have to tell you, Kate," her boyfriend had said, "no one wants to work with you. You killed a horse. We've all seen the bloody pictures. It makes people uncomfortable, especially me. A beautiful woman like you isn't supposed to be a killer, to be able to do things like that."

She'd been hoping for a comforting hug, for reassurances that life would return to normal. Hadn't realized her co-workers were uneasy until Andrew had pointed it out. "So it's not because I'm afraid of heights?" she'd asked.

"Well, your ridiculous fear is obviously an issue. But since the boss considers you a hero"—his lip had curled at that absurdity—"nobody will admit the truth, even if you ask them. But you can't do your job feeling the way you do. It's dangerous for everyone. And let's be honest, you're bad luck. The decent thing would be for you to quit."

And so she had. She didn't want to endanger anyone. Had experienced enough blood and guilt to last a lifetime.

She'd packed up her clothes and saddle and the remnants of her pride and found a job where she didn't have to venture into the mountains. Where nobody knew what she'd done, or even cared. And if her new co-workers heard a little gossip, they certainly refrained from judging. As Allie once said, everyone at the ranch was trying to escape something. The pay was far less but so were Kate's needs. And the Mustang River Ranch had become her home.

But now a trail ride had ended in the biggest disaster in the illustrious ranch's history. Deadly for horses as well as humans. She'd carved a bow and shot an arrow at a man's throat. Notorious stuff. Even the federal agents were shaking their heads. No way could Sharon Barrett afford to keep Kate on staff. Her survival classes had never been popular. They'd be less so now. Guests wanted to relax at the ranch, not feel threatened.

She squeezed her eyes shut, fighting a wave of despair. The agent beside her refused to tell her anything, only that Courtney and Tyra were safe. While that was a relief, the fact remained that Kessler might still be alive if she had only trusted the man a little more. If she had just reported the slashed trees on the very first day.

Would the negative publicity bankrupt the ranch? No doubt, reservations would be cancelled. Bookings would plummet and fellow employees—her friends—would be laid off. And Sharon Barrett had been nothing but kind, the only person who had stepped forward and offered a job. While the guest ranch was an established business, capable of surviving a few lean years, insidious shadows would remain. A terrorist stigma was always a downer.

As well, the White House might be vindictive. Who even knew the President's thought process? He'd be more bitter if Courtney were left traumatized. The poor girl would probably never want to ride a horse again. She'd only escaped because Jack was there. He was the one who'd sent her off with Monty, then acted as a decoy, leading Logan and his men in the opposite direction. He'd been prepared to sacrifice his life for Courtney, for all of them. He might have saved Kessler too if Kate had just told him about her suspicions. She dropped her head in her hands, her mind aching with images and questions and alternate scenarios.

But the "what ifs" didn't help. Kessler was still dead, his broken body lying out there, alone and exposed to scavengers. So were the loyal horses who hadn't done anything wrong except be obedient, and nobody would even tell her how the mules had fared. Those bogs to the south were belly deep and treacherous. If a mule had become stranded, Monty wouldn't have had time to stop and free them. Maybe Belle was sinking in a bog right now, too smart to flail around but sinking nonetheless. Predators quickly sniffed out the weak and helpless.

Her mind jumped from images of animals ripped apart by wolves to Kessler's bloody eye sockets being ravaged by the beaks of hungry crows. And all she could do was keep her back to the agent and fight the helpless feeling that she could have—should have—done more.

She felt the agent tug the blanket higher over her shoulders, but that wasn't the kind of comfort she needed. Besides, he didn't care about the animals or the ranch or Monty and Tyra. He only cared about the President's daughter. She realized she was looking down as they passed over the foothills, no longer disturbed by her elevated view. And a tiny sob escaped, because even though she might be able to handle heights better now, that small triumph seemed trivial.

She already knew how this would turn out. Best to do the ethical thing and quit before she was asked to leave. That would make it easier for everyone—bosses, workmates, lovers. She didn't even know how to categorize Jack, but she couldn't deny he was behaving exactly the way her last boyfriend had. Distancing himself before the blowback started.

She and Jack had barely spoken since he'd used Logan's radio to call in their coordinates. She'd been giving Logan medical aid when the first helicopter arrived, spilling out a load of grim-faced men. Jack had been swallowed in a blur of commands and harsh questions. She remembered a steely-eyed agent confiscating Jack's gun, and all she could think about was that it didn't even have any bullets.

The agent nudged her on the elbow, yanking back her thoughts. "Don't touch those bandages," he said. She realized she was picking at her hands, her agitation apparent.

"I've got this," a familiar voice said.

"No," the agent snapped. "I understand you work directly for the President but it's important to follow protocol."

"Move," Jack said, and the steel in his voice could have cut glass.

Then his strong arms wrapped around her, his chin positioned over the top of her head.

"You okay, sweetheart?" he asked, his voice much gentler than it had been mere seconds before. He spoke as if he had all the time in the world, as if a hostile agent wasn't hovering two feet away, making sure they didn't discuss the events. "Would you like to move to a seat with no window? Maybe back with the medic?"

"No," she said. "I'm fine. It's not the h-height." It was the fact that her lungs didn't seem to work, were struggling to push out air. And that panic was beginning to sweep over her in waves.

She couldn't formulate any more words but Jack seemed to understand, taking over the conversation, pondering about the blue of the river in between telling her to hold her breath and asking her to guess the color of the pilot's underwear. Slowly her breath came easier, simply from the absurdity of his questions, or his proximity, or maybe it was his total ease with the situation.

"Sure is nice grassland," he was saying. "That's great you can look down now, appreciate the view." She felt his teasing smile against her hair. "Maybe we'll finally see those wild mustangs."

Her breath escaped in a choke then disintegrated into help-less sobs. He just held her, keeping her turned toward the win-dow, shielding her from the other agents, his compassionate hand stroking her head.

"I'm okay now," she whispered, after a minute of silent cry-ing, or maybe several. She really didn't know how long they sat. Jack seemed in no hurry to vacate the seat, even though the blond agent was hovering, his disapproval radiating in waves.

Jack reached around and stroked her wrists. "They're taking you directly to the hospital. Two of your fingers are broken, and you're going to lose some nails. And that cut on your forearm will need stitches. Do you want anything more for the pain?"

She shook her head, dismissing her injuries. Once she'd de-cided to climb that rock wall, she hadn't felt a thing. Still didn't. There were too many people, and animals, who had fared much worse. "Did they find Kessler's body?" she asked.

"Yes," Jack whispered.

"What about Logan?" she asked, following his lead, keeping her voice low so the agent wouldn't hear.

"Already in surgery. Looks like he's going to live, thanks to your first aid."

"That's good, I guess," she said. But she didn't feel much emotion. She'd held his wound, prevented him from yanking out the arrow while Jack searched for Logan's radio. The man was no longer a threat and she hadn't wanted him to die. But she would have shot another arrow if necessary, and she knew she shouldn't admit *that* during her interrogation.

She probably would though. Last year, her lawyer had cautioned her to only answer the specific questions. But evasiveness didn't come naturally. The inquiry had dissected every one of her thoughts and actions, forcing her to relive the experience in the most agonizing detail. She'd already accepted that she could, and would, do what was necessary to save a life. And that made others uncomfortable.

Actually it was rather surprising Jack still sat beside her. He'd tilted her back in the seat and was studying her hands, his ambivalence obvious by his expression.

"What kind of freak could climb a rock wall?" Had he heard those comments? Maybe even participated in them?

He shocked her by gently picking up her wrists and kissing them, first the right, then the left, then the right again. Respectfully. Reverently. Certainly not hiding his actions. "I can't believe you were able to climb out of there," he said. "You saved my life."

The muscles in his throat moved and he lifted his head. "I don't want you to worry about the interview," he said. "It won't be like your last time. And the girls are fine. Stiff but grateful. Monty took good care of them."

"What about the mules?" She shot a wary peek over his shoulder. The other agents had shut her down, refusing to answer any questions, only saying an information officer would meet her at the hospital. But as usual, Jack seemed to be operating under a different set of parameters.

"The mules are fine," he said. "They'll be picked up and hauled back to the ranch. Monty insisted they not be asked to walk another step. Two agents will stay with them until the trailer arrives. Right now, they're enjoying the long grass around the fire tower."

She gave a wobbly smile. Belle, Gus and Bubba were safe. Once again Monty had returned with all his animals. Not her though. Her smile faded and she wondered if Monty even knew about the horses yet. Or Sharon.

Of course, her boss was fair, reasonable. Animals should always be sacrificed for people. But once the dust settled, Sharon would grieve. Banjo, Dusty and Oreo had been bred on her ranch. Banjo was Monty's favorite. Each horse would be missed. Even Slider—who had proven remarkably loyal—had looked at Kate with something akin to hurt when she'd chased him away. As if he knew Logan's men were lurking, waiting to pick him off.

"May I talk to my boss?" Kate asked, squeezing the words through her thickened throat. "Just for a minute. To explain...why we had to let them go?"

"No." Jack shook his head, every bit as emphatic as the agents. "Not until you answer a few questions. Officials will meet you at the hospital."

"Will I be able to see Courtney and Tyra?"

"No. Sorry. They've already been whisked away."

"What about you?" she asked. "Will you be there?"

"No," Jack said. "They're escorting me directly to Washington."

"I see." Even though he was still holding her, she felt alone. "I should have told you about the tree blazes," she said, her voice small. "Should have trusted you. This could have been so different."

"Hey." He turned her around, his expression shocked. "You did your job, way beyond. You and Monty were incredible. *Are* incredible. And this is on me. I saw those trees too."

"Oh," she said, feeling a bit better. Then she sobered. "Aren't you worried about your job future? I'm surprised you're even allowed to talk to me."

His look of disbelief changed to something entirely different. He wasn't smiling but there was definitely amusement in those golden-brown eyes. "Your boss said you were conscientious. That you'd worry. But you need to understand you're a hero. You can expect to be treated as such. And I don't care if I ever get another government contract... Although I'm quite sure I will. Everything's fine, sweetheart," he added. His head dipped and he gave her a swift but reassuring kiss.

She shifted away the moment he lifted his head, despite the urge to wrap her arms around his neck and never let go. "Aren't you afraid they'll see us?" she whispered.

"Are you kidding?" He really did grin then. "I *want* them to see us. They're all calling you the warrior princess. And every one of them, including the female pilot, wants to ask you out."

She scanned his face, wondering if he was joking. But his smile had already turned to a scowl. "I don't advise accepting," he said. "These agents are all based in Washington. And I don't think you'd like the city. I, on the other hand, live in Idaho."

Her heart gave a hopeful kick. Maybe he *would* want to see her after the dust settled. At least that's the way it sounded. The helicopter rotors might be garbling his words.

But he was looking at her the same way he had last night—before she'd shot an arrow in Logan's neck. When there'd been nothing but desire in his eyes. Only now there was something else. Longing and an endearing mix of uncertainty, so at odds with his usual confidence.

"What about the pilot?" she asked, pretending to purse her lips in thought. "She looks nice. And we already established she wears red underwear. Where does she live?"

The sides of his eyes crinkled in a smile. "Montana. But she doesn't like horses. For a woman like you, I guess that rules her out."

A woman like you. She'd heard those words before. But Jack spoke them differently. Like she was something good, even special. He didn't seem to mind that the other agents were watching, that their relationship would be reported. Or that she might be bad luck.

"I probably won't have a job soon," she said carefully. "So I'll have more time. And I'd like to visit your ranch, see Suds open that beer. But don't feel you have to ask me out, you know...because of what happened."

"You mean because you saved my life?" His gorgeous smile flashed again.

Clearly he knew exactly what she meant and though she smiled back, her face felt frozen. She'd helped people before, and obviously he'd rescued many more. That left feelings, ties and obligations, especially when it involved the opposite sex. She didn't want him that way.

She nodded again, determined to show her understanding of the situation. She even forced a careless shrug. "You know what I mean," she said "Don't feel we have to get together because of what happened."

"Because I want to be with you?" he said. "Because I'm falling in love with you?"

She was still nodding even as his words filtered to her brain, and then to her heart, until it was beating double time. "Oh," she managed.

"Not quite the response I was hoping for," he said dryly. "But I intend to work on that. How about I come by the ranch, soon as I leave Washington?"

If I'm even there. But she didn't want to get into that, not with the blond agent hovering. Besides, this time it didn't hurt so much about her employment situation, or any of the other repercussions. Just knowing she'd see Jack when it was over left her flushed with optimism. Maybe he'd return quicker than expected. Although by the look of things, the feds didn't plan on giving him much freedom any time soon.

The blond agent leaned over Jack's seat, as if trying to hear their conversation. This time though, he tapped Jack on the shoulder and gestured at the window.

Jack inclined his head and turned back to Kate. "I couldn't convince them to stop," he said. "And I'm not authorized to answer your questions. But they all agreed you deserve a little detour. This is better anyway. It will end the day on a more positive note."

He was grinning and even the blond agent looked oddly satisfied. "Take a look down," Jack prompted.

She turned toward the window. The foothills had leveled into a mix of rolling fields and pasture, dotted with clumps of trees and grazing livestock. Then familiar outbuildings and a long rectangular arena sprouted into view. If she peered to the right, she'd see the dining hall where the cook was no doubt preparing a special cake to celebrate Monty's return. And there was the dance hall where she'd first met Jack. When she'd discovered dancing wasn't such a chore, as long as it was with the right man.

The helicopter slanted then straightened, hovering near the barn. The holding pen was empty except for six horses. Five of the animals placidly munched hay. But the sixth horse, a palomino, lifted his head, eyeing the helicopter with open suspicion. A blaze ran down his face, accentuating his white mane, showcased against his beautiful golden coat.

"Oh, my," Kate breathed. "Slider! He made it home?" Her incredulous gaze shot back to the other horses. "They all did?"

"Every one of them," Jack said, a grin splitting his face. "Logan was lying through his teeth. The four-wheelers never caught them. Never even saw them. The horses have some superficial cuts and tore some shoes off but they're fine. It was Slider who raised the alarm."

"What do you mean?"

"He didn't stop by the pasture with Banjo and the others but jumped the fence. They found him waiting outside the barn early this morning. That's when all hell broke loose. And the reason the helicopters arrived so quickly. They're safe," Jack said, squeezing her hand. "And I just wanted you to see them."

Her lower lip quivered, her heart doing a delighted tap dance in her chest.

"We can't talk about details yet," the blond agent warned, his voice still authoritative but not quite so harsh.

Jack raised his index finger. "One more thing," he said, turning back to Kate. "Courtney and Tyra insisted on sending a message. Your friends at the ranch volunteered to deliver it."

He tilted her head back toward the window.

They were flying low over the south field now, where wranglers clustered around a tractor and hay wagon. But not just wranglers. There were loads of other workers too: the cook in her big apron, Allie wearing her striped swimsuit cover-up, and sweet Charlie from the fire pit. Even Sharon Barrett was there, distinctive in her white cowboy hat. She stood a little apart, not waving quite as madly as the others, but instead holding her arm up, as if in salute.

Jack pressed closer and even the blond agent leaned over Kate's seat, until all three of them were craning to see out the window. The agent's holster trapped Kate's bandaged hand against the steel frame of the seat, but the pain was miniscule, soothed by her flood of happiness.

She stared down at the upturned faces, her eyes misting as she absorbed their excited waves and the huge message they'd painstakingly printed in the field, using forty-pound bales of hay.

Only one word but it conveyed plenty. THANKS! it said.

EPILOGUE

Jack anchored the nylon rope, waiting for Kate to slide down to the cave floor. As soon as her feet touched the bottom, he turned her around and gave her a long and lingering kiss. He'd been watching her all weekend, admiring how she calmed Slider when the helicopters arrived, the way her eyes sparkled as she pointed out the mustang herd, and how easily she'd conversed with the President.

It seemed last year's abduction attempt hadn't tarnished Courtney's interest in the wild horses, not one bit. In fact, she'd persuaded her father to rebook her graduation present, returning less than a year later with a plucky Tyra in tow—who'd agreed to come only on the condition that she be allowed to ride a mule, preferably Bubba.

Of course, this time the President had insisted on far more elaborate security. In addition to a huge Secret Service team, he'd also employed three of Jack's associates before dropping in to join Courtney for a portion of her wilderness trip—the part where they all enjoyed steak and lobster within a virtual fortress.

It was a measure of Kate's talent that she'd been able to lead such a clumsy entourage around the valley without spooking the mustangs. However, she'd been able to guide the girls remarkably close to the herd. Courtney had been ecstatic with the experience, staring so long and intently that the binoculars left an outline on her face.

Even Tyra had been entranced, especially delighted with observing the foals and how their stubby tails twitched contentedly when they sucked milk from their dams.

The girls had spent hours giving the mustangs names, based on their color and behavior, peppering Kate with questions ranging from wild horse slaughter to how the mustangs protected their foals from predators and why the stallion was so mean to some of the colts.

Jack remained on the inner security perimeter, hiding his amusement behind a poker face. But sometimes he felt like running off other males too, before they tried to steal Kate away. He'd admitted that once and she just looked at him, her eyes incredulous. "But you're the gorgeous one," she'd said.

She had no idea how amazing she was, and he couldn't fathom why she considered herself an oddity, rather than truly exceptional. Hadn't understood it until her ex-boyfriend had dropped by the ranch for a "visit."

It was obvious the ex had made things much worse with Kate's job last year. The pretty boy was clearly a narcissist, craving the limelight and suddenly keen to have her back in his life. But only after the White House had championed the Mustang River Ranch as a top-notch vacation destination, with exceptional staff, animals and adventure opportunities. The President had even mentioned Kate and Monty by name, putting them firmly in place as top guides in the industry. Now everyone clamored for her services, whether it be carving classes, trail rides or the new women's survival program.

Thankfully, for the next twenty-four hours, Jack had her to himself.

He lifted his mouth from Kate's, carefully studying her face. Her cheeks were flushed from her descent into the cave but colored for all the right reasons—not shadowed by fear from the recent climb.

"I think everyone had fun," she said, still pumped with success. "It's especially good for the mustangs. A high profile visit like that will help safeguard their future. You were talking to Sharon a lot this morning. Does she still think the Mantracker packages are a good idea?"

"Absolutely," Jack said, unclipping her safety harness while Kate removed her lightweight climbing helmet. "She has more requests than the ranch can handle. Guests are stoked about matching their wits against you and Monty. It's not just locals either. They've had calls from Canada and Australia as well as a sheik from the Emirates."

Giving guests a head start and then sending Kate and Monty out on horses to track them down had been Sharon Barrett's idea. No doubt it would be a surefire winner, providing adrenaline-seekers with the ultimate challenge. There were enough scenarios to fit almost everyone. And one of Sharon's suggested variations was to have him—a former SEAL—partnered with Kate.

Only Jack didn't want to horn in on Kate's success. He loved seeing the happiness in her eyes, along with the occasional look of disbelief, as if she still couldn't believe she'd landed her dream job for life.

"Sharon asked if I'd be interested in filling in for Monty on occasion," Jack said, gauging Kate's reaction. "When I'm between jobs... But only if that's something you'd like. She wants us to think about it."

"Think about it? But that's wonderful!" Kate rose on her toes and flung her arms around his neck. "Imagine! Paid to ride together!"

"Yeah. And she'll throw in the guest cottage by the helipad in exchange for some security work."

"A cottage too? Unbelievable!" Kate was literally hopping now, her reaction exactly what he'd hoped. "I can't believe she agreed to that. Only Monty has a cottage, and he's worked here for ages."

"Negotiations were tough." Jack felt the side of his mouth twitch. Sharon Barrett was a shrewd businesswoman but she also knew how important it was to ride the crest of free publicity. He'd taken full advantage of her desire to keep Kate on staff and to use him as part of her tracking team.

"The women will *want* you to catch them," Sharon had said, rubbing her hands in glee. "That is unless you're frowning. Then they'll be shitting their pants in fear. And that wouldn't be good for my ranch. You will be charming with them, right?"

"A little fear is a good thing," Jack had said.

"I suppose. But it doesn't matter." There'd been an imp of mischief in Sharon's voice. "Because Kate will make up any of your deficiencies. We all know how the men feel about her, including the President."

The idea of Kate tracking men who might *want* her to catch them had made Jack scowl. "And me," he'd said. "Remember how I feel about her. In fact, I'd be just as happy to have Kate live with me in Idaho...rather than be worked to death at your ranch."

Sharon had shot him a pained look. "I already agreed to the cottage. What else do you want?"

"It'd be nice if you gave her Slider. Maybe surprise her on her birthday."

"That's not necessary. None of the other wranglers ever ride him. They all know he's Kate's favorite."

"Then it won't matter if you give him to her," Jack had said, keeping his voice reasonable. "And I'll be bringing along a couple horses, and of course my rescue dogs. I expect they'll be welcome."

"Long as they don't bite," Sharon had said, blowing out a theatrical sigh.

But they both knew she was ecstatic with the turn of events, and her expression had remained satisfied beneath her cowboy hat. The White House had covered up Courtney's abduction attempt but they'd been lavish with praise of the Mustang River Ranch and even more glowing about the competence of the ranch guides. The last thing Sharon wanted was to lose Kate's services.

"You're good at getting what you want," Kate said, nibbling at Jack's lower lip, the pleasure of her touch jolting him back to the cave. "First, Sharon gives you a cottage, then a job, and now she agreed to let us make this little detour."

"I wanted to sleep in your cathedral cave," Jack said. "See firsthand where you climbed out. Check out that inscription." And he'd needed to whisk her away and grab some privacy. The last nine months had been a whirlwind, with both of them working and only able to snatch limited time alone.

And before she started chasing people around the mountain, he needed to make sure she was truly ready. Simply for his peace of mind.

He slid his hands beneath her shirt, skimming his fingers over her velvety skin, drifting over the sensual curve of her backbone. His fingers dropped, patting a trail over her hips, her ass, her thighs... And lower.

"No knives on me," she said, correctly realizing this was actually a search. "Security was much tighter this time. Did you see those sniffer dogs yesterday? One of them reminded me of your Shepherd."

But she was speaking a little too fast, as if trying distract him. And seconds later he pulled her tiny red jackknife from the inner side of her climbing boot.

"Oh?" he said, holding up the jackknife and pretending to scowl. "Then what have we here?"

"Okay, so you found it." She clearly saw past his scowl and gave him a mischievous grin, and then an even more delightful hug. "But that's all," she said. "And it's just my tiny knife. I don't need my big one anymore... Not when you're around."

He dipped his head, smiling against her hair. She made it sound like he walked on water. And to find a woman who cherished his lifestyle—who actually reveled in it—made him feel like the luckiest man alive.

They had some differences. Her tolerance for people was much higher than his. Over the last few days, she'd been in her element: helping Courtney and Tyra with their horses, keeping the animals calm when the fleet of helicopters arrived, then guiding the girls close enough to the mustangs so they could snap some truly spectacular pictures. She really didn't seem to mind the mountains anymore. Her face had been glowing and if the Mustang River Ranch gave her that kind of fulfillment, then he had no intention of ever asking her to leave...as long as they had enough quality time together.

"Great idea to sleep in the cave tonight," she said. "But I thought you weren't superstitious?"

"I'm rethinking a lot of things," he said. He unhooked the clasp of her bra and finally was able to wrap his hand around her perfect breast. Oh, God, and now if they never moved, he'd die a happy man.

"Don't you want to read the inscription first?" she asked. "Take the ten-second tour?"

"In a minute, sweetheart. I'm happy just standing here."

She tucked her head against his chest and gave a contented sigh. "See what I mean?" she said. "This cave really does have a mystical feel."

"Yes," he said. "It does."

He lifted his head, checking over her shoulder, eyeing the jagged crack that separated this chamber from the main cave. Most men would never have been able to squeeze through the opening, only a very small one... And possibly the man named Peewee.

Neither Kate nor the feds had ever questioned why he'd used his last bullet on the wiry sidekick instead of Logan. But his decision to protect her, at the risk of exposing Courtney, had marked a change in his values. Kate was his priority now.

Over contract and country.

"Do you think the saying is true?" she asked. "That anyone that makes love here will stay together?"

"I do," he said. "At least as it relates to us."

She gave an affirming nod and snuggled against his chest. They remained locked, absorbing the warmth of the sun as it spilled molten gold over their linked arms, neither of them feeling the need to speak. And he gave fervent thanks for finding this remarkable woman, someone who delighted in the activities he relished and who made his heart sing.

It was clear she didn't yet comprehend the depth of his love. But she would, eventually. He'd make sure of it.

About the Author

Bev Pettersen is a three-time nominee in the National Readers Choice Award and a two-time finalist in the Romance Writers of America's Golden Heart® Contest as well as the winner of other international awards including the Reader Views Reviewer's Choice Award, Aspen Gold Reader's Choice Award, NEC-RWA Reader's Choice Award, Write Touch Readers' Award, a Kirkus Recommended Read, and a HOLT Medallion Award of Merit. She competed for five years on the Alberta Thoroughbred race circuit and is an Equestrian Canada certified coach.

Bev lives in Nova Scotia with her family—humans and four-legged—and when she's not writing novels, she's riding. If you'd like to know about special offers or when her next book will be available, please visit her at www.BevPettersen.com where you can sign up for a newsletter.

Also Available From Bev Pettersen:
Jockeys and Jewels
Color My Horse
Fillies and Females
Thoroughbreds and Trailer Trash
Studs and Stilettos
Backstretch Baby
Riding For Redemption
A Scandalous Husband
Millionaire's Shot
A Pony For Christmas (Novella)
Repent (Thriller Novella)
Strange Behavior (Thriller Novella)

www.ingramcontent.com/pod-product-compliance
Lightning Source LLC
Chambersburg PA
CBHW061611190726
48288CB00007B/2267